HEARTW

*Mending the
Doctor's Heart*

—

Sophia Sasson

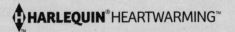

Recycling programs
for this product may
not exist in your area.

ISBN-13: 978-0-373-36820-4

Mending the Doctor's Heart

Printed in U.S.A.

"Where are we?" Anna's eyes were wide with confusion.

"We're in that old stone church off Chalan Road," Nico told her.

She sprang to her feet. "I went to Lucas's grave."

He nodded. "We tried to reach you on the sat phone but you didn't answer, so I got worried and came after you. There's a hurricane going on outside—I needed to get you to safety. You passed out there."

"I..."

Despite everything, he was glad she'd gone to Lucas's grave. She so desperately needed closure, but it was clear she hadn't found it. He fought to breathe. How was he going to help her?

"Do you have any emergency supplies?" she asked. He pointed to his bag and she rummaged through it, coming up with a handful of pills and a water bottle. "Hand me the radio." The battery-operated device turned on, but there was no signal.

"I guess we're stuck in this dungeon until the storm passes," he said. Not that it was a horrible prospect. This might be the last time he'd get to have Anna to himself. "Let's just hope there aren't any dragons."

"Just those we brought with us," she said wistfully.

Then the lights went out.

Dear Reader,

This story has been in my heart for nearly a decade, since the first time I visited the beautiful island of Guam. I fell in love with the people there and the seeds of this story were sown. *Mending the Doctor's Heart* is the story of Captain Anna Atao, a woman who must find the courage to forgive herself and find a way back to love.

This book explores the depths of deep pain and sacrifice, against the backdrop of a paradise island decimated by natural disaster. I cried when I wrote Anna's story and every time I've read it since. It's a story to immerse yourself in, and the tears you shed will be worth it to see Anna complete her journey.

To get free book extras, visit my website, sophiasasson.com. I love hearing from readers, so please find me on Twitter (@SophiaSasson) or Facebook (SophiaSassonAuthor) or email me at readers@sophiasasson.com.

Enjoy!

Sophia

Sophia Sasson puts her childhood habit of daydreaming to good use by writing stories she hopes will give you hope and make you laugh, cry and possibly snort tea from your nose. She was born in Bombay, India, and has lived in the Canary Islands, Spain, and Toronto, Canada. Currently she calls the madness of Washington, DC, home. She's the author of the Welcome to Bellhaven and the State of the Union series. She loves to read, travel to exotic locations in the name of research, bake, explore water sports and watch foreign movies. Hearing from readers makes her day. Contact her through sophiasasson.com.

Books by Sophia Sasson

Harlequin Heartwarming

The Senator's Daughter
First Comes Marriage

CHAPTER ONE

FIVE YEARS, TWENTY-SEVEN DAYS and ten hours since she left and swore never to return. Anna watched the swirls of aquamarine, green and royal blue surrounding the little patch of island she once called home. A tiny drop of land in the bucket of the great Pacific Ocean. At ten thousand feet, the view was breathtakingly beautiful, but as the helicopter dropped, the serene vision gave way to the carnage of broken buildings and debris-littered streets. She swallowed hard.

Anna was the only passenger on board, so as soon as they touched down, she unbuckled, grabbed her duffel bag and hopped out. Her boots hit the muddy ground with a squelch. She pulled down the sunglasses parked on top of her head and raised her arm to shield her face from the stinging wind kicked up by the still-revolving helicopter rotors.

This was the golf course where she and Nico were married. It looked far worse on the ground than it did from the air. The pristine green lawn with perfectly planned hills and flower beds was gone. Tree branches were everywhere, strewn about with random garbage. *This is the* least *damaged part of the island?* A crushing vise gripped her heart. *Is Nico alive?* She hadn't been able to get through to their house on Tumon Bay; the landlines and cell towers were out.

"Captain! You okay?"

Anna turned to see the pilot carrying a box. He tilted his head toward the rest of the cargo, which he had unloaded from the helicopter and set on the ground. How long had she been standing there? She looked toward the medical camp. Tents were set a hundred feet from where she stood, their dull beige forlorn against the calm blue sky.

Anna swung the duffel on her back, looping the handles around her shoulders so she could carry it like a backpack. Her arms protested as she lifted a heavy box. It had been more than a month since her last deployment, and her muscles were a little out of shape.

She carried the box to a waiting staff member, then set down her bag and helped the pilot carry the rest of the supplies from the makeshift helipad. When they were down to the last box, the pilot stepped back into the cockpit, waving to her as he started the rotors.

The helicopter rose and disappeared from view. There was no way off the island now; she was stuck here. Again. The permanent ache in her heart gnawed at her.

Picking up the remaining box, she walked back to the bright-faced staffer. His crisp uniform, regulation lined badges, and chipper hello told her it was his first deployment. She nodded to him and handed over the box.

"Where do I report?"

He pointed her to the medical command tent. She unzipped the outer pocket of her bag to remove her papers. As she entered the tent, her eye caught the big digital clock that hung from a wire. Forty-five hours and twenty-two minutes. That's how long ago the tsunami had struck. It was also the clock that would determine when she could leave. Around the time it struck 168 hours, the actively wounded would slow to a trickle, mostly limited to those hurt as a result of the rescue efforts. When the red digits ticked to 381 hours, the rescue operation would be over and the focus would turn to recovering bodies. By then, plenty of relief organizations would crowd the small island with their staff outnumbering the injured. She'd be replaced by social workers who would stay here for months dealing with the mental trauma that would haunt people for generations to come.

"Took you long enough to get here."

She whirled to come face-to-face with a woman dressed in blue scrubs. Rear Admiral Linda Tucker was Anna's height, around five foot six, and had red hair streaked in spots to faded copper. Her face sagged with exhaustion but her gray eyes sparked as she surveyed Anna.

The Public Health Service was a uniformed division but worked more like a health care service than a military unit, so Anna didn't salute and was happy to note that her new supervisor was wearing scrubs. Some PHS field commanders insisted they wear their uniforms, which inevitably made the days uncomfortable. Yet despite this concession, she knew Linda Tucker's reputation and braced herself.

"I got here as soon as I could," Anna replied evenly.

"I expected you yesterday."

Anna had flown from Washington, DC—where she'd been visiting with her sister,

Caro—to Japan, where she had to wait for the long-haul military transport helicopter to bring her to Guam. She'd been traveling for twenty-three hours and fifty-three minutes straight.

Shrugging, she settled for a nonchalant. "I was delayed." What she didn't say was that she'd come close to being discharged from the PHS for defying orders to board the first transport to Guam. It had taken a call from the surgeon general's assistant with a plea from the SG himself to get her on board. She was the only PHS officer who spoke Chamorro.

"Well, get changed and meet me back here, we have a lot to do." Dr. Tucker turned and bent over the newly arrived cardboard boxes, efficiently slicing through the tape. Anna handed her papers to the clerk, a young man with a pockmarked face who looked pained to be there.

Anna scanned the tent while the clerk typed her details into the computer. The tent looked like every other medical command center she'd seen. Every available inch of space was being put to use. Corners were stacked with cardboard supply boxes, the center dominated by U-shaped desks cluttered with laptops and assorted materials. A large fan blew in fresh air from a makeshift window, but the heat was still oppressive. She ran her finger under her collar and twisted her neck, trying to get some air between her sticky skin and the wilted cloth of her once-starched khaki uniform. She scanned the faces in the room but quickly stopped and chided herself. *Why would he be here?* Nico would be out in the community, helping people defy the odds of survival. *If he's alive.* Closing her eyes, Anna took a breath. She'd have to go to the house in Tumon Bay to check on him, find out for sure. From what she'd seen in the air, the roads weren't passable by car, so she'd have to walk the five miles there. At her typical walking speed, she could do it in an hour and fifteen minutes, but given the condition of the terrain, she figured she'd have to budget at least four hours to get there and back.

"I'll show you to your tent. That way you can get changed while I process your paperwork," the clerk said suddenly. Anna turned to see Dr. Tucker motioning to him to hurry things up.

"I need you to get to work." She bent over

the boxes again before Anna could ask when she might be able to go check on Nico.

Anna followed the fast-walking clerk out of the tent and down a narrow pathway. No matter where she went, the sounds of the aftermath of a disaster were always the same. Moans of people in pain, shuffling of fast-paced boots, generators and battery-powered machines rumbling to life, the smell of wet earth and the incessant buzzing of insects.

Nico has to be okay. I'd know if he wasn't. Wouldn't I?

The clerk led her to the tiny tent that would be her living quarters. She groaned inwardly at the paper sign in the plastic sleeve on the door-flap indicating she would be sharing the tent with Linda Tucker. So she wasn't going to get a reprieve on this deployment.

She changed quickly and found Admiral Tucker waiting for her outside the tent. She motioned for Anna to follow. "We don't have enough wound care supplies or topical and IV antibiotics, so we need to ration them. I understand this isn't your first deployment?"

"No, ma'am, I've been through twenty deployments in five years. My last one was in Brazil for the Zika virus after I returned from

Liberia, where I was dealing with the Ebola outbreak."

The rear admiral's eyes widened with respect. "Good, then I don't have to orient you. Feel free to call me Linda." She continued her brisk pace, weaving through the narrow gaps between tents, dodging pieces of machinery and carts carrying supply boxes from one tent to another.

"The locals are just now mobilizing, so we get about ten new patients an hour. Tent space is at a premium. Anyone who doesn't need to be monitored gets sent to the high school, mall or the hospital, where they've set up shelters."

Anna's throat closed. "Is the hospital operational?" she choked out. The last time she'd been at the Guam General Hospital, she'd lost everything she ever loved. She hadn't used her pediatrics training since then, staying as far away from children as she could.

Linda shook her head. "Not as a medical facility, but the building is still standing so they're using the space to house people." Linda slowed and turned to make sure Anna had heard her.

"A local stopped by a few hours ago to say someone's managed to set up a field hospital in one of the newer buildings. A local physician is helping them, but they have over a hundred people there. If we get through our current patients, I'd like you to go. They can't get those patients to this side of the island."

Anna nodded. It would give her a chance to go to Nico's house, her old house, and make sure he was okay. "Did they tell you where on the island?"

"Talofofo. It's on the Pacific side, so I'm not sure how well it fared."

A brick fell through Anna's stomach. *Talofofo*. That's where Nico had bought land. Right after they'd buried Lucas, the piece of herself that would forever be in Guam. Nico had tried to convince her it was the way to heal, a desperate attempt to get her to stay. What happened to his plans? Had they washed away like the rest of their life together?

"Dr. Tucker, I have a request." Before she could continue, Linda stopped abruptly and Anna almost bumped into her. One of the patients had come out of a tent screaming at her.

"I'm going to die!" A man scarcely over five feet tall stood in front of Linda, his chest puffed out.

"Sir!" Linda's voice was firm and laced

with annoyance. "I've told you already—you're not getting pain medication, so stop the racket."

Linda turned to her. "He's yours. Sixty-some-year-old male, leg laceration, five stitches, prior undiagnosed first-degree heart block. He's been having arrhythmias, which is why he's still here. Not even close to the worst of the wounded."

Anna took in the broad, wrinkled forehead, the firm purse of the man's lips, the gray in his hair and the slight stoop to his back. He was an elder, a man used to getting what he wanted. She stepped up to him and bowed slightly, making her frame smaller so she wouldn't tower over him, then spoke softly in Chamorro. "We don't have supplies, the hospital is damaged, we're saving the pills for people who are badly hurt."

The patient nodded, thanked her, then went back to the tent.

Linda shook her head. "He speaks English. I heard him talking to the others. These people!"

Anna bristled. "He needed to know that you weren't making a judgment call in denying him pills. People here understand shortages and rationing…" She muttered under her breath, "They understand it all too well."

Linda pressed her lips together tightly, and Anna reminded herself that the woman was a superior officer. While Anna wasn't interested in climbing the career ladder, she had to work and live with Linda for the foreseeable future, and she still had to ask her for a favor.

"He should be grateful we're here to help him," Linda said irritably. "But I'm glad you speak Chamorro. Follow me—I think I'll put you in this tent."

Anna opened her mouth, then shut it. Linda had already resumed her purposeful walk. Most of the doctors she worked with didn't appreciate the local cultures. They were adrenaline junkies who went into deployment to feed their hero complexes and left with little understanding of the place. They were dispassionate about the very people they supposedly came to serve. While people like Linda annoyed her, at some level Anna understood the need for emotional distance from the patients they were serving. She had come to Guam and ingrained herself in the community. If she'd treated her time here for what it was, a temporary medical rotation, she never would have married Nico, never would have had Lucas.

Linda went through the open doorway of one of the tents, talking as she went. Anna pushed her attention to Linda. She needed to stop thinking about her past and snap into the present. This could be Liberia, or Sri Lanka, or Thailand. The tents all looked the same, the misery around her was no different. *Pretend you're not in Guam.*

"...but I need someone who has a background in pediatrics," Linda was saying. The sound of crying babies and high-pitched little voices made Anna freeze. Filled wall-to-wall with children of all ages, the tent suddenly spun around her. Older children were sitting on cots, while younger ones played and crawled around on the dirt floor. Mothers held tiny babies and stared at her as she took it all in. She shivered. The flash of a sweet face burned her eyes, and she jolted at the memory of a cold little body in her arms. *No. No, no, no, no!*

Linda kept talking. "I have my hands full. No one has evaluated these children since they were brought here, and most of the—"

"I...can't." *Is that my voice?* "Listen, I'm not sure what you were told, but I don't treat children. That's the only thing I won't do. You can assign me to the burn unit, send me out into the field to do body recovery… I'm game for anything else, but I don't treat children."

Linda put her hands on her hips. "Dr. Atao, you're a pediatrician! Need I remind you that we're in the middle of a disaster here? You don't get to pick where you work, and we have a tent full of children who need attending to."

Anna's chest tightened, but she forced herself to meet Linda's eyes. "I have an understanding with the PHS that I don't treat children anymore. I—"

"Are you refusing an order?"

A child's wail pierced through her. Her muscles tightened. Technically her understanding with the PHS was just that, an unwritten agreement. Her boss knew what had happened with Lucas, and her orders usually had a note attached about not assigning her young children to work with. It had never been an issue, not once in all her deployments. And perhaps in another place she could have handled it… *But not here on Guam*.

She shook her head. "I'm really sorry, I'll do anything else. I just can't…"

Linda wasn't listening. One of the staff in

the tent had handed her a writhing infant. "The paramedics are a little concerned about this baby. You're the only one who has any pediatrics training."

Linda extended her arms, ready to transfer the little body into Anna's.

Anna stepped back. There was definitely something wrong with the infant; she looked a little blue around the lips. A cold hand squeezed her heart and her brain shut down. All she could see was a still little body, his skin cold as ice.

"Give her oxygen now, check blood gases and listen to her heart for murmurs," she choked out.

She couldn't breathe. Her lungs were squeezed shut, no air would go in or come out. She turned and ran outside, desperate for oxygen. As soon as she'd cleared the tent, she put her head between her knees trying to calm down enough to get air into her lungs.

"No. No. No. No. *No!*" She barely realized she was chanting the words.

Her chest burned as she gasped for air. Everything spun around her. Her knees buckled and she fell, scraping her hands. She sat on the muddy ground and closed her eyes, picturing herself in the depths of the ocean, imagining the schools of fish going about their business, corals moving with the currents. One of her PHS colleagues had suggested taking up scuba diving. The hobby had given her the muscle memory she needed to control her breathing and the ability to close her senses and focus on a visual. A way to cope. To be a functional human being again.

Three hundred and thirty-six hours, and then she could leave.

She opened her eyes. Linda was standing with one hand on her hip, the other holding out a little cup of water.

Anna drank even though she wasn't thirsty. She knew the act of swallowing would force her diaphragm to relax and slow her breathing.

"Are you dismissing me?" Anna wheezed out.

"I should. But besides you, I'm the only doctor here. The local nurses and paramedics have barely enough training to help. I haven't slept in over a day." She blew out a breath. "I have to deal with you until reinforcements arrive. But this will be noted in your record."

Anna didn't care about a reprimand in her file. "I'm a competent doctor. I can deal with just about anything other than children. It's personal."

Linda sighed, clearly frustrated but resigned. She gave a dismissive shake of her head. "Guess I need to go treat those kids." She pointed to an area where people were erecting more tents. So far the camp had about twenty, but just in the time Anna had been walking around, a new one had been put up.

"I've already checked on everyone to this point." Linda gestured to the tents at the periphery. "I need you to start with those who arrived in the last two hours. They've been put in tent twenty-four. The paramedics who've been helping triage have been instructed to start putting people in tents as they're built."

Linda turned to walk away.

"Dr. Tucker, I have one more request."

Linda turned, her brows furrowed with impatience.

"I have some family here in Guam, and I don't know whether they're okay. Can I go check on them?" Anna hadn't meant to sound desperate, but Linda's frown softened.

"Start by checking the roster to see if they're here." She glanced at her watch. "Can you go in after seeing the backlogged patients? I need a few hours of sleep." Her tone was almost pleading.

Anna nodded. She'd been waiting for almost two days. A few more hours wouldn't make a difference. Not to Nico.

She parted ways with Linda and went to the medical command to ask the clerk for the roster of patients.

"I'm still transferring the paper logs to the computer. Check in later."

"Can you see if there was anyone by the last name Atao?" she said softly. The clerk looked up, eyeing the nameplate on her right breast pocket. He nodded, then tapped on the keyboard and shook his head.

"No one so far. I'll come find you if I see that name appear in the paper logs or the new arrivals."

Anna thanked him.

"We're not the only medical camp around the island. I'll ask the others when I make my status calls."

Tears stung her eyes at the pity in his voice. She stood straight, thanked him, then turned. Despite her best efforts, she hadn't been able to sleep on the plane. Couldn't stop herself from imagining all the scenarios she would face on Guam. Still, she was alert and eager to get to work.

The tents were filled to capacity. A standard issue tent could comfortably take twenty patients, but there were easily more than forty per tent. Each person shared his or her narrow cot with one or two others, taking as little space as they could so there was room for everyone. Anna introduced herself to the local paramedic, Jared, who was assigned to watch over the tent, and got right to work. Most people had broken bones and wounds of various sorts, which the paramedic had bandaged. A dialysis patient was worried about how he would manage. Anna figured the patient could comfortably make it another day or two before he would get toxic; hopefully resources would arrive by then. The first days after a disaster were always the hardest.

The young paramedic with curly black hair and dark eyes followed her from patient to patient, chatting away.

"My cousins are helping get the airport fixed," Jared told her. "There's so much junk on the runway, Lando—that's my uncle—had to go get a garbage truck to haul it all out."

Anna knew that one of the reasons so few resources had made it to the island was that helicopters were very inefficient. They could only carry so much weight to conserve fuel for the long journey back to Japan or the Philippines. The neighboring Marshall Islands and the Commonwealth of the Northern Marianas Islands—CNMI—had also been badly damaged in the tsunami.

"What about the military base?" Anna inquired as she drained the infected wound of an older woman.

"They were also damaged. They're repairing the base and sent an engineer to direct the efforts to fix up the airport, but there aren't a lot of people on base."

Anna nodded. Five years ago she had pleaded with the garrison officer on the air force base and each of the two navy bases, but they hadn't been able to help her. They'd been stretched thin with troop surges in Iraq and Afghanistan and there were no helicopters to transport Lucas off the island, no cardiac surgeons at the military hospital to perform the operation that could have saved his life.

"Have there been a lot of casualties?" Anna asked out of earshot of the patients as they went to get more supplies.

Jared shrugged. "It's hard to say right now. We had a brief warning from Hawaii saying they detected an earthquake off their coast, so we told everyone to take shelter inland, but not everyone made it. We're seeing a lot of rescuer injuries."

Her stomach roiled. Knowing Nico, he'd be out there putting himself at risk.

Once she was done gathering supplies, she moved on to the next tent, scanning every face for the one she knew so well. Yet another paramedic assisted her as she checked each patient in the overflowing tent. The hours sped by as more tents were put up, additional workers arrived and patients who'd been waiting in a triage area outdoors were moved to shelter.

Anna was surprised to see it was already dark when she came out of the last tent. People were still coming in, but she'd visited every patient at least once and discharged several after bandaging their wounds. She rolled her shoulders, trying to ease out the tension. She'd been on the island for five hours and forty minutes. She wondered whether she should try to find Linda or just inform the medical command clerk that she was heading to Tumon Bay to check on Nico. *He's probably okay.* Still, she couldn't shake the uneasy feeling in her stomach.

A shout grabbed her attention. "We have incoming, they need a doctor. Now!"

Anna ran to the triage area, where a group of new arrivals were gathered. A man yelled, *"Ayuda, ayuda."*

Anna stepped up and placed a hand on the man's shoulders. "I will help you. Tell me what's wrong," she said in Chamorro.

The man blinked rapidly. "A car fell on this man." He pointed across the field. Anna turned and asked the clerk to go find Linda and anyone else who was available. The damage from the tsunami was astounding; she'd seen a boat perched on top of a tree. In such cases, secondary accidents after the disaster injured more people than the event itself. She followed the shouting man away from the camp. They got to the main road, which was blocked by a big tree. On the other side of the trunk was a farm tractor with a wagon attached.

"Anna?"

She turned toward the familiar voice, momentarily blinded by the lights of the tractor. *Is that really her?* She shielded her eyes from the glare. Her chest squeezed painfully.

"Nana?" she said. Nana was what Nico called his mother. What Anna had once called the small woman standing before her. Nana stepped forward, blocking the light from the tractor. She looked exactly as she had five years ago, her curly gray hair pinned in a bun, standing tall in her five-foot frame.

"Anna!" She closed the distance between them, then reached out and clasped Anna's hands, her eyes wild. "Please, you must help Nico."

CHAPTER TWO

ANNA RAN TOWARD the tractor. The giant tree that blocked the roadway lay there, dark and ominous. Branches and limbs tore at her bare arms as she scrambled over the trunk. The thin cloth of her scrub pants tore as she made her way over the top. She barely felt the sting of the scrapes on her knees. Still blinded from the glare of the headlights, all she could see were shapes of people milling about. She scooted her way down a branch; it was too high to jump down. A shadowy figure approached at a run.

She used her hands to propel her body downward a little faster, ignoring the protests of her damaged skin. Just as she got close enough to jump the rest of the way, a pair of powerful hands grabbed her around the waist and pulled her down, slamming her into a hard chest. The smell of Irish Spring soap and sweat filled her nose, a scent as familiar to her as her own perfume. He held on to her even after she had a firm footing on the concrete.

"Anna!" Her heart thudded against her chest. She collapsed against him, relief flooding through her like someone had hit the release valve on a pressure cooker about to blow. He was alive. His strong arms held up her boneless body. Drawing her close, he rubbed his cheek against her head and her heart flooded with warmth.

"Oh God, Anna, it's really you." His voice was husky, and he pulled her even closer. The feel of his body against hers, so familiar and yet so distant, tugged her back into reality.

She pushed away, the words out of her mouth before she raised her face to look at him. "Nico!"

He stared down at her. His height had always been the talk of the island, a trait no doubt inherited from his white father.

Their eyes locked, her blue-gray ones pinned to his soft brown.

"You came back?" His voice was low, the words a little broken.

Something burned through her. Her legs weakened, threatening to buckle underneath her.

She stepped back, out of his reach. "I had to

come for my job." There was a slight tremor in her voice.

His eyes shifted. She stared pointedly behind him, eager to look away. "You need to come with me, Tito is hurt."

She followed him to the wagon behind the tractor and climbed up to the platform. Nico's cousin Tito was on the back of the wagon. He had an obvious open femur fracture, the bone protruding from his leg at an odd angle. Someone held a cloth to the wound, pressing on it to stop the bleeding.

"Anna, is that you?" Tito groaned in pain.

Anna smiled reassuringly at him. She'd been fond of Tito. He was slightly shorter than her but what he lacked in height, he made up for in width. "Yes, it's me, Tito. Looks like I'm gonna have to save you again."

"You came back for Nico?"

Anna shook her head, wishing she'd had the forethought to bring her medical bag. Her stethoscope was still miraculously around her neck. She took it off and began listening to his chest.

"Good! 'Cause he ain't available no more."

Anna took the stethoscope out of her ears. *Did I hear him correctly?* Tito groaned again and Anna cast around for something she could use to reduce the fracture. She spied a blanket in the corner of the wagon and pieces of rope, used to secure animals, hanging from the side rails. She picked up the blanket and wrapped Tito's fractured leg. He howled in pain, but Anna knew there was no other way. They wouldn't be able to safely transport him to the camp if she didn't reduce the fracture first.

As she untied a rope, she spoke to the group of men who had come with Tito, avoiding eye contact with Nico.

"Okay, we need to make a manual hare traction splint." She took the rope and tied it to the ends of the blanket. This wasn't the first time she'd had to reduce a femur fracture in the field. The last one had been in a rice paddy in Thailand. At least she was on dry ground this time. She finished constructing the makeshift splint. "I'm going to pull on this rope. I need you men to hold Tito down."

"What? No! This woman is gonna kill me!" The men ignored Tito and two of them kneeled on the floor, bracing themselves on either side of the injured man.

Anna grabbed the rope and balanced her footing. She pulled as hard as she could, keeping an eye on the bone, watching for the shift in the bulge telling her she'd snapped it back into place. She grunted, increasing the pressure on the rope. Tito screamed.

Nico wrapped his arms around her from behind, pressing his body close to her with the familiarity of a husband. Heat spread through her but she ignored how well she fit against him. He put his hands on top of hers and yanked with her. The bone fell into place and she held the rope taut. She could feel the warmth of Nico's body against her back. The hair on his arms pricked her skin.

"Okay, Nico, take this blanket and hold traction while I go arrange for a stretcher." She was glad her voice was businesslike. Ducking, she crawled underneath his arms and over Tito's legs. He had ceased howling and was now moaning and mumbling incoherently. Anna checked his breathing and pulse. Tito was in pain but would be okay until they got him to camp and gave him something to dull it.

Anna stepped down from the wagon to see a few of the men had run ahead to the camp and requested a stretcher already. She instructed the men to find two pieces of wood and nail a makeshift cross to the board.

They rolled Tito onto the stretcher and with

Nico's help, she tied her traction splint ropes to the cross to hold the fracture in place.

Someone lifted one end of the stretcher and nearly dropped it. Nico teasingly reminded Tito to lose weight and picked up the front end. That's when she noticed the blood on his T-shirt, right around his waist.

"Nico, you're hurt!"

He shrugged and adjusted his grip on the stretcher but she heard the unmistakable groan and saw the shift of his body. He was injured.

Two other men lifted the back of the stretcher, and a couple others held the sides as they maneuvered it down from the wagon and made the long walk around the tree trunk, since there was no safe way across. Anna followed, watching Nico shift his weight every few seconds. He was in pain.

They found Nana on the other side of the tree and she fell in step with Anna, reaching out to squeeze her hand. Anna let the woman take it for a moment, but pulled it back on the pretense of needing to check on Tito.

When they arrived at camp, Linda was waiting. She inspected the hare traction splint. "Not bad for fieldwork."

Linda took over Tito's care, instructing

Anna to manage the rest of the arrivals. Anna opened her mouth to protest but Linda was long gone.

NICO WOULD HAVE gone with Tito but they wouldn't allow him. It was just as well. He had a lot to do, and that was without knowing Anna was back. *What is she doing here, anyway?*

She turned to Nico. "Let me look at your injury."

He began shaking his head; the pain would subside eventually. He needed to get back to Talofofo, but one look at her face and he stopped. Maybe fate had intervened to give him the courage to do what he'd been putting off for more than a year. A jab in the arm caught his attention and he looked down to see Nana, her eyebrows raised at him. He didn't need her to speak to know what she wanted him to do. She'd been bugging him for months to get in touch with Anna.

After nodding to his mother to let her know he understood her silent message, he followed Anna silently to a tent that had just been erected. A man was delivering boxes.

She opened a zippered bag and one-handedly pulled out a folded cot. Anna had always been self-sufficient, preferring to do the hard work herself rather than ask someone else for help. It was her strength that he'd been drawn to when they'd first met, and also what he had counted on to get them through their son's death.

"Sit," she said sternly.

He was lower than her on the cot, so he tipped his head back to take her in. She looked the same, yet different. The luscious brown and golden locks that had hung all the way to her waist were cropped short now, close to her earlobes. Once vibrant blue-gray eyes were tired and had crinkles around them that hadn't existed five years ago. Her face held more definition, less of the fullness that used to be there. She was far more beautiful, but hauntingly so. Sadness shrouded her.

"You've lost a lot of weight." He winced as the words left his mouth. *Didn't mean to say it out loud.*

She pressed her lips together. "Yeah, well, I haven't had your relatives stuffing food down my throat."

His gut twisted at the bitterness in her voice. One of his favorite memories was right after she'd given birth to Lucas. Her face had a plumpness to it, her skin shone brightly, her normally slim figure had a wonderful feminine roundness. His relatives had showered her with attention and food, and she'd welcomed the nurturing for herself and baby Lucas. It was the only time in their marriage she'd embraced the presence of his extended family.

"Remove your shirt."

He wasn't going to make this any easier on her than it was on him. She had left him. Nico had done everything he could to get her to stay. When he finally let her go, it was with the hope that distance would heal her. He'd emailed her. Once a week for the first year, then monthly until he'd given up two years ago when she still hadn't answered. Not a single text, email or call. Not even to tell him she was okay. She'd even shut down her Facebook page, so he had no idea where she was or what she was doing. He'd finally resorted to emailing her sister Caroline, who at least had the decency to give him regular updates on what was happening with Anna, and let him know that she wasn't lying dead in a ditch somewhere.

He grabbed the bottom of his shirt and lifted it, wincing at the stab of pain across his belly. She inhaled sharply as he slid the shirt across his head and balled it up.

"How did you get that cut?"

"Tito got himself trapped under a car. The door had a jagged edge I didn't see when I was pulling him out."

"It's dirty and likely to get infected."

"It'll be fine."

"Some things never change," she muttered.

"Anna."

When she was upset at him, her eyes would normally turn an icy blue, a color he loved so much he would sometimes needle her just to see it. But now there was nothing but darkness. The same one that had been there when she left the island. He had hoped time would heal her. That leaving him would somehow bring her comfort. It hadn't.

"I'm going to stitch it up, then give you antibiotics."

She went to leave, but he grabbed her hand. Her skin felt soft, her hand small and fragile in his. "Why aren't you at peace with what happened to us?"

Her eyes flashed. "Because it didn't happen to *us*, it happened to me." His chest burned. No matter how hard he tried, she had never let him share her pain. Looking at her now, a familiar tightness choked his chest. He had grieved for Lucas, but he had moved on with his life. Taking a breath, he tried to shake off the suffocating feeling. What was wrong with him? He was at peace with what had happened. It was Anna who obviously still needed closure.

"Anna, you have to stop blaming yourself. You're not the reason Lucas died."

"I'm not the *only* reason. This island is the other reason. If we had been in California, he never would have died."

He let go of her hand and she stepped away. After Lucas's death, she had begged him to leave Guam, to come with her to California where they could start a new life. When they married, he'd thought she understood the man he was, a family man, one who wouldn't leave his home, his land. Not like his father. But ultimately she hadn't understood. She'd left without him and he'd let her go, thinking she would come back after time healed her wounds. But she hadn't come back. Nor had she healed.

Anna rummaged through some boxes and returned to him. He started to say something but stopped when a man entered the tent and began unpacking medical supplies.

Anna held up a needle in one hand and an upside-down bottle in another.

"Lie back," she ordered.

Nico lay on his back and felt her pouring liquid over his belly. It stung. He closed his eyes; there was no point in repeating the same conversation they'd had for months after Lucas's death.

A needle pierced his stomach, sending a sharp pain through his body, but then everything went blissfully numb. He opened his eyes and craned his neck. Anna was bent over him, stitching away. He remembered the last time he'd seen her like this and a different pain speared his chest.

"Anna…"

"Not now, Nico."

He waited patiently until she was done and saw her place a dressing over his wound. When she turned away, he sat up.

The man who'd been unpacking boxes left with an armful of empty containers.

"Anna…"

She turned to him, her eyes wet. "I can't do this, Nico. Not here."

He stood, then reached out and took her hand, pulling her close to him. She rested her face on his chest. Wrapping his arms around her, he placed his hand on her head, feeling her soft cheek on his bare skin, weaving his fingers into her silky hair. The years melted away as he felt her body against his. She belonged to him, always had. But her wounds were still as raw as the day she left. This island had never been her home because she hadn't let it be. And never would.

"I've missed you, Anna."

She nodded against his chest and he knew she still loved him, had felt the agony of their distance just as he had. Lifting her head, she stepped back, eyes shining, cheeks wet. He felt what she wanted to say. The very words that were on his lips. "Anna…we…" They were simple words, yet they stuck in his throat, threatening to choke him.

Her big, wet eyes stabbed at his soul. "Nico, I can't do this. I can never come back here for good. We…we…we need to divorce."

CHAPTER THREE

SHE FELT HIS *pain more acutely than her own. Yet Anna stood poised to cut into the delicate heart of her two-month-old son. Her hand trembled slightly as she touched the precision steel blade to pale pink skin. Right before it pierced, she retracted the scalpel. Closing her eyes, she took a deep breath. Even a minuscule tremble could end Lucas's life. She wasn't a cardiac surgeon, but if she didn't correct the big hole in his heart, he would die. If she made the tiniest of mistakes, he would die. If any one of a thousand things went wrong during the surgery, like the electricity going out again, he would die. She was six thousand miles away from California and they were out of time. There were no other options.*

She opened her eyes and looked up to see Nico's tall frame fill the viewing gallery window. His hair was disheveled, his eyes bloodshot, the normally smiling face creased. He put a hand on his heart, then onto the window that separated them. The gallery was meant for medical students and other physicians to watch surgeries. No father should witness his wife cutting into their son, but Nico had insisted on being there. Even across the room, she could see the wetness in his eyes. He mouthed, "I love you," then kissed his fist, relaying confidence she didn't feel.

She lowered her eyes from the viewing gallery to see the entire operating room staring at her. The panic in her chest was clearly visible in their eyes. The cold, sterile air reeked of desperation. They weren't going to stop her, tell her how foolhardy this whole thing was. Not today. They were used to letting their babies die.

"Dr. Atao, you need to begin."

The gentle but firm voice of the nurse anesthetist reminded her that the longer she waited, the more her son's life would be at risk. The hospital didn't even have a physician anesthesiologist. No one in their right mind would do this surgery. She looked at Nico one last time. His brown eyes reached into her soul, filling her with love. I have to do this. *Lucas couldn't die.*

She took a deep breath, willing her heart

to slow its frantic beating. She looked down at the small square of exposed skin, the rest draped with a blue sheet, as if the sheet could hide the fact that her little baby, the one she had nursed only an hour ago, was lying underneath. He was totally still, his normally wiggly, giggly, crying body as still as the air in the room. Ice seeped through her bones.

She pressed the scalpel into the skin above her son's heart.

ANNA SAT UP with a sharp pain in her chest.

"Dr. Atao?" Her brain registered someone calling her name.

"Dr. Atao!"

She rubbed her eyes. A hazy face slowly came into focus. "Sorry, Doctor, you asked me to wake you. It's eight o clock." Anna thanked the clerk and checked her watch. Three hours had gone by fast, but at least she'd slept. *The dream!* She hadn't had it for 392 days. But then she shouldn't be surprised it had returned. It wasn't so much a dream as a replay of the worst day of her life. The day she had performed surgery on her two-month-old son, hastening his death. It was technically a routine surgery; had she been in California, it would have been performed by a team of pediatric surgeons and Lucas would be a happy child today, five years, three months and four days old. But she'd been here on Guam, basking in the glory of being a new mother, ignoring the early warning signs.

She swung her leg off the cot, went to the latrine and splashed water on her face using the jug she'd brought. *Time of death, 10:56.* She'd done CPR for more than an hour, until finally the staff had pulled her away from Lucas and another physician had been called in to pronounce the death of her little baby.

For days after, his cries still woke her up at night.

She wiped her face with a paper towel. It was time to get back to work. There were still only two physicians, and patients were coming in by the truckloads as roads were getting cleared. Linda and Anna were taking turns sleeping. Anna had to keep moving; it was the only way to get through the remaining 319 hours on Guam.

A canteen hadn't been set up yet, but the medical command tent had a corner stocked with a box of MREs—military grade "meals ready-to-eat"—instant coffee and hot water. She made her way there and was surprised to find hard-boiled eggs and basic bread. Compared to the MREs, any real food was a treat.

The PHS personnel and several of the local firefighters who had been helping were huddled around the cardboard box that served as a table. There was even fresh coffee, courtesy of a French press. Anna helped herself to a cup.

"Dr. Atao, thank you for the treats," one of the firefighters said.

"What?"

"Your husband brought them in."

Anna choked on the lukewarm coffee she had just sipped.

"Excuse me?"

"The man with the same last name as you."

"Hi, Anna." She turned to see Nico, all six feet three inches of him, looking strong in a fresh T-shirt and jeans.

"Um…thank you. You didn't have to do that."

"Actually, it's a bribe."

Anna grabbed his arm and pulled him outside the tent. She didn't want her colleagues overhearing their conversation.

"I have no problems signing the divorce papers, but you might have some trouble getting them drawn up and adjudicated today given what's going on," she said. Last night after she'd asked for a divorce, he had sighed with relief, telling her that's what he wanted to talk to her about.

"Oh, I already have them drawn up, but you're right, it'll be weeks before the courthouse is open for us to file them. That's not what I was going to ask."

He already has the papers drawn up? How long has he been thinking about this? While she had considered divorce many times, the thought of calling a lawyer and actually having papers drawn up had never crossed her mind.

"What is it, then?" She shifted on her feet, eager for him to leave. She had work to do and the last thing she needed was Nico hanging around distracting her.

"I have a hospital building in Talofofo. People who can't make it to the camps on this side of the island have been coming there. Dr. Balachandra—you remember him, don't you?"

How could I forget the doctor who pronounced Lucas's death?

She must have nodded because he continued on. "He's been treating those patients, but he went to Cocos Island late last night to see a woman in labor with a breech birth and the currents are too strong this morning. He can't make his way back on the little boat he took out there."

Anna took a sip of the now cold coffee she was still holding and studied him. The only sign that he'd aged were the stray gray hairs around his temple. Nico was four years older than her, which meant his fortieth birthday was just around the corner. Yet aside from those wisps of gray, nothing else had changed. His face remained smooth, his milky-brown skin, inherited from his mother, unmarred. His high cheekbones gave him the kind of exotic handsomeness that made women swoon, and he hadn't lost any of his legendary charm.

"You built a hospital?"

"It's the private hospital I told you I would build in Lucas's memory. It's three months from opening." He looked around. "Maybe a little longer now."

Don't leave, Anna, I'll build a hospital in Lucas's memory. We'll make sure no one ever has to sacrifice like we did. I need you to do this with me.

He gave her a small smile. "It took a few years, but I built it to the best hurricane standards so it fared pretty well. It's damaged but still standing."

The pride in his voice cut through her. Before she left, he had tried to show her the land he'd bought in Talofofo, vowing to make enough money to build a private hospital where specialists from around the world would be invited to care for the locals so they would never have to rely on the substandard facilities of the chronically underfunded public hospital. It had been his way of making sense of Lucas's death. As if anything could make sense of Lucas's death.

"I need you to come see the patients who aren't in good shape. I used the tractor we brought last night to clear off the road to Talofofo. It won't take more than a few hours."

Spend the day with you? Go see the hospital that memorializes the fact that I couldn't save our son?

"I'll see if Dr. Tucker can go out. I have patients to see here." She somehow managed to keep her voice steady.

"I already talked to Dr. Tucker—she asked me to get you."

Anna stared at him. *How dare he?*

"It was her decision to send you." His voice was hard, his eyes dark and unreadable. There had been a time when his open face couldn't hide the emotions in his soul.

Anna shifted on her feet. *How am I going to get myself out of this one?*

"Dr. Atao."

She turned to see Linda walking toward her, and sighed in relief. "Dr. Tucker, just the person I was hoping to see."

"I see you found Nico, and what's this I hear about him being your husband?"

Anna opened her mouth to answer, but Nico jumped in. "We're actually separated."

Linda looked from Anna to Nico. "Well, I hope that doesn't make working together awkward."

"Dr. Tucker, I think it might be better if I stayed here, I…"

Linda glared at her. "Dr. Atao, I've made a lot of concessions for you. I'm expecting additional staff and supplies today. In case you've forgotten, I'm in charge here."

Anna pressed her lips together.

"There are no kids at the Talofofo hospital," Nico bent down and whispered in her ear.

Her face warmed. They were all but divorced; he needed to quit acting so familiar with her.

Before Anna could find the words to respectfully tell Linda and Nico to shove it, Linda was gone.

"Come on, Anna, the whole family is at the hospital helping out. They want to see you."

Why? She almost asked, then stopped herself. His mouth was stretched into that broad smile that used to melt her heart. But even his smile had changed. It was more reserved.

"Doesn't seem like I have much choice, so let's go gather up supplies."

It didn't take them long to fill a box with the things she needed. Anna lifted the box and Nico reached over to take it from her, his hands brushing hers.

She stepped back. "I can carry it." One thing she could never fault in Nico was his chivalry. There was an incident once when they had hiked up to the Fonte Dam, and she'd twisted her ankle. Even though she'd been able to walk on it, he'd carried her on his back the entire four miles home. He hadn't listened to her objections.

He raised an eyebrow. "Fine, then."

They made their way back to the road. Anna's arms protested. The box hadn't felt that heavy back at camp, but walking through mud and debris was wearing her down.

"You okay with that box?"

She nodded. "It's pretty light."

His lips twitched but he graciously pointed to a pickup truck parked down the road. She saw that the big tree she'd climbed last night had been chopped up and moved to the side so cars could pass in single file. The locals weren't going to sit on their hands and wait for help to arrive. She remembered when Nico had first introduced her to the island he'd said, *No one comes for us. We're more than twelve hours flying time from the US mainland. We fend for ourselves.* At the time she'd been enchanted with the idea of living on a remote island and awed by the spirit of the people who charted their own course.

Branches and leaves still littered the road. As they crossed the fallen tree, her foot caught an errant limb and she reached out to keep from falling. Nico grabbed her arm to stabilize her, then wordlessly took the box. He walked to the passenger side of the pickup, opened the door for her and set the box in the truck bed.

She got herself into the seat, then shut the door before he could come around to do it for her. Nico placed his hand on the steering wheel but didn't start the engine. Anna stared at him. He turned to her. "Before we see my family, there's something I need to tell you."

She waited. His face told her she wasn't going to like what he had to say. Her heart slowed until she could barely feel it beating inside her chest. He tried to smile, but it was his fake smile, the one he gave when he was trying to put a good face on bad news.

"Nana has breast cancer."

She gasped and instinctively placed her hand on his.

"She's not in a lot of pain yet."

A small ray bloomed in Anna's chest. "Have you considered taking her to Hawaii or California for treatment?"

Nico shook his head. "I've begged, but she doesn't want to leave the island. She's convinced that it's better to spend her last few days dying here than to waste away in a hospital on the mainland. Besides, Guam Hospital can do some basic radiation and chemo."

Anger sparked through her. Couldn't he see that his mother might have a real chance at treatment? *Why are they so obstinate about staying on this island?*

"That's why you've been working so hard to get that hospital up and running?"

"She was only diagnosed a month ago. The hospital was well underway, but yes, my hope is that it'll be open in time to help her."

She squeezed his hand. His frozen face told her he was fighting back tears.

"There's one more thing."

She waited, watching his Adam's apple bob as he swallowed. Her heart kicked up a notch. More bad news.

"My mother has asked me to marry again. She wants to see grandchildren before she dies. You'll be meeting someone who's very special to me."

CHAPTER FOUR

As THEY DROVE down the littered road, Anna clung to the handhold while Nico swerved to dodge branches, pieces of furniture and random objects. At times, he had to go off-road to bypass a section.

"This is what you call passable?"

He gave her a half smile and wiggled his brows. Despite herself, she smiled back. It was Nico's mischievous smile. Like the time he'd surprised her with their honeymoon. She'd thought they were going to Tahiti or Fiji. Instead, he'd driven her to a run-down house in Tumon Bay.

"What's this?"

"It's our new home."

She stared in horror. They had talked about buying a house so they wouldn't have to live in his family home, with his mother and the rest of his family constantly in their faces. Anna had pictured one of the cute cottages by the sea with a front porch they could sit on and enjoy breakfast as they watched the tide come in. While this house was on the sea, it looked like it would fall into it any second. The railings on the front porch were broken. A section of the roof had caved in. Trash littered the front and side yards. While she could hear the ocean, there was no sight of it. The whole thing looked like a crumbling heap that would collapse if she poked it with a finger.

"You bought this?"

He nodded and she turned to see his eyes shining, his mouth turned up in a brilliant smile.

"Now, I know what you're thinking. This place is a dump and if we combined our salaries, we could've had something much better. But I wanted to buy this for you, with my own money, and fix it up the way you want it."

Fix it up? This place needed to be bulldozed. Before she could say anything else, her feet left the ground as he lifted her. Automatically, her hands went around his neck so she could rest her face in the nook between his neck and shoulder. It was the best vantage point to breathe in the scent that was uniquely Nico. Earth, sweat and clean soap. Somehow the feel of his solid chest tempered her anger. It always did, and he knew it. He was still dressed in the cotton shirt and pants he'd worn to their wedding. She had chosen a plain white dress that fell to her ankles. Somehow a big wedding dress didn't appeal to her. They were married in the church where Nico had been christened, then had a luncheon at the golf course. Her sister Caro had come with her two-year-old toddler and the rest of the guests included nearly every person on the island. Nico and Nana were connected to everyone somehow, either by blood or friendship.

Stepping onto the rickety porch, he kicked open the door, which nearly fell off its hinges. The inside of the house was only marginally better than the outside. They entered through a foyer with peeling paint and years of grime and dirt on the hardwood floors. Miraculously, the stairs didn't crumble under their weight.

He toed open the door of a bedroom and set her down. Anna gasped. The room looked like it belonged to another house. There was a big wooden four-poster bed, complete with white gauzy drapes. It was covered in rose petals. A dark wood dresser held several candles, their flickering lights dancing along the mirror. The wide plank floors gleamed. Sky-lights let in the soft glow of the evening sun and big French doors led to a balcony.

Nico walked over and opened the doors. She followed him outside and gasped again. The balcony looked out to the calm waters of the bay and the waves of the Philippine Sea beyond.

"There is no other home on this island with this view. When we fix up the rest of this house, it'll look like this bedroom."

This was why she loved Nico. He dreamed of things she couldn't even imagine and made them happen. She turned and put her arms around him. "I love you, Nico, and I can't wait to make this our home and raise our children here."

He gave her that half smile and wiggled his brows as he carried her to the bed.

"Did our house in Tumon survive?"

While Nico had done most of the work to restore that house, Anna had put in her fair share of sweat equity. She remembered sitting with a toothbrush cleaning the grout in the kitchen floor, hauling trash to the industrial-sized bins in the yard, spending days scraping wallpaper off the walls and hand-cleaning inches of mud off the floors. It had taken them the better part of a year to make the house livable, and more often than not, she'd spent the time yelling at Nico for the slow pace with which things got done on the island. But when it was all finished, the house was even better than what she'd ever imagined. She'd been bounced from one rental to another as a child, and this was the first place that had felt like home.

He gripped the steering wheel. "I don't know."

"You weren't home when it happened?"

"I don't live there anymore."

Her stomach lurched. Had he sold their house? How could he? Even as the thought flew through her mind she realized how unreasonable she was being. She had left him, and their life. Why would he stay in their home? Of course he'd sold it.

"We still own the house, I didn't sell it, but I couldn't live there anymore."

His eyes were fixed on the road ahead. "I gave it to you in the divorce papers I had drawn up."

Pain ripped through her chest. How could she have forgotten about the asset division in the divorce settlement? While she had never been divorced herself, she had seen her mother through five of them, each one impossibly more contentious than the last. In the last one her mother had fought with her ex-husband for two months over a painting they had acquired during travels overseas. The painting wasn't worth as much as they each spent on lawyer fees.

"You bought the house, and it's probably worth ten times what you paid for it. You should keep it."

He shook his head. "I haven't been there since the day you left. Tito has been going once a month to do some basic upkeep. I paid the insurance, so any damage from the tsunami should be covered."

"What will I do with the house? I don't even live here. You should sell it." As she said the words, her breath stuck. The house was not a commodity; it wasn't a car or jewelry that you sold and split the proceeds, even though she knew that's what most divorced people did. The house had been home. Their home. One they built together.

Nico swerved hard to avoid an upturned car and Anna slammed into the side door. His jaw clenched. "The house is not for sale. If you don't want it, we'll figure out another solution."

Why did she feel relief? He was being totally unreasonable. Not that she wanted any
money from him, but if he wasn't going to
live there, he should sell it. The firm line
of his lips told her he was done with this
conversation. One of the many things about
him that irritated her. It wasn't that his mind
couldn't be changed. When they were married, a kiss in that crook between his neck
and shoulder or a nip on his earlobe melted
his resolve. Fights didn't last long. Until she
had Lucas.

After more than an hour of driving, he
pulled up to a white building. At least three
cars were on the roof and a good-sized yacht
was on its side on the front lawn.

"The building was in the direct path of the
tsunami. The roof will be an expensive repair." Nico's voice was grim, as if he was
surveying the damage anew.

The windows were blown out but the building seemed intact, which was far better than
what the other buildings in the area looked
like. Most of them were missing walls and
had roofs caved in.

"Will insurance cover it?"

He nodded. "They should, but they'll be

dragging their heels with all the claims that'll be hitting them."

They picked their way across the lawn. The revolving door at the hospital entrance had been blown out, so all that remained was a gaping hole. Still, Anna didn't miss the etched brass sign next to the door.

In memory of Lucas Michael Atao. The baby who remains in our hearts.
All are welcome, all will be served.
We save lives here.

Hand on her mouth, she staggered and gasped. He was right there as her knees buckled. She waited for the panic to hit but it didn't. All she felt was Nico's strong chest on her back, his arms holding her upright. It had been 1,923 days since he'd died. Yet the vise that gripped her heart was as strong as it had been the day it happened.

"I've never forgotten him, Anna, and I never will. Your sacrifice, and his, will not go in vain. Good will come from his death."

She couldn't talk about this. Nothing in the world could take away the hole in her soul. Not a new hospital, and definitely not Nico. Leaving his embrace, she steadied herself for what waited inside. Silently, he walked in first and she followed. Several people were in the lobby mopping and piling litter into large garbage bags. They waved to Nico and Anna, automatically greeting them with *"Hafa Adai!"*

She knew a few people, but not well. Some frowned, obviously trying to place her. She walked past them before recognition dawned.

Unfortunately, that luck didn't hold. "Anna, is that really you?" Before she could stop him, Nico's uncle Bruno enveloped her in his arms. Never mind that he hated her and they'd never gotten along. He greeted her like she was his long-lost daughter, kissing both cheeks and wiping tears from his eyes as he gushed over how good it was to see her back on Guam.

"Uncle, enough now. Mrs. DeSouza is critical—Anna needs to attend to her."

Bruno patted her on the shoulders. "It's so good to see you."

Anna shook her head as they walked away. "What's come over him?"

"Aunt Mae died last year and he's been going on these emotional extremes ever since."

Anna stopped. "Aunt Mae died? How?"

Anna had been quite fond of Bruno's wife, who had taken Anna under her wing and shown her how to fit in with Nico's family. She had taught Anna how to make Chamorro food and perform the rituals at church. Aunt Mae had even shown her what to plant in her garden to deal with the briny air. The woman was no spring chicken but she couldn't have been more than sixty.

"She had a heart attack." Nico's voice was matter-of-fact but Anna knew how much he too had cared for Aunt Mae. "I wrote you an email to let you know, but you never replied."

Anna had set her account so emails from Nico went to a special folder automatically. It was the only way to make sure she never saw his name in her in-box. After returning to California from Guam, she'd been sitting on a bus and checked her smartphone, mindlessly scrolling through emails. She'd read the email from Nico even before her brain had fully processed who the note was from. Crying uncontrollably for the rest of the bus ride, she had almost packed her bags when she got home. Luckily her brain kicked in. So she'd made sure she never accidentally read his emails again. Keeping him out of her mind was the key to her survival.

"I didn't see the email," she said sheepishly. "I'm sorry about Aunt Mae, she was a good woman. If we have time, I'd like to go to her grave and leave some flowers."

"She's buried near Lucas."

He might as well have dropped a boulder on her. Since the day she buried him, Anna had not seen her son's grave. On that horrid day, she'd buried a piece of her soul along with him, a part that she'd never get back. It was the same part that once loved Nico.

"What's this about Mrs. DeSouza?"

Nico got the hint and led the way. Anna noticed that though the hospital wasn't quite functional, the inner core was intact. It seemed the entire community was there fixing beds, rolling medical equipment, tending to sick patients. An old man bent low over a cane handed water to a young man who was sitting with a towel over his head. *We take care of each other. No one comes to help us, we only rely on each other.* Nico had explained this to her when they'd first met; it was what had first made her fall in love with Guam. She had traveled the world and seen a lot of close-knit communities, but never had she witnessed the kind of kinship that existed here.

Nico left her in what would eventually become the ICU. Right now, a generator was powering the few pieces of equipment that weren't waterlogged. A gap-toothed man sat at the nurses' station taking apart a defibrillator. Far from a sterile environment, but Anna was used to that now. In Liberia, she'd been lucky if there was a tent available to deal with a patient gushing blood. It was a minor miracle she hadn't gotten sick.

Mrs. DeSouza had suffered a stroke. Anna vaguely remembered her from community parties. If her memory served, Mrs. DeSouza had never been married, so she fostered little children. Teen pregnancy was common on the island and young mothers often needed child care while they studied for exams or took courses at Guam University. Anna did the best she could for the sick woman.

She moved on to the next patient on a bed, thankful she'd never seen him before. He was in better shape, though he'd obviously had a heart attack. Someone had used a defibrillator but he still had an arrhythmia. She administered some medication and hung an IV bag for a continuous drip. The man would need more invasive testing but he was fine for now.

Nico returned as she finished with her fifth

patient. "Mrs. DeSouza won't make it through the night," she said without preamble.

Pinching the bridge of his nose, he nodded. "Dr. Tucker said there were surgeons on the way."

Anna shook her head. For once it wasn't an issue of resources. "She's too far gone. It's time to say goodbye."

Nico nodded. "She has two teenagers she's been fostering for four years now. They're really close, I'll ask someone to go get them."

"The patients here are good for now. Where do you want me to go next?"

"We have some with burn injuries from fires that broke out." He grimaced as he said it, and Anna knew why.

She nodded. "Let's go. They are probably more critical than some of these cases."

He took her to another unit that was set up like a general hospital ward. Several individual rooms surrounded a nurses' station, where Nana sat. She stood and came to Anna. "I didn't get to properly greet you yesterday." Giving her a hug, she took Anna's hand and patted it. "Welcome home, my child. I am happy to see you are well."

Tears stung her eyes, but she blinked them away. She had never gotten along with Nana.

While Anna understood why some of the extended family took issue with the fact that she was white and not Chamorro, she didn't understand why Nana disliked her. Nico's father was white. He had been a marine stationed on Guam. Sometimes Anna wondered whether Nana had been taking out her husband's betrayal on Anna. Still, like Uncle Bruno, her smile held genuine warmth and her eyes welcomed Anna sincerely.

Nico motioned to the first door, but before he opened it, he paused. "Are you sure?"

"I'm a doctor—I've seen pretty horrific things."

He opened the door to a darkened room. The figure lying on the bed looked barely human; he'd been burned from head to toe. Anna slipped on gloves and a mask. Burn patients were highly susceptible to infection and she was glad that Nico had had the foresight to put the man in a relatively clean, secluded room. The patient was unconscious but breathing on his own, with a weak but steady heartbeat.

She examined his burns and determined that most of them were first degree with some second degree. The total mass of burns was concerning, so she dressed as many as she could, started an IV and gave him medication.

Each room held its own disturbing picture. Anna dealt with it the way she'd learned: one at a time. Compartmentalized. If she allowed herself to think of all the patients at once, she wouldn't be able to stand.

"How do you do this?" Nico was helping her with bandages. There was only one nurse at the hospital, and she was working on the less critical cases. No one else could stomach being in the rooms with the smells and sight of burnt flesh. They were on their third burn victim, who was also unconscious.

"I take it one patient at a time. I stay in the moment. My heart cried in the last room. I'm going to grieve for this one now because I don't think she'll make it."

"And when you walk out of the room, will you think about this?"

She shook her head. "I expend my emotions when I'm with the patient so when I leave, I have something left to give the next patient. I have to compartmentalize."

"How do you do that?"

"It's a learned skill. I've been working one disaster after another for the past five years. In Liberia, nearly all my patients died. My mentor there taught me how to be compassionate without losing myself."

"Is that what you did with me and Lucas? Compartmentalized us?"

Her head snapped up.

"Not a day has gone by when I haven't thought of Lucas."

"Then why haven't you been back?"

Because being here makes me want to bury myself with my son. She wished she could have left Lucas and Nico on Guam, but she carried them with her wherever she went.

She went back to bandaging the wound.

"I blame myself too. I blame myself for letting you do the surgery. Not because it didn't go well, but because I know you will never let go of the responsibility. I knew that when you made that first cut, that no matter what happened, you would never be the same."

"You would've let him die."

"Not because I wanted to, but because that was his fate."

Her hands were trembling too much to continue with bandaging. "It wasn't his fate. It was this island. If we were in California, he'd be getting ready to go to kindergarten."

"Sometimes, Anna, you have to accept what befalls you."

"And sometimes, Nico, you have to take control of your life and leave the man who refuses to do what's right for his family. You are not responsible for righting every wrong your father did."

They'd had this conversation before, said the same hurtful words to each other, and yet it seemed they couldn't stop. She took a deep breath and looked at her watch. Three hundred and seventeen hours before she could leave.

They finished attending to the rest of the patients in silence. She asked for a chart at the nursing station so she could document what she'd done. While the normally painstaking medical notation was often forgone in disasters, Anna wanted to leave a treatment plan for whichever nurse or physician came in next. The hospital had a working helipad, which meant rescue organizations might be able to transport patients off island to the Philippines or Hawaii for further care.

When Lucas had been diagnosed, the commercial airline pilots were on strike so there had been no outbound flights. They'd waited for a month but there was no sign of the strike resolving. That's when she'd begun researching other means of transport. With her mother's and sister's help, she'd cobbled together the money to hire a private helicopter. By then it had been too late. A storm system had come in, making helicopter flight impossible. Lucas had gotten worse and time ran out.

"You must be Anna."

She looked up to see a pretty young woman with dark hair and dark, luminous eyes.

"Have we met?"

The woman shook her long, lustrous hair. "I'm Maria."

The name was obviously supposed to mean something, but Anna couldn't place it. Then it hit her. Nico's new girlfriend. Her throat closed.

"You're Nico's…" She couldn't choke out the words.

Maria nodded. "Fiancée."

They're already engaged?

"Well, almost fiancée. We haven't made it official yet—he wanted to make sure things were squared away with the divorce."

Maria was sucking up all the air in the room. Anna looked around to see if there was anyone who could save her. A patient crisis, another tsunami, anything?

"I see you've met Maria." Nico appeared and put an arm around Maria. She smiled adoringly at him like he was her teenage crush. Then realization struck.

"Wait, are you the same Maria he went to high school with?"

They both nodded and Anna felt sick to her stomach. Nico's second cousin, who had also gone to the same school, had told her all about the girl Nico dated who had moved away in their junior year. While Nico had been nonchalant when he described the relationship, his cousin told her that Nico had long considered Maria to be the one that got away.

"My parents moved us to Hawaii when I was sixteen, but once I got my master's degree in administration, I decided to come home and work here."

"Maria is our hospital administrator. She came back to do some good for the island." The pride in Nico's voice made Anna feel like a three-year-old whose lollipop had been taken away. She wanted to hit the other woman. Of course Maria was his childhood love who had returned home to make the island a better place while Anna would continue to be the white woman who'd left her husband for her own selfish reasons.

Maria snuggled against his arm, then turned

to Anna. "I want to thank you for going to see Congresswoman Driscoll-Santiago."

Anna looked up in surprise. She didn't know anything had come of all the conversations she'd had with the congresswoman about supporting more medical infrastructure for the island.

Anna had met the congresswoman when she was Kat Driscoll, a professor who had recently discovered that she was the secret daughter of a powerful senator. At the time, Anna had set up a meeting with the senator's chief of staff, Alex Santiago, to make a plea for funding for Guam. Alex had rebuked her, but Kat, who was a silent witness to the meeting, had come up to her afterward to ask for more details.

Eventually, Kat had become a congresswoman—and married Alex. Kat's chief of staff was her half-sister, Vickie Roberts. Vickie was the one who often called Anna to get specific information about Guam on Kat's behalf.

"That's how we got this hospital built so fast and were able to buy state-of-the-art equipment. The congresswoman got us special federal funding. Ironically, it was disaster preparedness funds. She came here to tour the island last year and emphasized that you were the one who compelled her to do something."

"I didn't do much, I just brought the issue to her attention," Anna said shyly, thrilled that Kat had actually kept her promise. She made a mental note to send the congresswoman a thank-you note. Kat had invited Anna on that trip to Guam, and Anna had flatly refused, ending their conversation awkwardly. Since then, their relationship had cooled and Anna was afraid she'd offended the congresswoman.

Nico cleared his throat. "I've been meaning to thank you too, Anna. It escaped my mind with everything going on."

Maria slapped him playfully. "Nico, I can't believe you. It's the first thing you should have said when you showed her this building. I bet he went on and on about how he built this place with the best stuff and that's why it's still standing." She gave Anna a conspiring look. "Isn't that just like him?"

Anna's stomach churned. "I should check on the other patients."

"I'll take you to the next unit," Nico said quickly.

As Anna stepped out from the nursing station that had separated them, Maria came and gave her a hug. "I'm so glad to meet you. I know you've been a big part of Nico's life, so you will always have a place in my heart. Will you please let me make you dinner one night?"

Is she kidding? Who invites the not-so-ex-wife to dinner? Anna searched for malice in Maria's eyes but all she saw was an open invitation. Maria was exactly the kind of woman Nico should be marrying. She shared his generous heart and his Chamorro hospitality.

"Thanks for the offer, but I'll be leaving in thirteen days and there's a lot to do between now and then."

Maria began to protest but Nico gently dissuaded her and walked out with Anna. The tense silence stretched between them until Nico finally broke it.

"Our wedding date is set for one month from now. As soon as I can, I'll get you those divorce papers."

CHAPTER FIVE

JUST WHEN NICO thought the day couldn't get any worse, Uncle Bruno showed up. Nico had tried to keep the older man away from where Anna was tending to patients but once Bruno had seen her enter the hospital, the man was on a mission.

"You listen, boy, I don't want your head turned again. Maria is a good girl. Your mama only has a good year or two left in her. I don't want you wasting them chasing that woman again."

"Uncle B, less than an hour ago you were greeting her like she was your long-lost daughter."

"Of course. What do you want? I should be rude to her? She was family—technically still is since you're too much of a sissy to get the divorce done."

Nico pinched the bridge of his nose. He loved his maternal uncle but Bruno had become quite insufferable since Aunt Mae's death and his mother's diagnosis. Bruno's anxiety was easy to understand. Nico's mother had five siblings. One had died in a car crash and two others had moved away to the mainland. They came home once a decade. Most of their children had also moved away as well; Nico hadn't seen his cousins in more than twelve years. Bruno and Mae's two daughters were living in Oregon and Washington. While they came to visit their father once a year, both were increasingly "westernized," as Bruno called it. Nico knew that he was effectively Bruno's only family. He and Maria had talked about the fact that they might one day have to take care of Bruno when he became too old to live by himself. It was a conversation he could never have had with Anna.

"What do you want me to do? Wave a magic wand and get the internet working so I can get to my files? On a good day we don't have a reliable connection."

"You can build this whole hospital but you can't get the internet working?"

Nico sighed and threw up his hands. "Uncle B, I got work to do."

Bruno grabbed his arm. "Listen, Nico, I see the way you look at her and I understand it. It's how I felt about Mae. But Anna

SOPHIA SASSON   79

is going to break your heart again, just like
your father did to your mother. The white
folks never stay. They come here and see the
glittering shops and beach resorts and think
that's what life will be like for them. Then
they realize that us locals don't live like that."

How many times had Nico endured that
lecture? Everyone knew the tired old story of
how his father swept his mother off her feet,
married her with a promise to build a life
together, then abandoned her when she was
several months pregnant. Nico's father had
been a marine stationed on the island, and he
simply left when he was reassigned. Teresa
Atao hadn't even had a chance to change her
maiden name. Divorce papers were sent before Nico was born.

When Nico fell in love with Anna, the
family was up in arms, worried that history
would repeat itself. And it had. He knew that
Bruno and his mother were close, and her
pain over his father's betrayal anguished Bruno's heart, but the knowledge didn't make his
uncle any less difficult to deal with.

"I will get those papers signed. It's a good
thing she's here. She's met Maria, she knows
where things stand with me. Don't worry."

Bruno heaved a sigh of relief. "Good. I

don't want her destroying your happiness again."

"I won't." Anna's voice cut through the air like a machete.

He really should stop asking whether the day could get worse. Apparently, it was careening downhill. How long had she been standing there?

"How could you think I mean him harm? I will not stand in the way of his happiness."

Okay, so she'd heard the worst of it.

"Nico, if the internet is what you need, the field hospital has a satellite connection. I'll ask the clerk to help you when we get back. The sooner we get this over with, the better it will be for everybody." She looked pointedly at Bruno.

"Oh, Anna, don't be mad at me." Bruno gave her one of his cuddly, toothy smiles. "You're well aware this boy needs a kick in the pants to get something done. You are a lovely girl and will make someone a very good wife—"

"I'll make a white man a very good wife, right?"

Nico flinched at the hostility in her voice and noticed Bruno did too.

"Anna, Bruno is a *Chamorro-ist*, you know that."

Although she tried to hide it, he could see the hint of a smile on her face. It was a term she had come up with to describe his friends and relatives who constantly berated the non-Chamorro people of the island. They were the ones paranoid about their culture being washed away by the increasing presence of tourists and foreigners on the island.

"You two go ahead and make fun of this old man—my poor Mae is rolling in her grave seeing how you treat me these days."

Nico rolled his eyes and patted his uncle good-naturedly. Even Anna's face softened. He grabbed her elbow and led her away before the situation ignited again.

"Don't mind Uncle Bruno, you know how he is."

"It's not just him—your entire family always looked at me that way, like I would get up and leave any day. And I guess I did." Her voice was thick and a heavy sorrow weighed on his heart. He knew it hadn't been easy for her in the beginning, but they'd built a home together. With Aunt Mae's help, she had settled into his culture, and he thought she'd embraced it. Had she always felt like an outsider in his home?

"For what it's worth, that's not what I thought." He peered deep into her eyes. The previous anger was gone, replaced by desperation so intense, it touched his soul. His arms automatically lifted to pull her close to him, but he let them drop back to his sides. Maria had been very patient with him. It was time to move on with his life, give his family some closure too. They had moped with him for five years. Nana had consoled him when he'd cried for Lucas, encouraged him when it seemed the hospital would never get built. The entire community had rallied around him. Anna had left of her own volition, and she hadn't come back. She had never shared in his dreams.

"I have no intention of standing in the way of your happiness with Maria."

"I know that."

"I'll sign the papers. You can have anything you want—the house in Tumon…whatever. We'll get them printed and signed today so it's done."

The lady doth protest too much.

"You're right about the house. We should sell it and split the profits," he said.

Is it just me or does she look disappointed?

"You bought the house, you should get the money from it."

Why was she being so forceful? Was it that she wanted nothing to do with him and Guam? Including any money that came from the house they'd literally built together?

"How about we go to Tumon when that road gets cleared up and then decide how to split it. If the house is totaled, it'll be a check from the insurance company made out to both of us."

She seemed to consider his proposal, then nodded slowly. He released a breath he hadn't realized he was holding. The house was yet another item on his to-do list. After they were married, Maria was going to move into his mother's house with him, so they could take care of her. Bruno and Tito had kept up the house in Tumon ever since Anna's departure. Nico had been dreading making a decision on it. Maria had offered to go out there with him several times, but it didn't seem right to take her. He and Anna would know what to do. Together.

The next hour went by quickly as Anna dealt with the less seriously injured patients. Nico had never really seen her in action like this. He watched the way she took care of people, assuring them they would be okay while dealing with the most gut-wrenching injuries.

He was exhausted after seeing the burn patients, despite being the one who'd brought them in from the field and knowing what to expect. Anna had walked in cold and not once had he seen her recoil like the tough-as-nails men who had carried the victims to the hospital. Anna always had been bullet-proof. One of the many reasons he'd fallen for her. Without question, she was the great love of his life, the kind the legends talked about. Most people never felt this kind of love, and he considered himself lucky to have had it. But now it was time to be a re-sponsible man and take care of his family; a family Anna didn't want to be a part of.

"Do you have your mother's chart handy? I can review it."

He hadn't asked, but of course she'd of-fered. Pointing to a computer terminal, he led her there. "Maria insisted that we have our electronic medical records that are backed up on servers in a fire- and waterproof room in addition to off-site data storage. We were able to restart our servers and find a machine that hasn't been damaged. I'll have a clerk type in all the handwritten notes you've left on the patients."

Her eyes widened in surprise and his chest bloomed with pride. For their entire marriage, she had been the more accomplished one; she was more educated, made a better salary, had more prospects than he did. She never let him feel it, but it was always there. He hadn't left the island to go to college. His degree in architecture meant a lot to him, but it wasn't from a prestigious university like hers. And it was just a bachelor's degree. He'd never earn as much money as she did. This hospital was his legacy, and he wanted her to be proud of it. That was why he'd begged Linda Tucker to send Anna with him today. He knew she would never have come of her own volition.

"Wow! There are clinics Stateside that still don't have electronic health records. How did you manage that?"

Smiling, he pointed to the computer and logged in. "The people in Washington, DC, have no idea how efficient we can be with money when we want to. The grant they gave us covered the EHRs, too. Instead of buying one of those expensive ones the companies sell, my friend George designed this database. The man went to MIT. He's settled in Boston now, but when I called him up to do us a favor, he flew over for two weeks, figured out the specs and then did his computer magic. We had the servers and computers shipped from Japan."

She nodded. "I always knew you could do anything you wanted. You've accomplished more here in a few years than people do in generations."

"It wasn't all just me. I hired Maria two years ago and she's been here right alongside me. She helped write the grant that let us build the hospital."

Anna turned toward the computer and tapped some keys, but not before he caught the pain in her eyes. Taking credit for everything was easy, but not truthful. He knew how to construct a building but he knew nothing about what it took to run a hospital—Maria had done all that. She had been his partner in every way; his dreams had become her goals. Being with Anna made him forget that, and he wanted to make sure he reminded himself. He owed Maria.

He pointed to various features of the EHR as Anna navigated his mother's chart.

"Looks like she has stage 3 breast cancer. That's serious, but not fatal. She hasn't seen a breast surgeon, which is what I'd recommend. They may suggest surgery or send her to a radiation oncologist. I know some good people in California if you fly her over."

Nico shook his head. "She doesn't want to leave the island."

Anna gaped at him. "Are you crazy? This is her life we're talking about. She doesn't have to move there forever, just for treatment. There are even some medical assistance programs if you can't afford the treatment."

He bristled. "It's not the money. This island has been her whole life—she wants to die here surrounded by family, in her home. She doesn't want to live out her last days thousands of miles away in a sterile hospital."

"But she doesn't have to die! The five-year survival rates are pretty good. Treatment means more years of life for her…"

"Yes, but at what cost? Being sick all the time, lying in a bed? She wants to enjoy her last days and go out as the vibrant woman she is. That's how she wants to be remembered, not as a sick old lady."

Her wide eyes and slight pout told him that she not only disagreed, but wanted to dig her heels in and make him see things her way. And he wanted nothing more than to pick her up and kiss the pout right off her face.

"It's okay, Anna, I appreciate what you're saying, but you know it's not the way we do things here. My mother wants to die with dignity. She doesn't want to linger on and be a burden to her family."

"As a doctor, it's my job to save people, and your mother is by no means terminal. If you want to be obstinate, fine. There's only so much I can do."

"It's not your place to say how I should or should not live my life."

Nico turned to see his mother standing there and groaned. Why couldn't he catch a break? First Uncle Bruno and now his mother. The look in her eyes told him he was in for a long lecture. Approaching her, he spoke softly in Chamorro. "Nana, Anna is trying to help. Please don't start something. We don't have to listen to her."

"You do know I speak Chamorro, and my hearing is perfect." Anna's tone reminded him of the time he'd taken her to see the Fish Eye Marine Park and she'd been asked to pay the tourist fee, which was twice as much as the residents' ticket price. She had planted her feet and given the baby-faced teenager working the counter an earful about how she was just as much a resident as Nico. The poor kid probably hadn't received that kind of scolding since he was a toddler.

He gave her an exasperated look, remembering why they'd had to buy the house in Tumon Bay to begin with. For some reason, Anna and his mother just rubbed each other the wrong way and he always had the misfortune of being caught in the middle.

Anna stepped up to his mother, and short of physically separating them, Nico realized he wasn't going to avoid an argument today.

"Nana, I understand that you want to die at home, I respect that. But you don't have to die at all. Women survive breast cancer and go on to have happy, healthy, productive lives. You can see your grandchildren grow up. Surely that's worth the sacrifice of getting treatment."

She'd called his mother Nana. That's what Anna had always called her. When he'd first introduced the two women, Anna had insisted on calling her Mrs. Atao. That had changed when they got engaged, but it warmed his soul to know she still thought of his mother as Nana.

"Child, when you're my age, you'll see that life is about quality rather than quantity. It's time for me to go. You mainland people fight to the end, painfully eking out every breath. That's not how we do it here."

He watched Anna blow out a frustrated breath. She didn't understand; never had.

"Thank you for looking at her chart," Nico said. "Let me drive you back."

She blinked up at him, then shuffled her feet. "Is there someone else who can give me a ride?"

It was just as well. They'd just fight all the way back, and it wasn't worth it anymore. "I'll arrange it."

CHAPTER SIX

"Is she gone?"

Nico didn't have to ask Maria who she meant. Even in a disaster with the phone lines and internet down, Nana had managed to inform the entire island that Anna was back. Everyone who had ever known or met Anna had stopped by or told a friend to go talk to Maria to rehash what they'd heard and to give her unsolicited advice. So, his normally level-headed Maria had become a little paranoid about what Anna's arrival meant.

"Yes, *neni*, I asked Lenny to drive her back to the field hospital."

He was sitting in the office he and Maria shared. Eventually it would be her office as the hospital administrator and he would only come to the hospital as needed. He didn't know anything about running a hospital, but he knew how to get a building built, how to get supplies on and off the island. When he met Anna, he'd been working for a retailer who was putting up new shopping centers to cater to the hordes of Japanese and Korean tourists who flocked to Guam on holiday. Putting up the hospital had taken every ounce of his focus and effort for the past four years; he hadn't thoroughly considered what he would do once it was fully operational in three months. As majority shareholder, he would be running the hospital's board of directors, but was that enough for the rest of his life? He'd been so focused on getting the hospital built that he hadn't contemplated long-term plans. The hospital was his way of getting closure for Lucas's death. A few months ago, when the building had passed inspection, he'd known that he'd finally paid the penance for letting down his family.

"She's not what I expected." Maria had set up this office so their desks were back to back; she wanted them to face each other while they worked. She continued to tap away on her keyboard.

"Out with it, Maria, whatever it is."

She looked up at him through hooded lashes, her dark eyes thoughtful. "First of all, you said she was beautiful." This was what he loved about her. There were no games, no innuendoes or interpretation required. She didn't hide her feelings. If she didn't like something, she let him know in fierce terms, if she was upset with him, he knew exactly why. An open book.

"I was honest with you."

"Beautiful is what I am. Easy on the eyes, considered desirable by most men. Anna? Anna is gorgeous. She's the kind of woman men fantasize about, pin up on locker walls. You could've warned me—I would have put on some makeup, maybe gone to Gina's salon for the tsunami special highlights."

"Maria!"

"I'm not fishing for a compliment. I just don't want you to embarrass yourself in front of her. There were all these drool stains all over your mouth." She made a big show of wiping her own chin.

He rolled his eyes and stood. Maria didn't want a compliment, but she was getting ready to drop something heavy on him. It was her style, to make him smile or slap his forehead before she got to the heart of the matter. He went to her side and she turned her face so he could drop a kiss on her cheek. "So you gonna tell me what's really bothering you?"

"She's still in love with you."

"Maria."

"Trust me, a woman can tell these things. She might be angry, and still hurting, and maybe she doesn't know it, but the look on her face when she saw me..." Maria twisted her own face "...and when she saw you come and put your arm around me. It was as if she was a drowning woman and I had just taken away her life vest. I can't explain it, just a feeling—" she tapped her chest "—I got in here. The look in her eyes was so... I can't even describe it."

Maria didn't need to say more. Nico knew exactly what she meant. It was the bitter sadness in Anna's eyes. It had wrenched his soul when he'd seen it in the field hospital. It was what had made him work all night with the tractor to clear the road so he had an excuse to bring her to the hospital, hoping she'd find some comfort in it like he had.

"She's still not over Lucas's death. Anna's a stubborn woman and she won't stop blaming herself. Until she does, she can't grieve for him."

Maria shook her head. "I don't think that's it."

"You know this how?"

"She regrets leaving you, Nico. I know it, I could see it in her eyes when she looked at you."

"You're reading too much into things. She's already agreed to sign the divorce papers."

"And have you given them to her?"

He stepped away. "How? The only printout I had is under a foot of water. And unless you've been hiding an internet connection somewhere, I can't pull it from my backup files."

Maria sighed in frustration. "There has to be someone on this island who has managed to get a satellite connection working."

There was. But he wasn't going to mention it to her.

"I'll get hold of my cousin Bitsy at the Maestro Hotel—I bet they have internet." Internet connectivity was an ongoing problem on Guam. The hotels seemed to have better luck using satellite services, so that's what Nico had installed in the hospital. But the dish had been damaged in the disaster.

"Don't worry—she's here for a few more days. I'll get the papers signed."

Maria raised one brow. "You sure you haven't changed your mind after seeing her? My booty's never going to be as skinny as hers."

He laughed and gave her another kiss. "I like you just the way you are, Maria. You're nothing like Anna, and I don't want you to be." And that was the truth. Nobody could replace Anna, and he didn't want Maria to be a stand-in. He planned to love Maria the way she deserved to be loved; for the wonderful woman that she was.

"Okay, then, I have some good news."

He went back to his desk and started his computer. Though the internet wasn't working, he needed to work on his spreadsheets to record and calculate the damages he'd need to submit to the insurance company. He also needed to figure out how long their opening would be delayed.

"The governor stopped by while you were out getting Anna. That's what I came to the burn unit to tell you, but then I thought I'd wait until you could focus."

He sat up. The governor was newly elected and was not well-known to the Atao family. They had gotten lucky with the previous governor because he happened to be a good friend of Uncle Bruno's and had helped them get the necessary permits and permissions for the hospital. Having the permit in place was what had clinched the grant money. Nico had been meaning to make friends with the new *maga'låhi* and get into his good graces.

So much on Guam happened because of who you knew and hadn't angered.

"Apparently Guam Hospital is beyond repair. The building will have to be torn down. There's an uproar in the community because a lot of their patients died when part of the building collapsed, not because of the actual tsunami."

"You call this good news?" Nico had been so focused on helping people near his home base of Talofofo that he hadn't really kept up with what was happening on the other side of the island. He knew Guam hospital wasn't operational; that was why he had opened up his building and hurriedly set up whatever equipment was still functioning with Dr. Balachandra's help.

"We need a hospital on the island, especially now, and the governor wants it to be this hospital. He wants to cut a deal with us— funding, staff and any equipment that can be salvaged from the other hospital."

Maria's eyes were alight with excitement but Nico's head was starting to throb. "Let me guess, he needs us to go operational now."

She nodded. "That's the downside. But we're so close. Hiring staff was the major problem, so if we get all of the old hospital staff, things can happen quickly."

"Maria, we don't have a chief medical officer. I don't want to put Dr. Gejan in charge here." Dr. Gejan had been the CMO at Guam Hospital for almost two decades. He had done nothing to progress medical care in Guam. Nico's vision was to bring in someone who would make sure the hospital could provide care that was equivalent to, or better than, what folks received on the mainland. Maria had put an advertisement in the major medical journals and they had two candidates they were interviewing in the next month. The CMO was the linchpin who would attract other medical specialists to rotate through the hospital. He didn't want the same old staff and the same old substandard hospital.

She bit her lip. "Could we use one of the other doctors on a temporary basis?" Nico couldn't think of anyone who was qualified. "Let me talk to Domingo and see if he thinks there's anyone good enough over there." Domingo was Nico's neighbor and had worked as a billing clerk at the hospital for nearly twenty years. Not only did he know everyone there, he had a beat on every nurse and doctor in the hospital. When they came to settle their bills, patients talked to him about the quality of the care they'd received.

"I told the governor we'll come see him tomorrow morning."

"Maria, that's not enough time." He tamped down his irritation. Maria was good at what she did, but she should have consulted him before agreeing to a meet. She still operated like a stateside girl sometimes, assuming that everything worked according to rules. That wasn't how Guam operated.

"It's just to talk generally about how this would work. How much funding he can give us, what we need—that kind of thing." She gave an exasperated sigh. "Look around, Nico. We're already functioning as a hospital. I don't even want to think about what will happen if someone sues us—we don't have our malpractice insurance squared away. Being officially designated by the government will give us some protection."

He wasn't worried about those things. People wouldn't sue him. Not for taking care of them when there was no other option on the island. "I don't want to go into that kind of meeting with back-of-the-envelope calculations. He'll ask us how much we want and hold us to the numbers we quote him. We need time to put together cost projections, timelines—"

"Nico! Come on! We're the only hospital around. People need a place to go. We get this done, one way or another. That's why you built this place."

He took a deep breath. She was right, that was exactly why he'd built the hospital, and even if the governor offered them nothing, Nico would still open the door—not that there was one right now—and make sure people got care. This was why Maria was good for him. She reminded him of his mission, kept him on track so he didn't let the details take away from the big picture.

"I don't want to take the staff wholesale from the other hospital. I want good people. See if you can get hold of those candidates we want to interview for the CMO position. Maybe we can move up the interviews, bring them in to run the hospital for a week and see how they do."

She slapped a hand on the desk. "Now, that's the spirit. If they can run this place in the middle of this chaos, they can do the job. But, my darling, where am I going to find a working phone?"

He grinned. "Do I have to solve all your

problems? Talk to Bruno. He knows someone who works at the utilities—they'll know
who has a working phone."

As he went back to his spreadsheets, a
fleeting thought took hold in his mind. There
was one person who would make the perfect
CMO for the hospital. He shook his head. It
would be playing with fire.

CHAPTER SEVEN

NICO HADN'T SHOWN up for three days. She should be relieved. Apparently, local nurses and doctors from Guam Hospital had taken over the care of patients at Nico's Talofofo facility since the regular hospital had collapsed. The airport had been cleared and more help was arriving daily, so Anna had the opportunity to get a rare eight hours of rest. Given the grueling hours of the past several days, she should be exhausted and ready to drop, but she couldn't even bring herself to lie down. Two hundred and ninety-seven hours before her deployment ended. She was buzzing with energy, and she knew why. She had to get closure. There was no other way.

Grabbing her duffel, she changed her shoes and clothes and set out. The locals were reporting that roads were still bad, but four-wheel drive vehicles could take detours across unpaved land, which meant she could definitely walk it. Congresswoman Driscoll-Santiago's office had called the camp to say she was lobbying for more disaster relief funds and planning to visit as soon as there was a seat available. With only one runway working at the airport, a limited number of flights could land. The congresswoman had enough sense to know that if she took a seat, that meant one less relief worker got to the island. Not all politicians had that understanding. Anna was grateful that she'd listened to her sister and gotten an appointment that led to her meeting the congresswoman—though at the time she'd just been Kat, the senator's daughter.

She checked out at the front desk so they'd know she wasn't on base. The clerk issued her a sat phone in case they needed to reach her.

As she began her hike, Anna's thoughts drifted back to Nico. Didn't he need divorce papers signed? Obviously he was in a rush to move on with his life, get married and start a family. What if she decided to leave early? He didn't know how her deployment worked. She had checked with the front desk and he hadn't called for her. Some of the locals who she'd known while she lived here had asked for her when they showed up to get their injuries tended to, but none of them had any news about him. They wanted to know more about why she was back and whether she still had feelings for Nico. How was she supposed to answer that? She had simply told them she and Nico were getting divorced.

She picked her way across the rough terrain using a compass and her memories as a guide. No telling what she would find, but one thing was certain, she couldn't leave Guam without facing her demons. The nightmare had come every night she'd been here and she was not going to live with that for the rest of her life. Nico was moving on, and it was time she did too.

By her calculations, it was a 2.6-mile hike. Doubling the time it would normally take her, she should've been there in a little over an hour. But she had underestimated the amount of detours she would have to take to avoid having to climb over fallen trees or blocks of concrete.

It took her well over two hours to make it to the cemetery. The energy she had when she'd left base camp was long gone, replaced with a weariness that made her legs leaden. Surprisingly, the cemetery was intact. Even Mother Nature had held back out of respect for the dead. There was some debris and a few fallen headstones, but none of the devastation she had just picked her way through to get here. Lucas's grave site was burned into her memory like an iron brand. It was slightly downhill from where she stood.

There wasn't much she could recall from that day. It was all a nightmarish blur. But in that fog, there was one image that played in her mind like a never-ending movie.

The funeral home didn't have any coffins that tiny, so Lucas was being buried with all of his stuffed animals and hand-knitted blankets. And then she remembered. How could she have forgotten?

"Stop!"

The priest looked at her in alarm. Nico tightened his arm around her but she pushed him away. They'd been about to lower the coffin, but she couldn't let them.

"I need to see him, he doesn't go to sleep without it!"

Nico held on tighter, but some unknown strength gave her the power to push away from him and fly to Lucas's side. The coffin was latched and there was a collective gasp from the crowd as she fumbled with the locks, trying to open the lid.

"Help me!"

No one moved. They all stood frozen, unwilling to help but too scared to stop her. She took a breath and focused, willing all her attention on working the locks. She managed to get two undone which opened the top half of the coffin. It was enough. She could see his face and most of his body. He was surrounded by all the things that had belonged to him in his little life. Nico's hands were on her shoulders.

"Anna, we have to let him go."

She slapped him away, then bent down and kissed her boy. He was so small. His body so cold and stiff. She blew softly on his face. "Night night, little baby, close your eyes..." Her throat closed so tightly, the next words wouldn't come out of her mouth. Nico gently lifted her from the waist. All she saw was a pair of hands closing the coffin door.

"But I haven't finished the song. He doesn't go to sleep until he hears the full song." The words were in her head but her voice box wouldn't work. She screamed silently as they lowered the coffin.

She made her way to his gravestone. It was

chipped and had an entire corner missing, but his name was clear. The ground was muddy as she sank to her knees, and it didn't take long for the dampness to seep through her jeans. But she didn't notice.

"Night night, little baby, close your eyes. Night night, little baby, no more cries. Sleep little baby, your mama's always near. Even if she's not right here."

This time the words came. The song flowed out of her and she sang it over and over, touching the earth like she was caressing his head. Over and over. She had no idea how much time passed or what was happening around her. She was back in her home in Tumon, with her baby in her arms, singing to him, lulling him to sleep. His fine hair felt silky beneath her fingers, his skin smooth and soft. Why did people say babies smelled good? Hers smelled of spoiled milk, but she didn't care. She loved that smell. Lucas moved in her arms, and she enjoyed the sensation of his little kicks.

It was her happy moment, when all was well. Before their world had turned upside down. She lay on top of the grave. Eyes closed, she stayed at the house in Tumon.

It had been a while since she'd been able to go back to that house and she didn't want to leave. She was going to stay with Lucas.

"WHAT DO YOU mean you can't reach her?" Nico glared at the desk clerk at Anna's field hospital.

"She's not answering her sat phone."

"How long has it been?"

"Five hours, give or take."

Nico swore under his breath. He'd come to the field hospital to talk to Anna and print divorce papers. His entire family was riled up, and the only way to calm them down was to show them signed papers. They were all convinced he was still hung up on Anna. They didn't understand that he wasn't going to forget her, or stop loving her. But he wasn't going to let those feelings stop him from moving on with his life. Even the tsunami wasn't enough of a distraction for his meddlesome family.

A broadcast had come over the emergency radio system that another storm was expected. Everyone was bracing. He'd left Maria in charge of making sure all the broken windows at the hospital were boarded. They'd already been well on their way to completing that task before the latest forecast. The windows would take months to replace since they had to be ordered from the Philippines. The governor had begged for help; Guam Hospital was so badly damaged, the building was condemned. The only medical care available—besides what little they could offer at Nico's hospital—was at two field hospitals, the one Anna was in and another set up by a relief organization. Those field hospitals were being moved to the school and a mall, but they could only do so much in temporary locations. And once the disaster relief efforts were over, there would be nothing on the island unless they got the Talofofo hospital up and running.

Nico had gone into the meeting prepared to say no. He'd done the numbers and the timeline just didn't work, but Maria had been right. It was the whole reason their hospital had been built. He had made a special request of the governor and had just gotten word that the man had managed to keep his end of the bargain. Nico had come here to talk to Anna about the divorce and his idea for the hospital, only to find that she was gone. Five hours wasn't a long time. There was no cause to worry. Except something in the pit of his stomach churned with such intensity that he couldn't ignore it.

"What's the storm update?"

"It's now a Category 5 hurricane. Models predict it'll hit in four hours. We're taking down our tents now and moving to the school. The hospital will have to continue there."

Nico nodded. His hospital was also being used as a shelter given that it had withstood the tsunami. With all the debris lying on the road, it wasn't safe to be outside. The hurricane-force winds would blow things everywhere.

"Can you try her one more time?"

The clerk sighed dramatically but picked up the phone and made a show of holding the receiver so Nico could hear the never-ending rings on the other end.

He had promised Maria he would be back before the hurricane came. While such storms were not rare on Guam, the damage from the tsunami would complicate things. Even buildings that were in good shape would topple. The hospital was filling up with people coming for shelter. Nico had built it to the highest possible standards, but he had no idea whether the tsunami had damaged any critical structural components. He hadn't had time to get an engineer to check the foundation. Nico needed to be there in case something went wrong. It was his hospital and he was responsible for the people inside it. Anna was a grown woman; she could take care of herself. She was no longer his problem.

He walked to his truck and slammed his hand on the steering wheel. There were only two places she would go. Nico was pretty sure he knew which one she'd chosen.

It was raining by the time Nico parked the car in a grassy knoll, away from any trees or other buildings. He'd have to walk the rest of the way. Picking up his emergency backpack, he began the trek. Normally he could run half a mile pretty fast, but the winds were starting to pick up and he had to dodge random items as they flew at him. Despite the cold air, sweat beaded on his forehead. What was she thinking, walking in these conditions? She could be lying injured anywhere between here and the field hospital. He'd kept his eye out during the drive, but she would've taken a different path if she was on foot. Time had obviously not softened her stubbornness.

Rain pelted his face, but he forged forward. He should've brought her here. They should have come together. It had been three months since he had visited Lucas's grave. He used to come every Sunday after church; sitting with Lucas brought him peace. But, as time went on, his visits seemed more hollow. Memories of Lucas had faded and all that remained were regrets related to Anna. The cemetery sloped downward into a valley, so he went to the highest vantage point first. It didn't take long to see her collapsed on Lucas's grave. Heart pounding in his ears, he raced toward her, almost falling several times as he tripped over debris.

"Anna!"

She didn't respond. His legs moved with such force that he got to her in no time. Lying sideways, her body was covered with mud and water. He lifted her shoulders, placing her pale face in his lap. He put his ear to her nose and nearly collapsed with relief. She was breathing, her pulse weak but there.

"Anna, wake up. Anna!" She stirred but her eyes remained closed. A gust of wind blew a tree branch in their direction and he lifted his arm to deflect the blow. He had to get them to shelter. It was too late to try and get to the hospital. The storm must be coming earlier than predicted. Lifting her, he draped her over his shoulder in a fireman's carry, grateful for his days as a volunteer firefighter. There was a stone church nearby. The building wasn't a designated shelter, but it had stood on the island for hundreds of years, so Nico hoped it could survive one more day.

The wind and rain slapped against him, making it harder to walk. Random litter swirled around his legs and every once in a while something came hurtling at him. It was like walking through a video game where projectiles were being thrown at you, any one of them capable of delivering a fatal blow. He protected Anna as best he could with his arms. The church was only a quarter mile away, but it might as well have been twenty miles. It was late afternoon, yet the sky was dark with thunderous clouds. Sparks of lightning lit the deserted streets in ominous flashes.

They were almost at the church when a jagged piece of metal flew right at him. Nico stepped sideways to avoid it but a gust of wind pushed him back. He rotated so the shard would miss Anna and it caught him in the side. The wound Anna had stitched a few nights before burst open, sending a sharp pain through his belly. There was nothing in front of him but darkness; his legs threatened to give out underneath him and he wanted nothing more than to collapse right where he was.

Then Anna stirred. He felt her move and his vision cleared. The church was less than half a block away. Summoning a strength he didn't think he had, he pushed through the wind and up the stone stairs. The metal door leading into the church was locked. He set Anna down and lifted the heavy iron knocker, letting it fall back on the door. No one used that anymore but it had the intended effect. The loud bang could be heard above the wind and thunder. His arms were killing him, but he lifted the knocker one more time and then another. Finally, the door opened.

"Pale'!" Nico's knees almost buckled with relief. While he and his family belonged to a different church, the priest knew Nico and urged him in. Anna's eyes were open and she stared, bewildered, as he helped her to her feet and half carried her inside. The priest shut the door behind them.

"Nico, my son, what are you doing out in this weather?"

Nico didn't have the strength to explain, he simply nodded toward Anna and the priest understood. He led them down a set of stairs.

Nico hadn't been inside this church before but couldn't focus enough to see anything other than the priest's flashlight beam.

"This is a room we use for visiting guests." The priest turned on the overhead light, a naked bulb hanging from the ceiling which illuminated the stone-walled room with a bed and nightstand.

"There's some firewood, starters and matches on the hearth. I recommend you start a fire—it gets really cold down here. I'll go see if we have anything left in the kitchen."

Nico let Anna sit on the bed and realized she was shivering. Her clothes were soaking wet and so were his. There was a thin blanket on the bed, so he wrapped that around her, then went to the fireplace. Shrugging off his wet jacket, he began stacking wood and kindling. His own hands were trembling. Whether it was from the cold or the red-hot pain burning through his body, he wasn't sure.

"You…you…you're bleeding." Anna's voice was so tiny, he wasn't quite sure she had said the words. He looked down but didn't see anything. He was soaked from the rain. Ignoring her, he stacked the logs as best he could, then lit the newspaper and kindling with a match. It didn't take. The room was drafty, the wind seeping in from the chimney. He tried again and this time the newspaper caught and the kindling with it.

"Ah, good." The priest had returned. "I see you've got the fire going. I don't have much in terms of clothes, but I found a bag in the donation pile. Hopefully something will work for you."

Nico made a mental note to say his prayers tonight.

"The kitchen is a little bare—you'll have to make do with bread and peanut butter."

"Thank you, Pale', this is more than I could ask for. Do you need help with anything?"

The older man shook his head. "This building has survived much worse, my son. I've been helping my congregation deal with everything that's happened. I'm going to go pray that everyone remains safe tonight." With a weary sigh, he handed Nico a flashlight and headed for the stairs. "You can find me in the rectory if you need me."

The logs had caught fire, bathing the room in a soft, orange glow. Anna was staring at him, her gaze a thousand miles away. He unwrapped the blanket to find that she was stone-cold. Her lips were a strange purple.

She'd stopped shivering. He helped her to the fire and sat her down. Turning her toward the flames, he lifted the edge of her top and pulled it over her head. She was still his wife, yet he kept his gaze focused on the hearth. There were no towels so he used the top sheet of the bed to dry her off as best he could, then pulled a sweater over her head.

"I'm okay," she whispered through chattering teeth. Breathing a sigh of relief, he handed her a pair of pants that looked like the only thing small enough to fit her and told her to get out of her wet jeans. She didn't move but he retreated to a dark corner and stripped his own clothes. The room was starting to spin around him. He managed to pull on a pair of sweats, but as he took off his shirt, he noticed it was sticky. Looking down, he saw that not only had the earlier gash come apart, he'd been newly cut by that jagged piece of metal. He took a spare T-shirt and wiped the wound as best he could, wincing as more waves of pain ripped through his body.

"You're hurt." He hadn't noticed Anna stand. She was wearing the pants he'd given her and looked remarkably better. Before he knew it, she was peering at his wound and directing him to lie down on the bed. She took a corner of the bedsheet and ripped it, then used it to bandage the wound tightly.

"You're going to need stitches. Stay here and I'll go to the hospital and bring them back."

What?

"Anna, are you crazy? There's a hurricane outside. I barely got us here."

For the first time, she seemed to consider her surroundings. The stone room was eerily quiet, buried in the ground with no windows. The only noise came from the crackling fire and the occasional draft of wind that made it down the chimney and blew sparks from the hearth.

"Where are we?"

"We're in that old stone church off Chalan Road."

"How did we get here? Why are we here?" Her eyes were wide with confusion, and he could see her trying to shake the cobwebs loose in her mind. His own focus was fading as the exhaustion of the day wore him down and the soft pillow beneath his head teased him with the promise of sleep. Grunting in pain, he sat up.

"Anna, do you remember where you went when you left the field hospital?"

Realization dawned and she sprang to her feet. "I went to Lucas's grave."

He nodded. "We tried to reach you on the sat phone but you didn't answer, so I got worried and came after you. There's a hurricane going on outside—I needed to get you to safety. You passed out there."

"I…" She stopped herself from saying the words that were on her lips.

Despite everything, he was glad she'd gone to Lucas's grave. She so desperately needed closure on his death, but it was clear she hadn't found it. Her eyes still held the haunted look of a woman struggling with ghosts of the past. He fought to squeeze air into his chest. How was he going to help her heal?

"I must've dropped my backpack with the sat phone. Do you have any emergency supplies?" He pointed to his own bag and she rummaged through it, coming up with a handful of pills and a water bottle. "A thousand milligrams of ibuprofen. It'll take the edge off the pain."

He took the pills, grateful he'd had the foresight to bring his waterproof backpack.

"Hand me the radio." The battery-operated device turned on fine, but there was no signal.

"I guess we're stuck in this dungeon until

the storm passes." Not that it was a horrible prospect. This might be the last time he'd get to have Anna to himself. "Let's just hope there aren't any dragons."

"Just those we brought with us," she said wistfully.

Then the lights went out.

CHAPTER EIGHT

THERE WAS A time warp in her head that Anna just couldn't shake. Staring at Nico in the soft glow of firelight took her back to the house in Tumon Bay. Before Lucas was born, around the time she'd gotten pregnant. A storm had raged outside their house and they both anxiously waited to see if the newly installed roof would hold.

"I bet you two kids that it holds," Nico said confidently.

"I see your two kids and raise you one more that there's at least one leak."

He stuck out his hand. "Deal."

She gave him her hand and he pulled her onto his lap. They were on their living room couch, firelight playing on the walls. The electricity had gone out hours ago but it didn't bother them. They were used to it. The old house had exposed power lines. Next on the never-ending home repair list was a generator.

"I think I'll miss it being just us. Are you sure you don't want to wait another year?"

She shook her head. "I want at least three kids, and it's medically optimal to have them three years apart. There's not a lot longer I can wait."

A bolt of lightning illuminated the entire house, then a new torrent of rain pounded on the roof. She snuggled into his chest and he wasted no time in taking advantage of the situation. Cupping her face in his hands he kissed her softly on the mouth, then worked his way down her jawline and to her neck. "Just promise me one thing."

"Hmm..." She couldn't think when he nipped her neck like that. Her brain became totally fuzzy. They'd been married for almost two years and yet every time he kissed her, butterflies danced in her stomach the way they had the very first time.

He lifted his mouth and she opened her eyes to look into his dark brown ones. "Promise me that when we have children, we'll still be us."

"Why wouldn't we be?"

"Just promise me that you'll still love me, no matter what."

It was such a silly thing to say. She had

always wanted children, but no child would ever take away the love she felt in her heart for Nico. He was her soul mate, her other half. "Of course I will. Nothing will ever take away the love I have for you."

He hadn't changed in the six years since that night. A man used to physical labor, he kept his body in shape. Any other man would've passed out from the pain of that gash. She ran her hand gently over his stomach the way she used to, feeling hard muscle beneath her fingertips.

"Why did you come for me?" Her voice was thick.

The glow from the fire danced around his face like it had that night in Tumon. Except now his dark eyes stared at her with such intensity, her heart shattered like a fine china glass dropped on the concrete floor.

He pushed himself up, placed his hand behind her head and brought his mouth down on hers. The moment their lips touched, time melted away. Her arms went around his neck, and she pulled herself closer to him, needing to feel his heartbeat. She felt a small tug of guilt inside her; he was with Maria now. But then every rational thought flew out of her mind and all she wanted, more than anything in the world, was to feel the warm glow of his love in her heart. She needed a salve to bandage the wounds that were killing her from the inside. And that's exactly what he did. He drew her closer and breathed new life into her. His kiss was so tender and at the same time so intense, she was reminded of the power of his love. How it had once made her feel cherished and whole. When she left Guam, she'd left her soul with Lucas, but she'd left her heart with Nico.

When their lips disconnected, he kissed her cheeks and then her eyes. She hadn't realized she was crying but tasted the salty wetness when his lips found hers again. She grazed his back with her fingers and savored the feel of smooth skin over taut muscles. *You were always my strength, Nico, the one who propped me up.*

He groaned, then disconnected their lips. He rested his forehead against hers. "Anna." His voice broke. And that's when her brain kicked on again and she remembered why they shouldn't be doing this.

Pulling her arms back, she moved away from him. "You came for me because you still love me."

He nodded, eyes shining.

"But love isn't enough, is it?"

His eyes burned through her soul. She wanted with all her heart for him to show her a way out. But he couldn't.

"What happened at Lucas's grave?"

"I didn't find what I was looking for."

"Forgiveness?"

"Release."

TEARS STREAMED DOWN Anna's face and Nico wanted nothing more than to pull her back in his arms. It was where she belonged. She held the other half of his heart. Always had. He would never be whole without her. Not once since he'd met her had he doubted that fact. But he couldn't be both the fire that burned and the balm that soothed. Besides, he'd made a promise to Maria, and to his family.

"I've seen some horrors in the past five years. That's why I signed up with the commissioned corps, why I only do deployments, and to the worst places on earth. I figure my pain can't be worse than what others have endured. I'm waiting for that something that'll make my heart understand that what happened with us is not the end of the world."

He ached for her. "It doesn't work that way, Anna."

"How did you do it?"

"Do what?"

"Move on with your life? Fall in love with Maria?" There was no malice in her voice, just a genuine question. Still, his breath stuck. It hadn't been easy for him, and still wasn't. When Anna left, his entire world had crashed down on him. He hadn't gotten out of bed for days. Bruno and Tito had to physically remove him from the house. They had taken him to the plot he'd bought in Talofofo and reminded him of what he needed to do. Lucas's death had to mean something, and he'd thrown all his energy into building the hospital. But he knew what Anna meant. He might have grieved for Lucas, but he'd never found a way to expunge her from his heart.

Had it not been for his mother's illness he might never have opened his heart to Maria. She reminded him of the man he hoped to be. Maria had been his high school sweetheart; she'd known the boy who hadn't yet failed his family, who hadn't lost his son or his soul mate. She reminded him of the confidence he once had, the dreams he'd planned when he was a boy, before fear gripped him. Maria had given him the hope he needed to continue on. For the first time since Anna left, he had felt something other than a bottom-less canyon of sorrow.

"I accept that there are things beyond my control, that I don't need to forget the old memories in order to make new ones." He held out his hand and she took it. "Lucas will always be a part of us. You will always be a part of me. I embrace it, I hold you close in my heart. Maria understands that and also accepts it."

She lowered her eyes. Wet lashes threw shadows over her cheeks as the fire flickered. His chest snapped and he wanted nothing more than to pull her back into his arms. If he did that, there would be no happiness in his future. As it was, the last soul-searing kiss would burn in his memory for eternity. But that was a kiss of closure, the kiss he hadn't been able to give her when she'd left the island.

He should've known better than to give her an ultimatum. Now was not the time to push her and yet that's exactly what he'd done. But what did she expect from him? She'd given him an ultimatum, too.

"I can't stay here, Nico. This is not my home. I want to go back to California." Anna's *voice was cold, matter-of-fact. Her eyes were so distant, he had no idea where she was.*

"We buried Lucas two months ago. Now is not the time to make big decisions."

"The strike's over, and there's room on a flight leaving in ten days. There are two seats available. All you need to do is tell me if you're coming with me."

He took a step back. "You'd go without me?"

She didn't answer, just looked at him with those vacant eyes that didn't belong to his vibrant Anna. He reached for her but she pushed him away.

"I need an answer, Nico."

"For how long?"

"One-way ticket. I'm not coming back."

"This is my home. Our home." He gestured to the house they'd built together, the crumbling heap that they had fortified, but she stared past him to a place in the distance where he wasn't invited.

There was only one way to reach her. He wrapped his arms around her, but instead of softening like she normally did, she stiffened, her back as hard as a board. Then she wrenched away from him with surprising force.

"Don't touch me!"

He staggered back like he'd been slapped.

This was not his Anna. She hadn't been since Lucas died. His entire family had rallied around them, but Anna wanted no part of it, so he'd let her be, to grieve the way she wanted to. And perhaps that's what she needed now, to come to terms with things. To be around her own family. For the first time since he'd met her, he didn't know what to do to make things better.

"Anna..."

"You come with me, and we go forever."

"You know I can't." His mother would never leave the island, so neither would Nico. She knew this. He had made it very clear to her before they married.

"I can't stay."

"Then you go." Perhaps a month or two in a different place would be good for her psyche and she'd decide to come back.

She turned and walked away from him.

He had spent the next week desperate to come up with a plan to save his marriage. By some miracle, he'd found the land in Talofofo and convinced the owners to sell it to him on a payment plan. The land belonged to a family that had long since moved to the mainland. The parents were dead and the children wanted nothing to do with Guam. He was sure his plan would talk Anna out of getting on that flight. If she left, she was never coming back; some part of him had known that, even then. When he'd told her about the land, she wasn't interested. Wouldn't even come see the place where he planned to build the hospital dedicated to their son.

Days later, he'd come home to take her to the airport only to find that she was already gone. Driving like a madman, he'd arrived to discover that she'd gone through security to the gate. He had stopped at the checkpoint. If he'd wanted, he could have found a way through. Guam was a small enough island that somebody would know somebody who worked in security and would let him past. Usually it took no more than two to three phone calls for a man as well-connected as Nico to find someone in the right job. But he'd just stood there. The way she'd looked at him at the funeral, and then again when she talked about leaving, haunted him. There had been more than just anger in her eyes. There had been blame, and hatred. She needed time to heal. He'd give her that time; he would go get her when he built the hospital.

In the months that followed, he'd regretted that decision. Not only had she not come back, she'd also refused to talk to him. His grand plan to build a hospital had hit several roadblocks, the primary being that nobody wanted to fund a hospital. There were plenty of investors interested in building hotels and shopping malls, but hospitals were a losing proposition.

By the time he'd figured out that he'd made a colossal mistake and shown up at her mother's house in California, Anna was in Africa and wanted nothing to do with him. Her mother had advised him to let her be, that time would heal. But it hadn't. That had become clear to him the moment he'd seen her at the field hospital. The pain in her heart was clear from the second he held her. She was not his Anna; that Anna had died with Lucas.

The kiss was for the Anna he'd lost.

He stacked more wood into the fire with precision. Anna's soft sobs were a relief after the silence he'd endured. The deafening silence that had greeted him for five years had ripped him into shreds. The Anna he knew was passionate and fiery. She wasn't numb inside, she wasn't a woman who went off to hide her pain in the horrors of the world.

"Why haven't you given me the divorce papers yet?" The catch in her voice nearly undid him. He squeezed his eyes shut, letting the warmth of the fire fortify him.

"That's what I'd come to give you before the storm hit."

CHAPTER NINE

MARIA BLEW OUT a sigh of frustration. "Let's move up one floor. There's no way we're going to control this water."

"How can I help?"

She turned to find the governor behind her. As if she wasn't stressed enough dealing with the hurricane and the hundreds of people who had shown up to take shelter in the hospital, the governor had also decided it was a good place for him to hunker down.

Maria knew full well why he was there. He wanted to make sure they were capable of handling the money he planned to give them. Great time for Nico to have disappeared. She knew her anger was irrational; the storm had come suddenly and hit much earlier than predicted. He'd likely gotten caught and had to take cover rather than return. It was the prudent thing to do and had he called her, that's what she would have told him. But it bothered her that he hadn't called. They had a new satellite phone and she knew the field hospital had one too because she'd been able to call there and confirm that Nico had indeed shown up. But he wasn't there anymore, and suspiciously, neither was a certain blonde doctor.

Control your green-eyed monster, Maria. There was too much to do. Turning to the governor, she put on her best, everything-is-all-right smile. "I don't think we're going to be able to keep the water out. The sandbags can only do so much. I'm moving everyone to the higher floors." What she didn't say was that there was likely a crack in the foundation, which was causing so much water to seep through. That was a problem for another day.

"Is there room on the upper floors?"

Hardly! We're packed full.

"We will have to make room."

"Leave it with me."

He turned and left before she could ask him what he had in mind. She had to return to the problem at hand, getting everyone out. Anyone who could walk was already being ushered out, the problem was the majority of the people on this floor weren't mobile. The elevators weren't working, so anyone who could climb stairs had already been relocated to higher floors. She directed her able-bodied volunteers to bring every available stretcher and backboard, and assigned patients to each team. Taking the steps two at a time, she broke into the emergency supplies and grabbed the stair chair. It was supposed to be used in case of a fire.

Directing an elderly woman into the chair, Maria wheeled her to the stairway and began hoisting her up. The woman was two hundred pounds, almost double Maria's weight, and her arms felt ready to rip out of their sockets. A pair of stronger arms grabbed hold of the handles. "Leave it."

She turned to see the governor and stepped aside to let him haul the woman up the stairs. When they were on the second-floor landing, she noted that he had gotten people to squeeze into the nursing station, moved some beds into the hallways and had patients sitting four to a bed. Peeking into the rooms, she saw everyone lined up on the floors, sitting knee to knee.

"We have ten empty rooms. If we carry the beds up from downstairs, we can fit four beds a room."

Maria nodded and they went to work, using the utility stairwells while the volunteers carrying patients used the regular route. It was backbreaking work, but the governor did most of the heavy lifting, letting her push while he pulled the beds up the stairs. The man was strong, like Nico.

"I guess you find time to work out in your busy schedule."

He laughed. "I used to be in the army. Five miles every morning, and I've gotten soft in my old age."

"Old? What are you thirty-four, thirty-five?"

Continuing to heave the bed, he smiled. "Forty-two."

The man didn't look it. Dark hair, dark skin, eyes black as night, he was solidly built with not a gray hair in sight. Maria figured he had to keep up appearances, being a politician and all.

"Must seem ancient to a young one like you."

Now it was Maria's turn to laugh. "How old do you think I am?"

"Twenty-five, twenty-six tops."

She stopped to catch her breath and he balanced the bed so she wouldn't have too much weight leaning on her. "Thank you. That's a nice compliment but a bit much, don't you think?"

He raised his brows. "I'm not playing you."

She motioned to the bed and began pushing again. "Oh, yeah, you are. I'm thirty-eight." Well past her reproductive prime, as the obgyn said. Still, Dr. Li at Guam Hospital had told her that if she started soon, she could have one, if not two, children. But the clock was not just ticking, it was clanking loudly.

Now it was his turn to stop, and he looked genuinely amused. "You're kidding."

"What, you think a woman likes to make herself sound older than she is?"

Once they were done with all the beds, she went to check on the patients with the governor following closely behind.

Lenny, one of the men who'd been helping them since the tsunami, ran up to them. "Maria, we have a problem."

"What's going on?"

"Ingrid isn't doing well, and she won't leave."

Maria went to talk to her. She'd been worried about the seventy-year-old woman since she'd gotten here. Ingrid had arrived after Anna left, and Dr. Balachandra still hadn't returned. The nurse had proclaimed her stable, but Maria could tell by her face that she was suffering. She wasn't a doctor, but she knew Ingrid and something was wrong.

Ingrid was sitting in a chair with old Leo Berman at her side. Ingrid and Leo had both lost their spouses years ago and rumors abounded that they were more than just good friends.

Ingrid was wheezing audibly. Maria turned to Lenny. "Go get Betty." Betty was one of the nurse practitioners and right now she was the most highly trained medical person they had on-site.

Leo shook his head as Lenny took off. "She's not gonna make it. It's her emphysema. Dr. Balachandra told her that all those years of smoking are catching up to her."

Maria crouched, noting that the floor, which had simply been wet an hour ago, was now covered in an inch of water. She'd changed into sandals but didn't enjoy the feel of cold water beneath her feet. Good thing she'd thought to wear capris so at least her pants weren't soaking.

Almost everyone was upstairs now, and she didn't like the idea of leaving anyone alone on the waterlogged floor.

"Let's get you upstairs where you'll be more comfortable."

Ingrid grabbed her hands. "I want to marry Leo."

"What?" Maria had been expecting any number of things, but this wasn't one of them. While everyone knew Ingrid and Leo were secretly dating, she had no idea they were that serious.

"I want to marry Leo before I die. I want him to be my husband. I want him to bury me."

"Please, Maria," Leo begged.

Maria stared at them. As much as she wanted to marry Nico, if today was her last day on earth, that would not be at the top of the list of things she'd want to do.

"Please," both Ingrid and Leo implored her.

She could do this. It was Ingrid's dying wish. She went through her mental inventory of everyone who was upstairs. No priests, no ministers. No judges. Who else could do it? Then it hit her. She turned to the governor.

"Will you marry them?"

He looked surprised. "I'm not a priest."

"But you're head of State. It's the Government of Guam that makes marriage legal, and you're the highest ranking official."

She silently pleaded with him. Even if he didn't have the proper authorizations, they could figure it out later. Right now, Ingrid needed to marry Leo. Seemingly reading her mind, he nodded.

"I'll be your witness," Maria said, closing the discussion.

Betty and Lenny arrived and Maria filled them in. Examining Ingrid, Betty conveyed with her eyes what Ingrid had already told Maria. She didn't have much time left.

"All right, then," Maria said. "Let's get this going before we have to make it a floating wedding."

"Do you, Ingrid…"

"Rodgers," Maria supplied.

"… Ingrid Rodgers, take Leo Berman to be your lawfully wedded husband, to have and to hold until death do you part?"

"Death do us part, I take him as my husband in this life and in eternity beyond. He's not getting rid of me that easy."

The governor smiled, and for the first time Maria noticed that the man was quite handsome. Unlike on the mainland, politicians in

Guam didn't get elected on looks. In fact, most were short, fat bald men.

"Okay then, Leo, Do you take Ingrid to be your lawfully wedded wife, to have and to hold for this life and the eternity beyond?"

"I do, and I'm gonna be right behind you, my darling."

"Then by the power I'm vesting in myself on behalf of the Government of Guam, I pronounce you man and wife."

They all looked at him. "You forgot to say 'You may kiss the bride,'" Maria whispered. He slapped his head.

"You may kiss the bride."

Leo hugged Ingrid, kissing her so hard that Betty leaned forward to make sure Ingrid could breathe.

Leo turned to them with shining eyes. "Can you leave us here? We don't mind the water, I just want some time alone with her."

Maria shook her head but the governor placed a hand on her shoulder. "I'll take responsibility. Let them be."

She gave them some drinking water and power bars along with a wrench that Leo could use to bang on the grate if they needed someone to come down and get them. With the wind howling outside, they might not hear screams or shouts. They established a signal of taps, but Maria had a feeling she wouldn't hear from him. Not until Ingrid died.

After checking on everyone upstairs, she sat in the stairwell. Her office was being used by the staff.

Ingrid and Leo! Everyone suspected they were a couple; why had they waited so long to make it public? All that wasted time that they could've spent living together and enjoying social life as a married couple.

The governor came and sat beside her, handing her a bottle of water. She shook her head. "Save that, we don't have a lot." Then she slapped a hand over her mouth. "Sorry, I shouldn't have told you that. Forgot for a second you're the governor."

He stuck out his hand. "How about tonight I'm just Tom." She took his warm, callused hand.

"Okay, Tom. Thank you for that, because every cell in my body hurts, and I don't have it in me to keep up appearances."

Grinning, he cracked open the bottled water and pressed it into her palm. "Drink. You need this. I brought along water filters from our emergency stash. We can use those to filter the water we collected in the containers before the storm started."

Right, that's what she'd forgotten to do. It was the kind of thing Nico took care of. Good thing the governor—*Tom*—had remembered.

"So where's your partner in crime?"

Somewhere safe, I hope, because I want to kill him myself as soon as I lay hands on him.

"He went to the field hospital and must have gotten caught in the storm."

"You two are engaged, right?"

"Kind of." She didn't want to get into it with him. "How about you? Married?"

He shook his head.

"Divorced?" She could've kicked herself. Why was she being so nosy?

He shook his head. "No, never been married."

Her eyes widened. "Seriously?"

"What you're really asking is what's wrong with me that I'm not married yet?"

She put a hand on her mouth. "Listen, I really put my foot in it. What I meant to say is that you're an extraordinary man and I find it hard to believe that someone didn't snag you. I waited, and before I reconnected with Nico, I was finding that most men my age married ten years ago."

Stateside, it wasn't unusual for women to marry in their thirties, but on Guam, that was considered downright ancient.

He smiled and leaned forward conspiratorially. "My third cousin advised me to tell people I got married overseas but that my wife divorced me rather than move to Guam. So everyone will stop wondering what's wrong with me."

She leaned back and laughed, and he continued. "My campaign staff went so far as to advise me to hire a wife for the campaign. They said no way a man without a family would get elected governor. And look at me now."

She hadn't followed the election or voted because she'd been too busy getting the hospital up and running.

"So what does *kind of* engaged mean, anyway?"

It was a genuine question, but suddenly she was too weary to give the pat explanation she gave her family and friends. Especially her sister, who was bugging her for a wedding date so she could arrange time off work. It wasn't as if Guam was a quick ride over; it took more than twenty hours to get to the island from most places.

"It means Nico is still hung up on his soon-to-be ex-wife and can't decide whether he's truly committed to me." The bluntness of her answer shocked her more than it startled him.

"Then why do you want to marry him?"

That answer was much simpler. "Because he's a good man, and I love him."

"Does he love you?"

She nodded. "He loves me as much as he will ever love anyone who isn't Anna, if that makes sense. I'm at peace with the fact that I'm not the big love of his life."

"Why?"

She looked at Tom, confused. "Why what?"

"Why would a woman like you want to be second choice?"

"That's not how it is." Her voice held more force than she intended. Perhaps because she'd never had this conversation the way she wanted. With Nico it was guarded, with her making sure she encouraged his honesty. Family and friends were already judgmental, so she kept it upbeat with them. She normally picked her words carefully, but this time she wanted them to come naturally. "I tell people that Nico is a good man and that I am thirty-eight years old, I need to stop being choosy.

But the truth of the matter is, I've been in love with him since I was fifteen."

Tom raised his brows. "You were high school sweethearts?"

She nodded. "At the time, I didn't really appreciate him. You know how it is when you're that young. My parents moved us to Hawaii. Here, I was this awkward girl, and Nico was my best friend. In Honolulu, I ran with the cool kids. I was enjoying my new identity as a popular girl and I wanted to fit in. So I broke it off with Nico to free myself to date the boys I needed to be seen with. But the more boys I dated, the more I realized what I had lost. First I chalked it up to young boys. Then I went to college and learned that what I had in high school with Nico was the best I was ever going to get. By the time I screwed up the courage to find him on Facebook, he was already in love with Anna. So I let it go."

"Did you return to Guam for him?" There was no judgment in Tom's voice. No silent admonishment reminding her that she was a woman of the twenty-first century and men should fall at her feet, not the other way around. Just a simple question, one to which she had hardly given herself an honest answer.

"Yes." It felt good to say it out loud. She'd

given herself and others a really nice story about needing to return to her roots, do something for the community, fulfill her need for public service. All those things were true. And she'd done many of them when she was in the Peace Corps. She'd spent time in El Salvador, in Indonesia. She could've chosen any place on earth to go work. But it had never been a choice for her. Then a photo of Nico on Facebook one day, with a caption from one of his friends about how Nico was finally getting dressed for a date, had her packing her bags. Not immediately, of course; she'd waited a year. She wouldn't have wanted Nico on the rebound; if there'd been any chance his marriage was going to work, she would not have been the one to stand in his way.

"I came to the island with no plan. I just wanted to see what it would be like here. I left when I was a teenager, and you remember things a certain way, but reality is always different as an adult."

"I know what you mean. I've lived here my whole life, but when I deployed for the war, I came back to the island seeing it in a whole new light."

She nodded. "I know. When we first moved to Hawaii, I remember thinking how nice Honolulu was, how much more developed it was. The people were nicer, there was so much culture. Then when I returned, I realized how much I missed the sense of community here, a feeling of belonging. We do things for each other, and not just in extreme situations like the one we're facing right now. Every day, we sacrifice for the collective good."

Tom nodded. "When I came back, what struck me was our acceptance. I know we have our differences sometimes, but nothing like what we see on TV and in the news. There's no major fighting over religion or the color of someone's skin."

They sat in companionable silence sipping water, taking a moment to reflect on their day.

"So was it love at first sight when you saw Nico again?"

Maria smiled at the memory. "Not quite. I had this whole thing planned—my cousin was friends with Nico's aunt Mae. They were having a get-together at her house and Nico was invited. So I was going to go get my hair and nails done, had even bought a new dress at the tourist mall. But wouldn't you know it, it's the middle of summer and my air conditioner breaks down. So here I am sweaty and smelly, my hair a total disaster and I go to Old Man Pete's shop to see if I can rouse him 'cause he hasn't been answering my calls. And who's there? Yep, Nico."

Tom laughed. "Why do I get the feeling that he fell in love with you the instant he saw you."

"He sure smelled me a mile away, and I couldn't even hide—he totally recognized me. But it was good. We started to chat and then we kept on talking. He had this land to build a hospital and he wanted me to come tell him what I thought, which I did. Then before I knew it, we were working together to get the funding."

"And the rest, as they say, is history."

"Hopefully. But I don't know for sure that there's a happy ending to this story."

"You think he'll go back to his ex-wife?"

With all of her heart, she wanted to say no. Nico had assured her over and over that there was no repairing his relationship with Anna. "Nico has only known a marriage with Anna, so he considers it something great. He clings to what he knows. All I can hope for is that he gives me a chance to show him a different life."

Tom held up his water bottle in a mock toast, and she tipped hers toward him.

"I sincerely wish that it works out for you, because that leaves me with hope that an old man like me can one day find a woman like you."

CHAPTER TEN

WHEN SHE WOKE, the room was pitch-black and she was on the bed. Rubbing sleep from her eyes, Anna tried to clear her head. *Nico!* Fumbling in the dark, she found the flashlight she remembered them using to get to the bathrooms. Nico was lying in front of the hearth. She kneeled beside him and touched his head. He was burning up. Lifting his shirt, she checked his wound. The torn bedsheet was soaked through. His breathing was shallow, but he seemed to have decent capillary reflex, so she ran up the stairs to find the priest.

The main hall was bathed in light. Out of the dungeon, she could hear the wind howling. Why hadn't she thought of this last night? She went through the church until she found the rectory and rapped on the door. The priest opened it right away.

"Everything okay, my child?"

"Do you have any medical supplies? Nico is injured."

Without delay, the priest rummaged through a cupboard and came up with two boxes. One was an automatic external defibrillator. Anna sincerely hoped she would not have to use that. The other box held a medical kit. Taking it from him, she raced back downstairs, hearing his footsteps behind her.

Back in the dungeon, Nico was awake and rubbing his head. Anna opened the kit to find more ibuprofen, which she gave him right away. There was also Betadine and bandaging supplies, and a QuikClot kit. It wouldn't take the place of proper sutures, but was far better than the unsterile, amateur dressing she'd done last night.

"What time is it? Has the storm passed?" Nico asked.

"It's five in the morning," the priest said. "They say we'll have strong wind gusts for the next few hours, but the rain seems to be dying down."

"Any reports from here or the surrounding islands?"

The priest shook his head. "I have a short-wave radio—that's how I've been getting weather updates—but all other communications are down. No cell, no landlines, and I don't have a sat phone."

Anna kicked herself for being so careless with her backpack.

"I'll have to go out there to see for myself."

"Nico! You're running a fever and I'm pretty sure your wound is infected."

"The people need me. I should've been at the hospital last night."

Instead of saving me. He was gathering the contents of his own backpack.

"I'll come with you."

"Oh no you won't. I don't need to be worrying about you. It'll be a trek to my car alone, then who knows whether it's drivable."

"I hiked it from the field hospital to the cemetery, I think I can manage."

"You collapsed at the cemetery."

"And you're injured."

They stared at each other. There was no way she was letting him go out with that injury. Who knew how much blood he had lost carrying her over here in the rain.

"Besides, I have to get back to the hospital. There's a shortage of doctors right now." That finally convinced him.

They thanked the priest and promised to return for services. The electricity was still out, but he had more jars of peanut butter and plenty of water to survive on. The church was somewhat remote. This part of the island once held small, locally owned shops that had closed once the big malls opened.

Nico had a rain poncho in his emergency backpack and gave it to her. His windbreaker was relatively dry. The wind whipped at them as they walked away from the church. The rain was lighter than it had been, but it still stung their faces.

"Let's see if my truck is still where I left it. It'll be our best bet."

For once, luck was on their side. The wind was at their backs and propelled them forward. They made it to the truck in less than an hour, but that was when their luck ended. His truck was flipped on its side.

"We'll have to hike back to the field hospital," Anna said.

He shook his head. "Let's flip it and see if it'll start."

She stared at him. "How are you going to flip this thing?"

He put his hand on one of the tires. "The old-fashioned way. Sometimes you just have to power through things."

"That QuikClot stuff isn't going to hold. I need to restitch you, Nico. It'll be safer to walk."

But would he listen to her? Of course not. Once he got an idea in his head, he charged forward with it. Like buying the house in Tumon, and the land in Talofofo.

"The field hospital moved to the school for shelter," he said. "That's four miles. We need the car."

He went around the side of the truck and began pushing. Sighing, she joined him. The vehicle wouldn't budge. Without waiting for permission, she lifted his jacket and shirt to check on his wound. As she suspected, he was bleeding again. An infection was a given, especially after her shoddy care last night.

What was going on with her? Even in the most austere environments, her medicine was always the best the conditions would allow. How could she have let him spend the night without properly dressing the wound? But she hadn't been herself yesterday. Years of exhaustion had descended on her like an avalanche. She hadn't been able to think or process clearly.

Now, in the cold, wet morning, her rational side was kicking in, and not just to assess her medical skills. She wanted to analyze the kiss they'd shared the night before. She hadn't kissed Nico goodbye when she'd left. At the time, she couldn't handle looking at him, let alone being near him. Knowing he would come to take her to the airport, she'd slunk away early. In the moment, it had seemed like the right decision, but as the years went by, she found herself longing for a proper goodbye. One where she could fill her heart with his love so she could remember it forever. He had needed it too.

"Nico! You have to stop."

But he wouldn't listen, so she pushed with all her might. As she felt the truck begin to tip, both she and Nico gave it everything they had. The rig crashed back onto the road, miraculously on four inflated tires. Nico brushed his hands on his jeans and retrieved the keys from his backpack. He turned the engine over and it coughed but didn't catch.

He popped the hood and bent over the engine. Just then she heard the unmistakable sound of a siren. It was a fire truck. She raised her hands and waved, and Nico did the same. The truck stopped.

"Nico!"

"Benito!"

The two men hugged and kissed each other

on the cheek. Anna smiled. All around the world, she'd witnessed men affectionately greet each other in a way that seemed completely natural. Yet Stateside, that kind of affection was a cultural oddity, replaced with chest bumps and weird handshakes.

"You crazy man, what you doing out here?" Benito was a big, burly guy who looked vaguely familiar. Anna was sure she'd met him at some point; Nico seemed to know everyone on the island, but she'd never been able to keep up.

"Rescuing a princess. Now, can you give me a ride and maybe tow this thing?"

"Sure thing, man. I've been towing idiots like you all night."

Nico punched him playfully.

"Yo, Anna!" Benito turned his attention to her. She nodded and stuck out her hand, but he gathered her in a bear hug. She didn't dare ask if they'd met before. Obviously they had, and he'd take it as a great insult if she suggested she didn't remember.

"I gotta drag your butts back to Talofofo."

"Talofofo? I need to get back to base camp," Anna said.

"Yeah, there ain't no base camp anymore. The school flooded so we've been moving all the patients to your new hospital."

That was apparently all Nico needed to hear to get into gear. He worked with Benito to fashion a tow hitch to attach to his truck. Once everything was ready to go, Anna got into the back of the fire engine while Nico sat in the passenger seat.

Benito had been tasked with driving around the island to see if anyone needed help. He had a working sat phone and Nico wasted no time calling the hospital, but the phones just rang.

"They got their hands full, man. Where were you all night anyway?" Benito looked pointedly at Anna, but neither of them was going to take the bait.

Benito's phone crackled. It was Maria, so Nico snatched the phone away.

"I'm heading back," was the first thing he said.

"Is Anna with you?"

"Yes."

"You need to take her and go to Troy Jenkins's house. They need help. He just called from an inland payphone that's still working. He's on his way back home now."

"Roger that."

Anna went into physician mode, thinking of all the supplies a fire truck would have on board for medical care. She noticed that the backseat had a bench where three to four firefighters could sit. All trucks carried a backboard, which she could lay across the bench to transport a critically ill or injured patient.

The fire truck was far more efficient at getting through the weather and over the terrain. Anna recognized landmarks as they passed. Memories of her and Nico exploring the island flooded her mind. The littered streets disappeared, replaced in her imagination by flowering bushes of bougainvillea and the sweet smell of jasmine. The roar of the ocean as it crashed into jagged rocks. Nico had seen every sight, but he'd marveled with her as if it was his first time too. Like they were discovering the island together. That was 2,787 days ago. A different lifetime for her.

They arrived at the Jenkinses' house and Anna jumped out of the truck at the same time as Nico. It was a rambler that looked to be in relatively good shape, which wasn't too surprising, considering it was inland and at somewhat of an elevation. The front door opened and a woman rushed out with a baby in her arms. It didn't take Anna long to recognize both the woman and the baby from a few days ago when she'd first arrived at the field hospital. The woman thrust the baby at Anna but her arms remained frozen by her side. The woman was screaming, but Anna couldn't hear anything above the pounding in her ears.

She watched as Benito took the baby. Nico turned her around and pushed her back toward the fire truck. He was saying something but it took her a moment to process the words. They wanted her to save the baby. Didn't they know? She couldn't be trusted.

Then Nico was face-to-face with her.

"Anna!" Through the intolerable pain seizing her chest, she heard his voice. Felt his arms go around her and squeeze her tightly. She gasped and a lungful of air went in. The pounding lessened.

"We need your help."

She looked into Nico's eyes; big, brown, warm eyes the color of dark chocolate. He cupped her face in his hands. "You can do this. We need you. The baby needs you. Please, Anna."

Blinking, she turned from him. He ushered her into the fire truck. Benito was in the back, adjusting an oxygen tank to blow air into a mask too big for the baby's face.

Something snapped inside her as she took

in the baby's blue lips. "Do you have a pediatric bag valve mask?"

"Baby's breathing."

"Not enough." Anna put her fingers on the baby's arm, checking her brachial pulse. It was weak but steady at about a hundred beats per minute, which was within normal range. She estimated that the baby was maybe five or six months old. Her breathing was shallow, though. Putting her mouth on the baby's she gave a small puff of air, then waited a few seconds and gave another.

"I don't have a pediatric bag valve."

"Then I suggest you get me to the hospital fast."

"Is she going to be all right?" Anna registered the speaker as the baby's mother. Nico gently steered the woman to the front of the truck.

"Aurelia, where's Troy?"

"He's not back yet."

"We need to go," Anna screamed in between breaths.

Benito didn't waste any time. He floored the accelerator. The baby had been on the bench but Anna picked her up to make sure she didn't fall or get hurt during the ride. Nico grabbed Anna and helped her into a seat, buckling her in as the fire truck rocked. He reached up to steady himself on a hand-hold and as his jacket lifted, Anna noted blood.

She continued blowing little breaths into the baby, her training overriding the painful contractions of her heart as she held the limp body in her arms.

"Nico, you're bleeding."

"I'm okay, Anna. What do you need?"

"Stethoscope."

He took the stethoscope from the bag Benito had left and put the earpieces on for her. He unbuttoned the little onesie the baby was in and placed the bell on the baby's chest. Anna positioned it in the right spot and listened. It didn't take long to find the problem, and her own chest tightened so painfully, she wasn't sure she had any air left to give.

Nico touched her cheek, and she felt wetness under his finger as he wiped her tears. "You can do this." She nodded and blew another breath into the baby who would probably die.

CHAPTER ELEVEN

ANNA DIDN'T KNOW what to expect when they got to the hospital, but it wasn't this. It seemed the entire island was here. Tents had been pitched on the front lawn and there were masses of people on the first floor mopping and cleaning out debris. Even Nico appeared taken aback by the chaos as they walked in with the baby.

Dr. Tucker was waiting for them. She had a pediatric bag valve mask and immediately put it on the baby's face and squeezed the bag. Anna handed over the baby to a waiting nurse and watched her carry the baby upstairs. At a loss for what to do, Anna stood frozen in the foyer.

She didn't know how long she just stood there, waiting for her heart to slow down, until a nurse gently shook her arm. "Dr. Atao, the echo confirmed your diagnosis. Come on, we have an OR ready for you."

What? She stared at the nurse, bewildered.

"The baby, she's critical. We need you in the surgical suites now."

No, I can't. I really can't. The words were on her lips but her voice box was locked. Then Nico's arms were around her waist, propelling her forward. "Anna, you're the only one here with pediatrics training."

Her legs moved on autopilot. Before she knew it, they were in a prep room and Nico was right beside her, helping her scrub her hands, fingernails and arms. He gowned her, then handed her a mask and cap for her head. "You can do this. You're the only one here who can."

How could he believe that? *I'll kill her. Don't make me do this.* She looked through the glass windows into the OR. The baby's unconscious form seemed so tiny on the large OR gurney.

"I need you with me."

He nodded, already scrubbing his own hands. She walked into the OR.

"Anna, it's good to see you again."

She turned to see Ajay Balachandra. The doctor who had pronounced Lucas dead. He was a short, bald man with dark skin. No one knew how old he really was; people joked that he could be forty or a hundred and forty. He'd been a staple on the island for over ten years, one of the most competent doctors they had. Hailing from India, the man had remained a bachelor, content to spend his days—and often nights—working. "Listen, I know this is difficult for you so I'm here to assist. As you remember, I'm an internist, so surgery is a leap for me. Pediatric surgery…" He shook his head. "No way. But I'm here to assist."

Why did he get to take the easy road but she had to step up? That's how it had been five years ago too. All of the resident physicians had shaken their heads at the idea of doing the surgery on Lucas. Even the one general surgeon had refused. Nobody wanted the liability of a pediatric death. So why did she have to be the one to take it on herself? If they could refuse, why couldn't she?

Then she looked at the little baby on the operating table. Dr. Tucker had already intubated her, and a small tube protruded from her tiny throat. A ventilator pushed the perfect amount of air into her lungs. Anna automatically checked the monitor. Her oxygen saturation was 91 percent. Not bad, but not the greatest. For healthy babies, it was 99 to 100 percent. She was hanging on, but wouldn't for long. Babies took a long time to decompensate, but when they did, they crashed hard. That's how Lucas had been.

"I have faith in you, Anna," Nico said behind her. "Please. This is Troy and Aurelia's first baby. Her name is Emma. They need you to try." He placed his hands on her shoulders and she leaned against him. She looked at the clock on the wall. One thousand eight hundred and fifty eight days and three hours since she'd been in an operating room. There was no viewing gallery here. But other than that, it was the same sterile space. The same expectant eyes looking at her to perform a miracle.

"Dr. Atao, I'm here, as well. We can do this." She glanced at Dr. Tucker. The woman nodded encouragingly. But it was Nico's hand on the small of her back that propelled Anna to step forward. The hole in Emma's heart was not as big as Lucas's had been. It was a small repair, but if she didn't do it, the baby would die. There was no ambiguity in this situation, Emma was already at death's door.

Anna asked for a scalpel. Her hands didn't tremble this time. She made a clean, smooth cut.

CHAPTER TWELVE

NICO WATCHED AS Anna cut into the baby's chest. He didn't know how she did it, but he knew she had it in her. Anna had incredible inner strength. Through the ordeal with Lucas, she'd been a rock. After the airlines went on strike, he'd lost hope and had begun preparing for Lucas to die. He'd gotten ready to say goodbye. But not Anna. When one plan failed, she came up with another. His Anna would never back down from saving someone; he knew she wouldn't have let Baby Emma die without trying to save her. No matter how hard it was.

When it was clear she didn't need him anymore, he quietly slipped out. Maria was waiting for him in the scrub room. He hesitated for a second, unsure of what to do. Under normal circumstances, he'd greet her with a hug and kiss but after all that had happened in the past twenty-four hours, seeing Maria put him off balance. As if sensing his uncertainty, she stepped back.

Taking off his mask, gloves and gown, he trashed them, then turned to her. "How did you pull this off?" The last time he'd seen this OR, the lights weren't working.

"Tom asked the US Disaster Management Assistance Team to set up shop here when the PHS lost their field hospital." Her eyes were bright with excitement. "You should see how these guys operate. They came with their own generators, communication systems and supplies. Oh, my god, you should see what all they brought. We have a full working hospital. Tom and I were up all night getting everyone situated."

"Tom?"

"The governor."

"You're on a first-name basis with him?" He quirked a brow, wondering whether the governor was the one who had put the brilliant smile on her face. Rather than feeling jealous, he was actually happy. For days now, he felt as if he'd been ignoring Maria, wrapped up as he was in everything going on with Anna and the disaster relief efforts.

"Yeah, after he spent the night with me." Her response was cheeky, and he smiled.

"Was he as good as they say?"

She sighed dramatically. "Even better." Then more seriously she gave him an update on what had transpired the night before. "Ingrid died early this morning. Leo's doing okay, but his blood pressure is high. Dr. Balachandra says he's not critical but I have a feeling he's not going to make it through tonight. He keeps talking about a double funeral."

"Any word from the coroner about getting us some space?"

She shook her head. "No, and our morgue is full. I hate to do this, but I told the orderlies to start double stacking bodies."

He pinched the bridge of his nose. "Is the governor still here?" She shook her head. Nico did not want to disrespect the dead, but it would be a while before the funeral home could come to take them away. His backup generator that kept the morgue cool would only last one more day. They needed more propane. Hopefully the incoming relief organizations would have some he could use but he knew they usually brought just enough to power their own equipment.

"And we have another problem."

Just one?

"Mr. Cooley needs his dialysis and our machine isn't ready yet."

His vision was getting hazy. Maria's lips were moving, but why wasn't he hearing anything? Then it all went black.

ANNA CHECKED THE CLOCK. Fifty-three minutes. It was time to close. Baby Emma had survived the surgery. She hadn't died on the table. As she stitched her chest, Anna realized something. "Dr. Balachandra." Her eyes were glued to the little square of exposed chest and the magnifying glass that let her use the teeny tiny needle.

"Yes?"

"You stitched Lucas closed, didn't you?"

She had manually massaged Lucas's heart, fruitlessly, until a team of nurses gently took her away. But Dr. Balachandra had done more than just pronounce her baby.

"Yes, I did." He said matter-of-factly.

"Thank you."

She finished the sutures and nodded to Dr. Tucker, who began bringing the baby out of anesthesia. They'd already successfully restarted her heart, now it was a matter of giving her some time, then turning off the ventilator, letting the baby breathe on her own and watching her for a couple of days to make sure she didn't get an infection. While the OR had been adequate to do the surgery, it wasn't perfect. In the urgency to get it set up, only the critical pieces had been sterilized. Ideally, the whole room was supposed to be prepared to create as clean an environment as possible. Anna reminded herself that she'd assisted surgeons who cut people open in tents with dust blowing around them. Sometimes it was not about doing it perfectly, but about getting it done.

Nico had left at some point, but while the nurses wheeled the breathing baby to the NICU that had been prepared just for her, Anna searched the corridor for him. She found Maria instead.

"He collapsed," the other woman said without preamble.

Before Anna could even process the words, Maria put a hand on her shoulder. "There are doctors here from the DMAT who are taking care of him."

"He's in shock. There's a wound on his abdomen. It's probably infected, he—"

Maria was nodding. "They found it, they're taking care of him. Nothing for us to do."

Anna bit her lip. *This is my fault.* He wouldn't

have been out there if it hadn't been for her. She'd been too self-absorbed to take care of him properly last night. And then instead of getting him medical attention when they'd arrived at the hospital, she had asked him to stay with her, to give her courage to do the surgery. How could she have been so selfish?

"I'm so sorry."

Maria stared at her. "What for? He cut himself saving Tito from the car."

Anna wanted to fess up to Maria, explain the whole situation, but somehow felt it wasn't her place. Nico had come for her; he needed to tell Maria what had happened. "I'd better go check on Emma. Where is Nico?"

"In the ICU."

Anna didn't need to hear any more. Dr. Tucker had gone to the NICU with the baby; she'd be fine for a few more minutes. She went straight to the ICU instead. It looked very different from when she'd been here a few days ago. She introduced herself to the physician in charge who was also a captain in the PHS. He was one of the new arrivals.

"Your husband is critical. We gave him a blood transfusion, repaired the laceration and started him on a course of antibiotics, but his pressure is still low."

"Have you given him vasopressors?"

The man nodded. "We have no idea how far the infection's spread. We need to give the antibiotics time to work, then see where we stand."

Anna knew all this already, but somehow she needed to hear it from someone else. She scrubbed her hands, put on a new mask and went to Nico's room. He was unconscious, a ventilator breathing for him through a tube. His pulse was strong, his EKG showing no arrhythmias. That was a positive sign.

"Nico." She went to his side and squeezed his hand. Tears fell down her cheeks. "I'm so sorry." He'd held it together for her. She sat with him until a knock on the door reminded her that she was on the job. Exiting, she came face-to-face with Maria again.

Maria gave her a hug and Anna returned the gesture. The two women sobbed uncontrollably, holding each other up.

"I can't do this without him." Was it her or Maria who said the words?

"Dr. Atao?"

She looked up to see one of the nurses standing there. "You need to come with me. Emma has crashed."

CHAPTER THIRTEEN

"You first." Maria's face mirrored the exhaustion Anna felt. She didn't even know where to begin processing everything that had happened in the past few hours.

"He's stable but still not out of the woods." Maria's voice was weary.

Guilt pierced Anna's heart. If she hadn't been so gutted by her own pain, she would've treated him correctly last night. They were standing in one of the corridors off the ICU that was blissfully empty. Between patients and the newly arrived medical staff, the entire hospital seemed to be crawling with people. Anna had been on her way to check on Nico when she bumped into Maria. She placed a hand on the wall to steady herself.

Maria leaned against the wall and slid down until she was sitting on the floor. Anna joined her. She didn't trust her legs to keep her upright.

"You love him, don't you." Maria hadn't asked it as a question, merely stated it as a fact.

Anna sighed. "He has a way of getting under your skin."

"Don't I know it. He's been under mine for twenty-three years."

"You've loved him since high school?"

Maria nodded. Anna could picture it. Once you had a man like Nico, it was hard for anyone else to measure up.

"He'll be happy with you." Anna truly meant it.

"I'm not so sure he can ever forget you."

"He will. You've helped him make his dreams come true. That counts for a lot. For Nico, it's about home—this community is everything to him. It's what defines him. I never fit in here like you do. Sure, we have history— that'll never change. But once I leave..." she squeezed Maria's shoulder "...and I *will* leave, things will go back to normal for you guys."

She could hear the relief in Maria's breath. Now came the hard part. Anna squared her shoulders.

"Listen, Maria, I know you're already stressed, but I need to tell you—Emma needs an ECMO machine. A heart-lung bypass. Her heart is too weak to heal on its own."

Maria gasped. "Where am I going to get that kind of equipment? Can she be transported?"

That had been Anna's first thought, too. *Get this poor baby off the island.* She had called a pediatric cardiologist on the sat phone to get his opinion. He had confirmed what she knew, that the baby was too unstable to transport. Her only hope of survival was to get an ECMO. And soon.

Anna shook her head. "She's not stable enough."

"Where are we going to get an ECMO in the next few hours?"

"Apparently one can be purchased from the Phillipines and be shipped here on helicopter. My colleague in the PHS found a company willing to sell one, but the price is steep. And we have to find a helicopter to bring it over."

Maria blew out a breath. "We can't afford it. As it is, I've gotten a loan from the bank just to buy the supplies we've needed to take care of basic wounds. The relief organizations are still mobilizing and the best places to purchase supplies are Japan and the Philippines because they're much closer than the US. But those guys want cash upfront."

"Isn't there any way to get an advance on

the insurance? Something?" An elephant was sitting on Anna's chest, but she took a deep breath. She couldn't let Emma die, not after she'd come as far as making it through the surgery. There had to be a way. Finding the machine had been next to impossible, but rather than letting panic seize her, Anna had called everyone she knew until someone gave her a lead.

"I also need to find a dialysis machine, a pharmacy's worth of medications, and a structural engineer to make sure this building won't fall on our heads. Everything seems to cost more right now, and everyone on this island seems to be on antiarrhythmic and blood pressure medications that washed down the drain." Maria blew out a breath. "I need to prioritize. I don't have cash on hand, and I don't know whether we will ever get reimbursed for any of this. With Guam Hospital out of commission, we are now the public hospital for this island." She waved her hands around. "What all am I going to get done?"

Anger bubbled through Anna. It was always about resources on the island. Someone got to live at the expense of someone else. The hospital would spend money to fly in a cardiac surgeon who could do surgery on adults but not one who could treat kids. "You want to ration care right now?"

Maria buried her head in her hands. "You think I want to make these kinds of decisions? I have to, or everyone dies. There will be more people who need the dialysis machine. The ECMO is just for Emma." She looked pleadingly at Anna, big, wet tears in her eyes. "Please try to understand. It's not how I want to do things, but I can't save everyone. Besides, helicopters aren't exactly available—there's a waiting list of patients who need medical transport out and those copters are all going to Japan. No way one can be spared to go pick up a machine in Manila."

Anna wanted to argue with her, to be mad and tell her there was always a way, but Maria was right. How many times had she made triage decisions, especially in Liberia? She would spend all of ten seconds evaluating a patient and then decide what color tag to put on them. Red tags for those who could be saved. They would get medical care as soon as possible. Black tags for those who were "expectant," meaning they'd die and there was no use expending resources on them.

But Anna wasn't ready to put a black tag on Emma.

The decision was obviously playing on Maria, as well. She wrung her hands. "Nico would know what to do. He's good at these things."

Had Nico known what to do with Lucas? At the time she hadn't thought so. When Lucas was diagnosed, they were both hopeful. She'd booked a flight to California and contacted every medical school friend she had to find the best pediatric surgeon possible. She hadn't started to panic until the pilot strike continued and all air travel out of Guam ceased. Then Nico had worked his contacts. He'd called every person he knew to see if someone would be willing to break the strike. It didn't matter. The airline made a statement with the union. They had taken all planes out of Micronesia. Nico had fought until Lucas worsened, and then he gave up and accepted their son's fate. That was when Anna's desperation had kicked in and a rift formed between them that grew and grew until it blew their marriage apart.

"Can your people pay for it?"

Anna had already explored that possibility and come up empty. The DMAT teams could not authorize expensive purchases; only the Office of the Assistant Secretary for Preparedness and Response could do that and they were already running low on their disaster relief funds.

Anna shook her head and stood. She had to go talk to Troy and Aurelia. Prepare them for what was coming. No one had done that when it was Lucas. She had diagnosed him and cared for him. At the time, she was the local pediatrician, the only one on the island. Calling on friends in California, she had sent over Lucas's ultrasound results and films and they had all confirmed her diagnosis with nothing more useful than "He needs surgery."

"We will get through this, Anna." Maria gave her a tight hug, holding on to her, and Anna squeezed her back. Anna didn't have close friends. She'd moved around so much as a child that her sister became her best friend. The only consistent person she had in her life. Without a doubt, if she'd known Maria when they were younger, they would have been friends. The woman had a goodness inside her that touched Anna's soul.

"He's going to make it. I know it in my heart," Maria whispered.

Anna nodded, not wanting to say what was

really in *her* heart. That Nico was going to die because of her. Just like Lucas had.

Troy and Aurelia stood as soon as Anna walked into the tent. Anyone who didn't need medical attention had been put in the tents outside. The wind had died down and even the sun was peeking out. Mother Nature was going to give them a break. At least for now.

For the first time, Anna took them in. They were both young, in their midtwenties. Aurelia was a petite girl with dark hair, cream-colored skin and soft brown eyes. Troy was a little taller than her, skinny with a goatee. Anna had already talked to them once, right after the surgery. Now she asked them to walk outside with her. The tent was noisy and distracting with crying babies, children playing games and people catching up with each other, sharing their stories.

Anna explained what was going on with Emma.

"So she's gonna die." Troy cut to the chase. Anna was prepared for the question, but none of her stock responses seemed adequate. Troy's fearful face made the knots in her stomach twist painfully. "I'm going to keep on trying to get that machine. I'll make some phone calls Stateside and see if there is anyone who can pay for it. If that doesn't work, I can…"

Aurelia put a hand on her shoulder. Anna forced herself to look into the young woman's tear-filled eyes. Anna was a doctor; it was her duty to put aside her own pain and console her patients. "Dr. Atao, if it's Emma's time, I need to know. I want to say goodbye, I want to hold her, I don't want her to go alone with all those machines."

The words hit her like a lightning bolt. *Don't do the surgery, Anna. You want Lucas to die in your arms, comfortably and knowing he's loved. You don't want him to die hooked up to machines.* This was the first time she'd really thought about what Nico had said. Back then she'd lashed out at him, accused him of giving up when things got really tough, of being willing to sacrifice their son's life rather than acknowledging that his insistence on staying in Guam was what would kill their baby. The last time she'd held Lucas when he wasn't cold and stiff was when she'd nursed him before the surgery. All she'd been able to focus on was the steps she needed to go through to conduct the procedure and the long list of what could go wrong.

She hadn't taken a moment to enjoy the

last moments of Lucas's life when she could just be his mother.

"Dr. Atao?"

She snapped her attention back to Aurelia. "Come with me. I won't take her off the ventilator and IV drips just yet, but I can let you hold her."

Back in the NICU where Emma was the only patient, Anna made Aurelia and Troy scrub their hands and arms, gown up and put masks on like they would if they were going into surgery, then led them to the incubator where Emma was fighting for her life. How could Anna have forgotten this? It was well-known that infants responded to touch and to being held. The kangaroo hold, named for the animal who carried her children in her belly pocket, was commonly used by pediatricians to help underdeveloped infants. Parents were encouraged to cradle them skin to skin.

Anna handed Emma to Aurelia and encouraged her to touch her cheek to the baby, to hold and talk to her the way she normally did. As she turned to leave, Troy grabbed her hand.

"Thank you, Doctor." The words were said with such sincerity that Anna couldn't hide her own tears. She didn't deserve their appreciation.

Unsure of what to do, she went to the ICU, passing through hallways crowded with people. Some sat on the floor, others stood waiting. Now that a number of other medical personnel had arrived, Anna's orders were less clear. She hadn't seen Linda Tucker since the surgery. All medical staff were wearing scrubs and name tags to indicate who they were, but Anna wasn't even sure who was in charge of medical command. It wasn't unusual in disasters. Normally she thrived in the chaos, letting it sweep her up in the moment so she didn't have to be alone with her thoughts for very long. But today she wanted quiet. She needed to think.

Nico was still on a ventilator, and a nurse that Anna didn't recognize was noting his vital signs from the monitor.

"He's stable," the nurse whispered before leaving. Perhaps because of who Nico was, or Maria's influence, they hadn't doubled him up. All the other rooms held two or three beds. Anna squeezed his hand, sitting on the edge of the bed. Why had she come here? She had nothing left to say to Nico. All the words in her heart, the hateful ones, the ones of love—she'd said them all. Yet something niggled at her. His chest rose and fell as the ventilator pushed air into his lungs. Her vibrant, full-of-life Nico with the strength of several horses was lying still.

"I need you to live, Nico." Perhaps she had come to feel his warm body, to know that he was still with her.

Then she realized what she hadn't yet said to him. With a stone weighing her heart to the floor, she leaned over and kissed his forehead. "I want you to know that I forgive you for what happened with Lucas. You were right. I should've accepted his fate and enjoyed the last few minutes of his life. I don't want to make the same mistake with you. Please don't leave me."

His hand twitched and she looked up, tears streaming down her face, but he remained motionless. It was just a muscle contraction. Patting his hand, she stood to leave. Despite the extra help they now had, there was still a shortage of doctors and she had a job to do.

Someone entered the room.

"Nana."

Nico's mother had aged since yesterday. Her gray hair was loose around her shoulders. Anna had only seen it like that when she stepped out of the shower. The woman always got herself put together every morning, hair, lipstick and immaculate clothes. She was not the type to be found lounging in pajamas past nine in the morning.

Sitting on Nico's bed, she placed her hand on top of her son's chest, then bent her head and began sobbing. Anna put an arm around her and squeezed her shoulders. The only other time Nana had cried was at Lucas's funeral. Even then, Anna got the feeling she was crying for Nico's pain, not necessarily for the loss of her grandson.

"Nico is all I have, all I've ever had. What will I do without him?" Her broken voice twisted Anna's stomach.

"He's going to make it through, I know it. Nico is a strong man." Her words were as much a prayer as reassurance. She held Nana until her sobs subsided.

"He went to California to get you back."

Anna knew this already. She had been in Liberia and not within phone or internet range, but her mother had sent a letter after the fact to let her know that Nico wanted her back, that he had come and begged for her. He'd even called the PHS to find out where she was, but of course they weren't going to reveal her exact location or allow him to visit.

"He told me he would leave Guam. If that's what it took to get you back, he would leave here forever."

What? Not once in their entire courtship or marriage had that notion been on the table. Nico had made it very clear that Guam was his home. Even after she threatened to go to California, he had never once considered leaving.

"His father, he didn't just betray us." The words were spoken so softly, Anna wasn't sure whether they'd been spoken at all. From the day she was introduced to Nico, she'd heard the story of how Nana had fallen in love with a marine who left her pregnant, then took up with another woman Stateside. Anna knew Nico felt responsible for his mother, who had sacrificed a lot to raise him.

"Nico's father left because he stole money from half the island. He convinced everyone to invest in this community center. It was supposed to have private tutors for children so they could be more competitive for colleges on the mainland, job training programs, computer classes, a place for kids to play after school so they wouldn't get into trouble. That's what attracted me to him, his spirit, how much he wanted to do something for the community. We all put our savings into it. They all trusted him because he was my husband."

Goose bumps prickled Anna's skin. She had never heard this part of the story. Not from Nico, and not from the community.

"One day I wake up and there's a note on the bed stand that he's been deployed. I didn't think much of it—we all know soldiers get sent away. After months went by and I didn't hear from him, I started to get worried. So I called his commanding officer. The man tells me he didn't even know Michael was married. By now I am seven months pregnant with Nico and people are starting to ask about their money. The land Michael said he had bought for the community center was being sold to a developer to build a resort. No one knew what was going on…"

The pain in Nana's voice was so raw, it was as if she were describing events that happened four months ago, not four decades in the past. "There was no money in our bank account. I had to get myself a job cleaning one of the government buildings. My fourth cousin gave me the job out of pity so I could

buy food. Then I get the divorce papers. I call
his CO again and he tells me Michael has
taken up with another woman and his tour of
duty is up with the military so there's nothing he can do."

Nana fell silent and Anna let the quiet linger in the room.

"I didn't have money to hire a lawyer.
Bruno's friend tried to fight for the money
Michael took from all of us, but it was long
gone. No trace of it. He was unemployed and
the court in Texas where he went wouldn't
ask him to pay child support. I was fighting the case from here, now with a baby in
my arms and no way to even pay for long-
distance calls."

Anna rubbed her back. The woman was
sobbing, reliving the worst pain of her life.

"The community helped me out. They took
care of me, bought me food so my baby could
eat, knitted me clothes for Nico. And when I
was well, the women watched him so I could
go to work and take care of us. No one asked
for their money back. No one filed a court
case against me. No one said a word. They
lost everything, their savings, their hopes and
dreams, and they said nothing."

Anna swallowed against the lump in her

throat. So that was why Nico wouldn't leave the island. He was paying everyone back for what his father had done.

"The only time in his entire life that Nico has said he would leave was after you went."

Anna closed her eyes.

"I don't know what it's like to lose a child. I thank the Lord every day that he gave me Nico. It's the only reason I've found peace in my heart for Michael. I understand why you wanted to leave, and I don't blame you."

Opening her eyes, she found Nana patting her hand. "When Nico married, you became my child too, and my heart still weeps for the pain you hold inside you."

Anna couldn't hold it back any longer. Tears flooded her face and Nana pulled her close and held her, stroking her head the way a mother would when consoling a small child.

It was as if a dam had broken inside her. Her own mother had been too focused on her various husbands to pay much attention to Anna when she was growing up. As the older sibling, she'd been responsible for making sure she and her younger sister, Caroline, made it home from school. There were always take-out meals in the refrigerator. Husband number two had been a decent man who at least tried to make them dinner. He hadn't lasted very long. Both Anna and Caro had gone to college as far away from home as possible. As children they'd been moved from one place to another with every husband upgrade. They never belonged anywhere; home was whatever apartment or house they happened to live in. Even their furniture was often rented. All of Anna's belongings could fit in a suitcase.

The community in Guam, the island itself, had filled a hole in her heart. But it had also ripped it to shreds.

"I won't take Nico away from here. I promise you that." And she meant it.

CHAPTER FOURTEEN

ANNA WAS SPENT physically and emotionally. Nico had been unconscious for twenty-two hours and six minutes. She had caught a couple of brief naps but hadn't had a full night's sleep since the night at the church two nights ago. Hopefully Linda Tucker would give her a few hours to rest so she could recharge and feel human again.

When she finally found Linda, Anna couldn't believe this was the same straight-backed rear admiral who had greeted her a few days ago. Her ginger hair was finger raked, eyes bloodshot and there was an indeterminate stain on her scrub top.

"Are you okay?"

Linda shook her head. "I'm running on fumes. The DMAT teams are helpful but they are still getting up to speed. Word has spread across the island that we have medical supplies and people just won't stop coming in. I just got a call that Congresswoman Driscoll-

Santiago is coming in on a military transport. Her helicopter lands in two hours." She blew out a breath. "I don't have time to be nice to a politician."

Anna bit her lip. While she'd been tending to one patient, two if you counted Nico, Linda had been running around picking up her slack. "Why don't you go sleep for a few hours," Anna offered. "I've met Congresswoman Driscoll-Santiago. We go way back— I can show her around. She's actually very reasonable and I think she's coming so she can ask Congress for more relief funds."

Linda looked at her gratefully. "How's your ex-husband?"

He's not my ex yet.

"Stable but still not able to wean from the ventilator." Anna didn't have to say the rest. It was understood that Nico would either heal or he would die. They had done all they could; now it was a matter of wait and see.

Grabbing a cup of stale coffee from the makeshift canteen, Anna got to work. The first thing she did was call the medical supply company in the Philippines and ask them to prepare to ship the ECMO machine. She wasn't giving up that easily. If Kat Driscoll-Santiago was coming, Anna had hope that they could make something happen. After checking on more than a hundred patients, she finally took a moment to wash her face. Her image in the mirror almost scared her. Heavy bags weighed down her eyes, her skin was blotchy and red in several spots. No amount of cold water would fix that, but she did manage to find a clean uniform to put on.

Kat Driscoll-Santiago was scheduled to arrive on the helipad, and Anna wanted to look presentable. From what she'd seen of Kat's governing style, she used the media to promote her message. There would definitely be pictures. Making sure her name tag and shoulder lapels were aligned, she walked out.

Anna had only met Kat once, when she'd gone to see Senator Roberts's chief of staff, Alex Santiago, who was now Kat's husband. Kat was the senator's daughter, and had been observing the meeting. Anna's sister, Caro, had talked her into approaching Senator Roberts. As a lobbyist, Caro believed anything could be done if you found the right sympathetic ear. So Anna had gone in to make a plea for more medical infrastructure on Guam while she was in Washington, DC, in between deployments. Alex Santiago had given her the brush-off but Kat Driscoll showed interest. Months later, when Kat Driscoll became Congresswoman Driscoll, she had called Anna to send her information and invited her to come to Guam. Anna sent the information but had refused to accompany the congresswoman on her trip. Even though she'd worried her refusal to come to Guam would jeopardize Kat's support, Kat had promised Anna she would do everything she could to change the situation, and she had.

As a territory, Guam didn't really have representation in Congress. They had a non-voting delegate who had little influence or power. All of the members of the House and Senate were responsible for representing their own constituents, so no one ever wanted to take up the problems of a Pacific territory that was far away from the hearts and minds of most Americans.

But not Kat Driscoll. The congresswoman from Virginia was out to change the world and the political system. She had made quite a name for herself by being the renegade who spoke out against many unfair institutional practices. The media loved her and she had a permanent entourage wherever she went. Unlike most people in that situation, she never promoted herself, but rather used it as a platform to get support for the issues she was tackling.

While Anna understood Linda Tucker's annoyance at the visit, she knew Kat wasn't coming to garner ratings or further her career. She was here to help, and maybe together they could save Baby Emma. Anna had checked on Troy and Aurelia, who were still holding their precious baby. While Emma was not out of the woods, she was hanging on, and Kat knew that if she got the ECMO machine within the day, she could save her. Just thinking about it gave her the adrenaline boost she needed to put pep in her step as she left the hospital.

The helicopter was landing when she arrived on the front lawn. The helipad was on the roof, where two cars had landed during the tsunami, so a temporary landing zone had been cleared on the front lawn.

Kat Driscoll-Santiago stepped off the helicopter in jeans and a T-shirt and Anna couldn't help but smile. Most bigwigs showed up in suits and immediately melted in the tropical heat and humidity. There was only one other person with the congresswoman.

She greeted Anna with a hug. Kat's blond hair was tied in a ponytail, which whipped around her as the helicopter rotors slowed. Her face looked a little fuller than before, and so did her figure. Anna had learned a long time ago never to make assumptions, but her medical training told her that Kat was pregnant.

"I'm so sorry, Anna."

Although the two women had only met once, Anna felt a kinship with Kat. She had given Anna hope when no one else would. Made Anna feel like she was doing something to make sense of Lucas's sacrifice.

"How much do you know?"

"Only that your ex-husband is critical and things are rough here."

He is not my ex. Not yet.

"Nico is strong, he will pull through." She said the words to remind herself to believe in them.

"I'm here to help."

"Good, because I need some."

Kat turned to introduce the woman who had accompanied her. She had green eyes and auburn hair. Even before being introduced, Anna pegged her as Vickie Roberts, Kat's half sister and chief of staff. "Vickie is here to make sure we understand what you need and try to make it happen."

Vickie stuck out her hand. "I'm also Tweeting and putting pictures on social media. The regular media will pick it up and ask us for comment. The Red Cross has started a collection fund for their relief efforts here, but the only way to get real resources is to make people on the mainland care."

Anna nodded. That was always the problem. Every hospital in the country was chronically underfunded and had its own community to serve. No one cared about a Pacific island that was closer to Asia than it was to the United States.

The pilot's door opened and a man hopped down. He was wearing a polo shirt and jeans, sunglasses shading his eyes. His sandy-brown hair shone in the sun as he strode up to them. Anna got the distinct impression from his close-cropped hair and fit physique that the man was military.

He stopped in front of Anna, then saluted. Laughing, Anna gestured for him to stop. PHS officers with medical degrees were automatically given a high rank and it was almost comical when hardened soldiers who ranked lower than her saluted. Anna still hadn't gotten used to it. She knew the uniform created that dynamic, which was why she hated wearing it during deployments.

"Captain Atao."

"Please, just call me Anna, especially since you're out of uniform."

He extended his hand. "Hi, I'm Luke." Anna smiled and took his hand. He wasn't the kind of stiff army guy she was used to dealing with and she liked him immediately.

"Anna, this is Lieutenant Luke Williams from the US Army, but he's not here in an official capacity. He's a personal friend and agreed to fly me over from Japan so we wouldn't tie up one of the relief organization's resources."

Adrenaline surged through her as she eyed the helicopter. "Can you fly that thing to the Philippines and bring back a machine?"

Luke grinned and lifted his sunglasses, mesmerizing Anna with clear, baby blue eyes. "Yes, ma'am."

And just like that, she felt a hundred years old, even though Luke was probably the same age as her. But it didn't matter. Clapping her hands, she resisted the urge to hug him. He might be the answer she'd been looking for.

Not wanting to waste any time, Anna ushered them into the hospital, explaining how they had gotten it running given the collapse of the regular hospital. She talked about the challenges of dealing with back-to-back disasters. Vickie was taking pictures with her smartphone, which apparently had a satellite connection.

"I'm already getting a bunch of re-Tweets and shares—this will get picked up by the media in no time."

Making a beeline for the NICU, Anna filled Kat in on the situation with Emma. "I know the ECMO is an expensive purchase, but we'll be able to use it on the island long after this situation."

"Do you plan to stay on?"

Of course not. My deployment ends in seven days.

"I will stay as long as I'm needed. Emma needs the machine now, and we don't have enough doctors yet"

Kat nodded. "I can't make Congress move that fast, but let me make a phone call to the Assistant Secretary for Preparedness and Response and see if she can repurpose some of the Ebola and Zika funds. Vickie, check if we have any chits with House Appropriations that we can use as a carrot."

Anna watched with a mixture of relief and horror as Kat and Vickie worked the phones, trading one favor for another. Anna lost track of how many deals they made to get to a point where they could promise the assistant secretary more funding for countermeasures in exchange for releasing the funds to purchase the ECMO.

"Why does Health and Human Services need countermeasures?" Luke had shared Anna's bewilderment at the entire process.

"Medication countermeasures. It's the assistant secretary's pet project. Drugs to treat radiation poisoning, for example."

"What a cheery thought." Maria had snuck up on them. Anna was glad to see the woman looked a little better than she had yesterday. There was a genuine smile on her face. Maria had brought "Governor Tom" with her. Once all the introductions had been made, Tom started chatting with Kat.

Luke pulled Anna aside. "I'd like to get going right away. I know it'll take some time to assure the Filipino company that they will get their money and to release the machine, and it's a three-hour trip there. I'll also have to stop at the base to get fuel. I don't want to waste time—that baby girl doesn't look too good."

Anna wanted to kiss the man. She gave

him instructions on how to check the machine to make sure it was the correct equipment and transport it as safely as he could given that he had to rig it in a passenger helicopter. There were still a million things that could go wrong, not the least of which was the fact that the machine itself might not work.

Troy and Aurelia were still in the NICU. After briefly introducing them to Kat and Vickie, Anna had shooed everyone back into the hallway so the parents could still have some time with their daughter. Until the machine was here and Anna had a chance to verify that it was in working condition, she was not going to tell the parents what was going on. The constant yoyo between hope and despair was worse than dealing with bad news. If Anna couldn't pull this off, she didn't want to have given them false hope.

After Luke took off in the helicopter, Maria pulled Anna aside. "Nico's stirring. He opened his eyes. Dr. Balachandra is going to take him off the vent."

Anna grabbed Maria's hand. "What are we doing here? Let's go."

They excused themselves, leaving Tom to continue charming Kat. He would escort her through the rest of the hospital, then take her on a tour of the island and stop for photo ops. Kat planned to stay the night.

When they got to the ICU, Dr. Balachandra was already there. "You made it just in time." Anna's heart thumped in her chest. Nico was awake.

As their eyes connected, she put a hand to her lips, silently letting him know that he was okay and to bear with the next few minutes. He blinked to let her know he was coming back to her. It took every ounce of energy she had to remain standing.

"Okay, Nico," Dr. Balachandra said. "I know you understand me, so I'm going to pull the tube out. I need you to cough when I pull to expel it. Blink twice if you understand."

Nico blinked rapidly, then looked at Anna pleadingly. Without thinking, she flew to his side. She grabbed his hand, squeezing it hard. He squeezed back. Dr. Balachandra deflated the balloon that kept the tube in place and pulled it out. Nico came up coughing, his hand crushing hers. After he was done, Dr. Balachandra checked his lung sounds and proclaimed him well and breathing.

"Anna," Nico croaked.

She picked up the paper cup of water and ice that the nurse had thoughtfully placed beside the bed and held it to his lips. He sipped carefully, swallowing with difficulty.

"Anna." This time his voice was much more discernible and Anna didn't bother to blink back the tears welling in her eyes. Nico was alive! She hadn't killed him. He was going to be okay.

"I'm here, Nico, what do you need?" But he just looked at her, and she didn't hesitate to bend down and kiss him on the forehead. He held on to her hand and Anna's heart had never felt as light as it did in that moment. Gazing into Nico's warm, brown eyes, everything that had happened between them melted away. She saw the man she'd first met, the playful, vivacious one who had pretended he was a tour guide just to spend the day with her. The entire room spun away from her and all she could see was that Nico, whose first kiss had made her fall head over heels for him. He smiled playfully.

"I love you." He whispered the simple words so softly, Anna barely heard them.

But what she did hear with resounding clarity was the unmistakable sound of a sob. She turned to see Maria run out of the room.

CHAPTER FIFTEEN

ANNA WASN'T SURE how she was still standing. Emma was deteriorating fast. Luke had been gone for ten hours now and there was no word on his whereabouts. Kat hadn't been able to get ahold of him, and Anna couldn't reach the company contact she had been working with. It was late evening in Guam, but they were two hours ahead of the Philippines so it was still the workday there.

"How much longer does she have?"

Anna couldn't bear to look at Aurelia. It wasn't the young woman's tears that affected her, but Aurelia's acceptance of the fate that lay in her daughter's future. She was at peace with Emma dying, while the little baby was still alive. Anna wanted that for herself.

Keeping her eyes on Emma, Anna replied. "It's really hard to tell. It could be hours or days, depending on how much fight she has left in her."

"Can we take her off the ventilator, let her go?"

Anna found it hard to keep from screaming, *how could you*? When she'd been in the same situation with Lucas, she had been working the phones 24/7, talking to everyone she could think of to try and save him.

The ECMO machine would give Emma a chance. She didn't want to give up hope yet. Against all odds, she'd found the machine, a way to pay for it and a helicopter to bring it back. She didn't know Luke Williams, but the sincerity in his eyes made her believe that the man would do everything in his power to return with that machine. He reminded her of Nico in that way.

Oh, Nico. He was still in the ICU. Although he was breathing on his own, he had a fever and his white blood count was high. Dr. Balachandra had given him pain medication to let him sleep and recover. Anna had looked everywhere for Maria but couldn't find her. When she thought about how that whole scene in Nico's room would have looked to the other woman, Anna's stomach twisted in a thousand knots. Anna had been so focused on Nico that she hadn't paused to consider that she was no longer the woman in Nico's life. It was Maria's job to be by his side. Nico was delirious; he probably had no sense of time and place. He'd seen Anna and latched on to her. She needed to find Maria and apologize. Set her straight.

But first, she had to convince Emma's parents to hold on without showing her hand just yet.

"Let's leave her on it for a little bit longer."

"Why? Dr. Atao, Troy and I don't want her to be in pain anymore. We are ready to let her go."

How are you ready to do that? I still haven't let go of my son who died five years ago.

"Just a little bit longer. Please, just trust me."

She left Aurelia and set a timer on her phone to return in half an hour. They couldn't spare the nursing staff to have someone monitor the NICU, so she needed to come back and check on Emma. Alarms would go off and draw staff if she crashed again.

Except she didn't know where to go. She was lost in more ways than one. Kat and Vickie were at Nana's house as her personal guests. There had been a minor brouhaha about where Kat would stay. The governor had offered his house, which then brought

Nana into the fray because she thought it was improper for a single man to be hosting two women. Kat and Vickie wanted to stay at a hotel, but of course no one would hear of that. While some hotels were becoming operational, locals considered it rude to let their guests stay there. So Nana finally won out and was hosting the two women. If Luke got back tonight, he'd be relegated to one of the cots assigned to the relief workers or go on base.

As if some unseen force was pushing her, she went back to Nico's room. She had passed by to check on him several times since he woke up.

He was awake when she arrived. "Glad to see you up."

"I don't know what you or Dr. Balachandra gave me, but I'm ready to get out of here," he said, sitting up.

"It's that kind of bravado that put you in this position to begin with."

"There's work to be done. This is my hospital."

"Nico!"

They glared at each other. He did look strong and healthy, like the old Nico. She knew it was only a matter of time before he'd pull out his IVs and get back into the thick of things. His eyes softened.

"I meant what I said earlier."

She sat on the edge of his bed and took his hand. He squeezed hers tightly, holding on to it.

"I know. I've never stopped loving you, Nico."

"Go on, say the 'but'…"

"But I can't picture a life on this island. And you can't leave."

"I…"

Before he could finish his sentence, she continued. "Nana told me about your father. About how he swindled everyone of their savings. I wish you'd told me."

"It wasn't my story to tell."

"Does Maria know?"

He nodded. "Nana told her, but she'd already heard the whole thing. She grew up here." It was a nice way for him to cover up the fact that Nana had never trusted Anna enough to tell her when they were together.

"I understand why you need to stay."

"I was ready to give up everything for you."

He'd said "was." He *was* ready to give up everything for her five years ago, when she wasn't ready to forgive him. Now it was her turn to do something for him. She leaned over and kissed his forehead.

"It's time for both of us to move on. When you're better, we'll go to the house in Tumon, decide what to do with it, then sign those papers. I think Maria has a working internet connection and printer now."

"When do you leave?"

It took her a second to think about it. She'd stopped keeping track. "Roughly seven or eight days."

"Then I guess we don't have much time."

Because she would never come back to Guam. A knock on the door finally made her look away from him. Nana walked in with a bag that smelled wonderful and Anna's stomach rumbled embarrassingly. She couldn't remember the last time she'd eaten.

Nana kissed Nico on the cheek, then gave Anna a hug. She stood to leave but Nana waved her down. "You sit and eat too. I have enough for the both of you. Look at how thin you've become. Keep going like this and you will pass out."

Anna hadn't eaten Nana's cooking in five years; she wasn't going to pass it up. Nana laid out bowls and poured hot soup from a thermos. Nico dug in and exchanged looks with Anna as Nana fussed about refilling their bowls and plating noodles when they were done with the soup. Nana was in her element. A shadow flitted across Nico's face as his mother groaned while bending to pick up a ladle that fell on the floor. Anna knew what he was thinking. It wouldn't be long before Nana couldn't do what she loved, feeding her family.

"Tomorrow morning, I'm having breakfast for Katerina." Pointing at Anna, she wagged her finger. "I want you to come so I can feed you proper food."

"Nana, it's Congresswoman Driscoll-Santiago," Nico said.

"That's what you call her. She's Katerina to me." Nico rolled his eyes but Anna gave him a brief nod and mouthed, "It's okay." She knew that Kat had probably insisted on Nana calling her by her given name.

"And you, Nico, you think about leaving this bed before Anna says it's okay and I'm going to bring my ruler and paddle your behind like I did when you were little." Nico looked pained and Anna laughed as Nana pretended to slap him. He held out his arms and mother and son hugged, laughingly wiping tears from their eyes.

Anna caught movement out of the corner of her eye and jumped up. She raced out of the room. "Maria, where are you going?"

Maria tried to hide it but there was an unmistakable shine in her eyes. "You guys look busy. I'll come back."

Anna grabbed her arm. "Your place is in there."

This time Maria couldn't stop the tears from rolling down her cheeks. Anna touched her shoulder. "He's yours, Maria. This is your home—I'm just a visitor. I'll leave in seven days, but you'll be here to put all the pieces back together."

"He still loves you." The pain in Maria's eyes was so raw, Anna felt a knife slice her heart.

"I'm his past, you're his future. He loves you too. Everything you've seen between us, it's closure, nothing more."

"I've loved him all my life, Anna. If you're going to take him back, tell me now while my heart is still intact, while I still have some dignity."

Take him back? Was that even an option?
She looked at Nico through the glass door.

He was watching them. Their eyes locked and he made a fist, kissed it and put it on his heart. She didn't know if the gesture was for her or Maria.

There was no choice. She knew what she had to do.

CHAPTER SIXTEEN

"Are you okay?"

Maria turned to Tom. She'd been sitting on a staircase. It was the only quiet place in the entire hospital. Somehow she knew he'd been looking for her.

She wiped her cheeks and nodded. "Just the stress of the past few days catching up with me."

He put his arm around her and she stiffened. It was a friendly gesture, totally platonic. He retracted his arm.

"Dr. Atao found a dialysis machine. I authorized payment for it from our general funds, so it should be here tomorrow."

That was one load off her.

"And the DMAT team has a contact for the heart medications we need more of. There's a distributor on the mainland that has enough supply. I'm hoping those will come in with the Red Cross shipment tomorrow."

"Thank you, Tom, I appreciate it."

"This is not just *your* problem. If anything, I'm responsible for everyone on this island. Tell me what you need and I'll do my best to make it happen."

"Can you get me a structural engineer? We need to get this building checked."

"Let me make some phone calls."

"How about a CMO?"

"Can't help you there. Nico asked me to make a call to the surgeon general's office requesting that Dr. Atao's deployment be extended. They agreed."

Her breath caught. Nico hadn't discussed it with her, but she knew what he was thinking and she didn't disagree with him. Just wished he'd talked it over with her first. *Typical impulsive Nico.* Except it was more than that. He wanted Anna to stay in Guam and hadn't discussed it with her. She'd have to deal with him later. She'd spent her entire night working with the plumber to fix leaks. Some of the local guys had reinforced boarded windows that had come loose during the hurricane. The water on the first floor had been mopped up and pumped out, but she was still worried about the foundation. The last thing they needed was for the building to collapse.

"How's Nico?"

"He's back to his old self. Dr. Balachandra said he can go home soon. Nico needs rest for a little while longer but we need the bed and the room."

"I'm glad he's doing well. Must be a relief to you."

"It is."

"And what about Dr. Atao?"

"What about her?"

"You were concerned that he was still hung up on her. Is that why he requested her tour be extended?"

I told this guy way too much. Should've kept my mouth shut.

"I think the two of them are still in love but just too set in their own ways to see that they need to sacrifice themselves for the love of their life." Her voice broke and a fresh torrent of tears wet her cheeks. Despite Anna's assurances that she was returning home and there was no way she'd be with Nico, the raw love for him in her eyes and the naked adoration in his face was so obvious that Maria would have to have been blind not to see it.

"Maria."

"Don't say it, Tom. I know I deserve better. Nico is a good man. If he marries me, he'll love me to the fullest and be a better husband than what 99 percent of the women in this world have. I should be happy with that. But I will always know that I don't have all his heart."

"And you need to decide whether you can live with that."

Right.

"Why don't you leave the hospital to me and go home and get some sleep, maybe take a shower."

"Do I smell that bad?"

He laughed, a deep baritone that came from his stomach, and she found herself smiling along with him.

"There is no way you could look or smell bad." His voice dropped and his eyes turned a warm chocolate brown. She wanted to melt into them. "You're the most beautiful woman I've ever seen. If you ask me, you deserve a man who thinks there is no other woman in the world for him, who will do anything you ask of him, a man who will worship at your feet." His gaze pinned her and she couldn't look away. "There are men out there who will love you like that, Maria." The way he whispered her name made her arms prickle with goose bumps.

His heart was completely open, and while

he hadn't said it, his eyes were clearly tell-ing her that she had an invitation. Standing, he extended his arm, palm out. She didn't hesitate this time. She placed her hand in his.

CHAPTER SEVENTEEN

A CHEER WENT up in the NICU when Anna plugged in the ECMO machine. She had two of the DMAT doctors and a few nurses helping her, and they'd set up a Skype connection with a neonatologist who actually knew how to work the machine. It had taken nearly the entire morning just to get the Skype working, but Anna needed the other doctor's guidance. Everyone clapped as the machine came to life and Maria faded away from the crowd. She needed to get used to this. Hospital administrators were not heroes. It was about the doctors and nurses who saved lives, and Anna was one of them.

Luke Williams, the army guy who'd brought the machine, sat in the corner while a nurse tended to the scrapes on his head and arms. Maria walked over to him. Obviously it hadn't been an easy pickup. She reintroduced herself and sat down beside him once the nurse was finished bandaging.

"You okay?"

"I'm made of titanium. This is nothing."

"Did the machine come to life and do that?" She motioned to the gauze wrapping on his head.

He laughed. "No, that was a pair of fake security guards who greeted me at the landing zone."

"What happened?"

He shrugged. "Just a few complications."

So he was a tough guy. "Yeah, it can be hard making a deal in the Philippines. We get a lot of fantastic nursing staff from there, but every once in a while, you run into a scammer."

Luke nodded and shifted in his chair. Maria could tell that he was uncomfortable and she made a mental note to have one of the doctors check him for internal injuries.

"The guards beat you up?"

He scoffed. "No, they tried to beat me up. They were a couple of thugs who wanted to steal the helicopter so they could sell it on the black market. I've seen urban combat in Iraq—these guys were nothing."

"So you went into ninja mode and kicked their butts?"

He gave a half smile, the kind that would

look smirky on most men, but somehow he pulled it off. Maybe it was the mischievous blue eyes.

"I'm surprised they handed you the machine without a bag full of cash."

"Yeah, that's where I got this." He lifted his shirt just enough to reveal another bandage. "The skinny guy from the company wanted hard US cash."

Maria had expected that. When she'd heard the whole plan to have Congresswoman Driscoll-Santiago sign a letter saying the US government would send money later, she'd tried to warn them that it wouldn't work. Kat had no authority to commit funds like that. Granted, the Filipinos wouldn't know that unless they were really savvy. The theory was that they would see a signature from someone in Congress and assume Kat had more power than she did. The Assistant Secretary for Preparedness and Response was working to get the money authorized for the machine and had promised to make it happen in a few days. Emma didn't have that kind of time. Even an assistant secretary at Health and Human Services couldn't get money to a foreign country that quickly. Maria understood how complicated it was to get their grant funding. It had taken upwards of seven months before they were able to draw down from the Treasury to build the hospital, and that was considered fast.

"So how did you convince him?"

"Well, the fake security thugs had a very nice Smith and Wesson that I threatened to use on a certain sensitive body part." Maria could picture it. Luke's sparkling blue eyes probably seemed very menacing when they were ice-cold and he was pointing a steel barrel.

"Well, whatever you had to do, it was worth it. You most likely saved that baby's life."

"No, Dr. Atao is saving that baby's life. And none of this would be possible if Kat hadn't put herself on the line by getting ASPR to commit the funds and sign that letter. She could get in a lot of hot water if word gets out that she did that."

The admiration dripped from his voice, and Maria wondered whether Kat and Luke had been an item.

"So you and the congresswoman are close?"

He turned his attention back to Maria. "We have history."

"Were you involved?"

It wasn't any of her business, but she wanted to know if he was in love with a married woman. It seemed relevant to her current predicament.

"We met in Iraq, and I was interested. But it was obvious she was in love with the guy she was traveling with, Alex. He's now her husband."

"So how did you deal with her being in love with another man?"

"There was no point in putting my heart on the line when she'd given hers to someone else."

It was like someone took a hammer and hit her right in the solar plexus, releasing every ounce of air she had in her chest.

"Listen, it's okay, I'm over it. Kat and I are good friends now. I would much rather have genuine friendship from her than halfhearted affection."

"How do you know it would've been halfhearted? She could have grown to love you." Her voice was thick and the slight frown and warmth in Luke's eyes told her he understood this was about more than just him. He turned to her, giving her his full attention.

"Love is a complicated thing, but it is a

two-way street. Someone doesn't love you with their whole heart, you let them go. My mother was the daughter of a general and she got set up with my father because he was going to be a future general. Now, most people would say we were a happy family—she cared for us, my father adored her. Picture-perfect army family. But let me tell you, I saw my mother wiping away tears when she thought no one was looking. She took pills that she hid on the high shelf in the medicine cabinet. When my father was deployed, there were nights when she left the house after she thought we'd fallen asleep and came back really early in the morning. My father was not the true love of her life, and she paid the price for it."

"What happened to her?" She could barely sputter the words, her throat was so tight.

"She killed herself. I guess there came a day when she couldn't take it anymore." He stopped and Maria could tell there was more to the story, but she didn't want to push him. Luke had shared more than any stranger deserved. And she didn't want confirmation of what she already knew to be true.

"I had a girlfriend once, and I told her I had enough love in my heart for the both of us." He hung his head and joined his hands, as if this conversation was as painful for him as it was for her. She waited, giving him the space to formulate the words.

"She told me that love doesn't work that way. Said I'd be miserable if I didn't have all her heart."

The question of what had happened with his girlfriend was on her lips, but she held back. When he looked up, his blue eyes were shining. Mr. Tough Guy had been hurt, badly.

Nothing was more painful than heartbreak, and Maria was setting herself up for a monumental one.

CHAPTER EIGHTEEN

TEARS SPRANG TO Anna's eyes when she saw
Baby Emma pink up, her oxygen saturation
rising on the monitor. The ECMO machine
had not only miraculously arrived thanks to
Luke Williams, but it was in working order.
The neonatologist and a mainland technician
had talked her through how to set it up and
use it on Emma. It had taken a few hours but
the machine was taking Emma's blood, oxygenating it and then pumping it back through
her body, a substitute for a heart and lungs
to give the hole in her heart a chance to heal.

Maria had made all this happen. Anna
would never have gotten the machine running without the Skype connection. When
Anna tried to thank her, she had shrunk into
the background. Anna wished with all her
heart that she could convince Maria that she
and Nico were done. There was no machine
that could heal her heart.

Anna sank into a nearby chair, every cell

in her body totally depleted. At least things looked good for Emma. Troy and Aurelia were back at their baby's incubator, holding her impossibly tiny hand. She'd lost weight, but that was to be expected.

"Why don't you get some sleep? We'll watch Emma and call you if anything changes." That was Linda Tucker. Anna smiled gratefully at her. It was now a matter of time. Emma's heart needed to heal, and there was nothing more Anna could do but wait. Some tents outside had been set up for temporary staff housing. There were more people than cots, so there were no assignments. She found an empty one and sank into it.

Despite the black night outside and the relative quiet of the tent, sleep wouldn't come. Somehow, she'd gotten roped into agreeing to come to Nana's breakfast the next morning. Kat had cornered her, and after everything the congresswoman had done for Baby Emma, Anna could hardly refuse. Nico had been discharged and suggested they go to the Tumon house after breakfast. It was time to say goodbye to her life on Guam.

LOOKING AT NANA'S HOUSE, one would never know that two disasters had recently hit the island. Anna had been through enough Chamorro events to know they were always over-the-top, with more food than the entire island could eat, but even she was blown away.

The front lawn was clear of debris. Anna recognized the tent that had been set up. Nana's house was modest, so she put up a tent every time she hosted a party. There was a long buffet table filled with dishes that close friends and family had contributed for everyone to share. As with any disaster, there was a shortage of groceries on the island. The Red Cross and other relief organizations had been distributing flour and sugar so the table was full of baked goods. The mismatched dishes included everything from casseroles to plain, hard-boiled eggs.

The community wasn't going to let Nana take sole responsibility for hosting Kat, or for thanking the relief workers. Tears welled in Anna's eyes as she recognized some of the houses around Nana's. Walls were caved in, roofs were collapsing. Nana's own house had wood boards where windows used to be. And yet there was a tablecloth covering the table and proper plates, some glued together.

Nico had come by the hospital to collect everyone who could be spared to join the breakfast. All uneaten food would go back there for those who couldn't make it.

"Are you okay?"

She turned to Nico, who put an arm around her waist to lead her in. This used to be her home. When she and Nico had gotten engaged, Nana wouldn't hear of Anna renting a room in someone else's house. She'd insisted Anna move in with her. It had been her not-so-secret dream that Anna and Nico would move in with her after they married. Nana had inherited a large plot of land to go with the house and suggested they build a house for themselves on the property. But two months in Nana's home had driven Anna crazy. She wasn't cut out to have neighbors and distant relatives constantly in her life, suffocating her with advice on everything, from how often she should go see her mother to the type of tea to drink.

On the pretense of greeting one of the neighbors, Anna stepped away from Nico. He and Maria were moving into the house soon. Anna was never going to make Nico's dreams come true. She had always been the wrong woman for him and should have seen that from the beginning.

Nico and Nana said the meal prayers so

everyone could begin eating. It didn't matter what religion you were. Everyone either prayed or stood silently in respect. It was a custom before any meal, even in large groups. Food was not eaten without saying grace. As they went through the words, Anna noticed tears flowing down people's cheeks. Until the relief organizations had arrived, several of the locals had gone hungry so the children on the island could get what little there was.

"Are you okay?" This time it was Kat who pulled her aside while everyone was busy lining up to dig into the food. Anna hadn't had a chance to really chat with Kat and was glad for the distraction.

"You're asking about me? I'm pretty sure you have some news to share that involves how you should not be traveling or standing on your feet so much."

Kat blushed. "I should've known you'd figure it out. Aside from Vickie and Alex, I haven't told anyone yet."

Anna gave her a hug. "When are you due?"

"I'm only four months along. The OB assured me it was safe to travel, and I brought a lot of bottled water and protein bars."

Kat's eyes were full of hope and Anna's heart welled up with joy for her.

"Thank you for everything you've done for Guam. I know you didn't have to do any of it, especially as a new congresswoman, but…"

Kat touched Anna's arm. "I ran for Congress because I want to make a difference in the world, and I'm glad you brought me to Guam. When I came here last year, I fell in love with the people and the island. There is such a great sense of community here."

Anna knew what she meant; she'd experienced the same thing when she first arrived. In fact, as she looked at everyone laughing and teasing each other, she couldn't help but want to be a part of it.

"Alex must be so excited."

Anna had only met Kat's intense husband once, when he was the chief of staff for Kat's father, Senator Roberts.

"He is over the moon and his mother has been spoiling me rotten. We finally convinced her to leave her little house and come live with us once I deliver so she can help me take care of the baby. I was so stressed trying to figure out how I was going to run for Congress again right after the baby is born, but Alex's mom is going to be a savior."

Anna knew what that was like. Nana had come by every morning after Lucas was born. She'd changed diapers, cleaned the house, washed clothes and cooked. Anna's own mother would never have done that. She hadn't even come to visit when Lucas was born. Instead, she'd asked Anna to fly to California when Lucas was older because the trip was just too much for her. But Nana had been there. She hadn't just looked after Nico and Lucas. Nana had taken care of Anna, too.

"What's Alex doing now that your father isn't in office?" Anna hadn't really followed the election, but from the little she'd read, she knew Kat's father had been a long-time senator with talk of one day becoming a presidential candidate. But he'd lost the last election, partly because Kat chose to run.

"Oh, he quit before my father lost. He's working for a law center that helps abused women. And hovering over me now that I'm pregnant. The only reason he didn't get on that chopper with me is he's fighting this big case against the former governor of Virginia. Apparently that sleazeball abused a number of his domestic staff and the women are finally coming forward to press charges. Alex used to live in that man's house when he was a kid, so it's really personal for him."

"How can the guest of honor not eat!" Nana

handed Kat a plate piled high with food. Kat looked at her sheepishly. "This is too much, I can't eat all this."

"I made sure everything was safe for your condition." Nana winked at Kat, who turned a deep red.

"How did you know?" she whispered.

Nana smiled. "A mother knows these things." She turned to Anna. "And you, this is your home, must I bring you a plate too?"

Nana's smile was so warm, Anna wanted nothing more than to give the woman a long hug and hold on to her as tightly as she could. Instead, she walked over to the buffet and got herself a plate. She returned with it empty and Kat looked at her gratefully as she pushed some of her own food onto it. At a time when people literally had no food, they couldn't waste anything.

When everyone was done eating, Nico offered to drive people back to the hospital. They all piled into his truck, which Tito had thoughtfully fixed while Nico was in the hospital. Anna hung back; he was going to return to take her to the house in Tumon.

"There's my girl." Bruno draped an arm around her. "Come on, we have something for you."

She looked up at Nico's uncle and shook her head. What did he have up his sleeve now? It was hard not to like the bear of a man. He was often obnoxious and usually irritating, but Anna knew he would give his life for Nico and Nana.

He ushered Anna into the house, which hadn't changed much in the past five years, though there were a few signs of damage from the storm. The rooms were pitch-dark from the boarded-up windows. They walked into the living room with the deep maroon corduroy couch where she and Nico had announced that they were getting married.

The entire extended family was there. Nana's best friends, Bruno, of course, and the immediate neighbors, all of whom Anna had greeted earlier. The couch was covered in plastic wrap, likely because it was damp and damaged. Anna was sure Nana would make Nico fix it rather than buy a new one.

They all stood and came up to her one by one and hugged her again.

"Sit," Nana directed. *What is all this?* The last time they'd done something like this was when they threw her a baby shower. On this very couch, she'd sat with a big belly while the women bestowed gifts of hand-knitted clothes they'd spent months creating just for Lucas. Her feet were so swollen at the time that she could barely walk, so some of the women had used a local oil to rub them while she sat eating cake. Why had she found that suffocating?

Everyone seemed to be talking, but Anna couldn't process their words. They were reminiscing about her wedding to Nico, and the baby shower.

"Bruno, how could you lose your shoes right before you had to leave? We had to wait half an hour with the sun baking us, waiting for you to show up." Nana jabbed Bruno in the side.

"Hey!" He pulled away from her, looking hurt. "I'm an old man, my memory isn't what it used to be. To this day, I know Mae moved them and didn't tell me. Besides, you got a chance to work on your tan."

Given Nana's milk chocolate complexion, everyone laughed. Suddenly, Anna realized that she hadn't visited Aunt Mae's grave when she went to see Lucas. She made a mental note to go drop off some flowers. Her heart clenched at the thought that she'd never see the woman again and hadn't even had a chance to say goodbye. All because she'd been too stubborn to read Nico's emails.

As the conversation continued, Anna relaxed into the chair, content to enjoy the banter that filled the room, to watch the love flow between everyone. Nobody seemed to care that the windows were boarded up and the carpet was damp. Or that the glasses they were drinking out of were badly chipped. The weather was nice and they were taking a moment to relax and enjoy each other's company. It was the way weekends and evenings were often spent on the island. Having come from the mainland where coming home meant retreating to her room to check emails, Anna had been perturbed when she moved in with Nana and had company nearly every night. Someone was always at the door with a homemade dish and a story to share. As much as it had annoyed her back then, she enjoyed it now, drinking it in for the last time.

"Anna, we made something for you but didn't get a chance to give it to you before you left."

Nana handed her a folded blanket. Anna stood and shook it loose, then gasped.

"After Lucas died, we each embroidered

a patch in his memory then made a quilt," Nana explained.

They had embroidered messages of love and hope into the squares. Wishes and prayers for Lucas and for her.

Sobs shook her body. Several women stood and held her while she cried, their own tears flowing with abandon. She clutched the quilt, convulsing with a pain unlike any she'd felt before.

A guttural moan escaped her lips. Bruno stood and wrapped his large arms around the whole group. She shuddered, her chest gripped in a crushing vise. Her heart wouldn't pump, her lungs wouldn't breathe, her legs couldn't hold her up. Yet she remained standing, fortified by Nico's family. They didn't rush her, didn't murmur platitudes or tell her it would all be okay. They let her cry, they let her scream.

Then they let her go, and a pair of strong arms enveloped her and her face was buried in Nico's chest. She pounded on it, asked him why Lucas had to die, why their perfect life had to be ruined. He squeezed her tighter and she felt the hiccupping sobs in his chest. They stood there, sobbing together. When the blood finally stopped pounding in her ears, she heard soft prayers. She lifted her head to see that everyone had joined hands and were silently praying. For her. For Lucas. And for Nico. Everyone in the room had lost or suffered damage to their homes. Many knew someone who had died. Yet they were praying for her. They were asking the Lord to bring her peace, to save her soul.

Nico's blue shirt was stained with tears, and so was his face. He bent and kissed her forehead, his wet lashes sprinkling her nose. Anna had grieved when Lucas died, and so had Nico. They had cried together, but never like this. As Anna pulled away from him she found her fingers still clutching the quilt. She spread it on the couch. Nico wrapped his arm around her shoulder and brought her close. Silently, they read the condolences on the quilt. In the middle was an embroidered likeness of Lucas. His sweet roundness was perfectly captured along with the small little divot in his chin.

For the first time since his death, Anna didn't feel the deep, dark ache that lived permanently in her soul. That knife that was permanently embedded in her heart had been removed. She was free. Finally, she had the release she'd been searching for.

She turned to Nico's family, her family. "Thank you." She didn't need to be more effusive or find words to make a speech. They didn't want any more. Closing in, they enveloped her and Nico again, and for the first time, Anna realized that they had always accepted her. She was the one who hadn't accepted them.

And now it was too late.

CHAPTER NINETEEN

NICO HELD HIS breath as they drove up the
gravel road leading to the house in Tumon
Bay. He hadn't been back here since that day
five years ago when he'd gone to the airport
for Anna. From the first moment he'd seen
the house, he had pictured himself and Anna
here. He had cobbled together every penny
he could and taken odd jobs around the island to buy the house, knowing that if they
bought it together, Anna would have spent
most of her savings on it. He'd wanted to give
her something, to show her that he could take
care of her.

It was his home, but after she'd left, Nico
hadn't even been able to come here to pack
his bags. Bruno and Tito had done that for
him.

The gravel road was littered with debris
and he had to go off-road to get close to the
house. He rounded the corner and the house
came into view. That was as far as the car

would go with the litter strewn across the road. They sat in silence, staring at what used to be their home. The sun shone down on it just as it had the first day he'd brought her here.

Anna threw her head back and started to laugh. Wisps of gold-brown hair escaped the clips holding her hair back, and her blue-gray eyes sparkled as a smile lit up her face. This was his Anna. The one without the heartbreak in her eyes, the one with the laugh that sounded like wind chimes, the one who saw humor in the world. Her laughter was infectious and he found himself joining in, a deep belly laugh that warmed his body and lightened his heart. He hadn't laughed like this since before Lucas was diagnosed.

"This is so not funny," she said.

"I know."

Still laughing, they exited the car and walked the last several feet to the house, picking their way over fallen branches and other odds and ends.

"Is that our kitchen table?" Anna pointed to a piece of furniture lying on its side.

"Yep, and there's the rocker I built."

The front door hung on one hinge, ready to fall off. Part of the roof had caved in on the left side. That was the side he and Anna had painstakingly repaired, then watched with bated breath when the first storm hit to see if it would hold. The house looked almost exactly as bad as it had the first time he had shown it to Anna.

They stood and took it all in, enjoying the soft lapping sound of the ocean on the far side. A stand of trees blocked the view from there, but it was visible from inside the house. He'd been drawn to that view from the beginning, like it was a hidden treasure only they could enjoy. "Do we dare go inside?"

She was gazing up at the second story, where the master bedroom stretched the width of the house. She'd stood there like that the first time he'd brought her there too. This time, there was no anger in her face, no hint of Anna's signature "I'm going to kill you, Nico" look. Just a reminiscent smile that lit up her face. Grinning, he stepped closer to her and picked her up, enjoying her squeal as he carried her like a baby up the front step, exactly the way he had on their first visit.

He toed the front door to nudge it open and stepped carefully inside. His boots hit an inch of water. Their rugs, lamps and assorted trash were floating on the first floor.

"Now, see, this makes it worth getting a ride. I hate wet socks," Anna said.

Laughing, he continued carrying her upstairs, stepping gingerly to make sure the floor wasn't going to give way under him. The stairs were solid. They'd stood for decades, even when the rest of the house crumbled. The door to the master bedroom was wide-open and Nico didn't hesitate. He crossed the threshold and set Anna down.

She gasped and he froze. He wasn't as religious as the rest of his family but in this moment, he had to believe this was a sign from God. It had to be. The bedroom was intact. The drapes that his mother and her friends had sewn hung neatly from the four-poster bed he'd built himself. Even the bedspread that Anna had picked out was still on the bed. There were layers of dust on everything and a few pieces of trash had blown in, but even the window was unbroken.

Appearing as bewildered as he felt, Anna ran her hands over the bed. She went to the nightstand and opened it. "I was reading this book before Lucas was diagnosed."

"I haven't been back since the day you left. Everything is exactly the same, waiting for you to return."

Closing the drawer, she went to the dresser and picked up the picture frame that sat there. It was from their wedding day. Neither he nor Anna was looking at the camera; they were both turned away, eyes only for each other. It was his favorite photo. Somehow Bruno had caught them in a moment that was just about them.

He knew where she'd go next. The small box in the dresser drawer. It was the first thing he'd checked when he came home and found her gone. She opened the drawer and found the antique silver box. She opened it and picked up the pearl ring inside.

Anna turned to him, her eyes wide, lips slightly parted. This wasn't the time to think, to analyze or to question. He'd spent five years doing that and had never come up with any answers. Pulling her into his arms, he brought his mouth down on hers. She melted into him, the way she always did. Her lips were salty from the tears she had cried earlier and he cupped her face.

Not for one second had he stopped loving her, and he wanted her to know how much he still needed her. That she was a permanent part of his soul. When he'd kissed her in the church, it had been a kiss of closure. He had conveyed the apology he'd never been able to give. This time there was no apology, just a plea. He kissed her cheeks, her nose and her forehead. "I will do anything, Anna, anything to take away your pain. To bring Lucas back to you. To bring you back to me."

"I'm sorry, Nico. I pushed you away, I never gave you the chance to..." Fresh tears filled her eyes and he held her, desperate for the warmth of her breath against his chest, the smell of her hair. His living, breathing Anna. Lately, he'd come to think of her as a sweet dream that had visited him in the dead of night but was gone by morning. "I need you, Anna. I can't be whole without you."

She took a sharp breath and pushed against him, but he held on to her. He wasn't going to let her go without saying everything he needed to say. That was a mistake he wasn't going to repeat. "You are my soul mate, the one woman who was made for me, who will live in my heart forever. Please, Anna, come back to me."

She pushed a little harder. "Nico, I'll never love anyone the way I love you. But we can't do this to Maria."

"No, we can't." He took a breath. "She came to me last night and asked how I felt about you. I told her the honest truth. That if I commit to her, I will love her all my life, no matter what. But she will never have my whole heart, because I've already given it to you."

Anna gasped. "How could you?"

"How could I what? Tell her the truth?"

"Break her heart."

"Because I can't break yours again."

She stepped back. "No. No, Nico, I never said I would stay, and I won't. I didn't ask us to get back together, I—"

He didn't let her finish. This time when he kissed her, it was with a passion he hoped would remind her of the love they shared, of the bond that could never break between them.

"You can tell yourself what you want, Anna, but you and I both know that what we have is the love of a lifetime. We can't throw it away."

He kissed the bridge of her nose, and then his lips found hers again and the love he'd kept locked away burst out of him. Anna wove her fingers into his hair and before his brain had time to talk him out of it, he and Anna were on the bed.

She didn't resist and, for once, he knew exactly what they were going to do.

Crack!

He froze and Anna stared at him wild-eyed. Before he could clear the euphoric haze from his mind, the bed gave way and he and Anna came crashing down onto the floor.

They looked at each other and burst out laughing.

"I guess this is a sign. Someone above is saving us from ourselves." Nico laughed.

CHAPTER TWENTY

"SERIOUSLY, NICO! WE need to get back, I have work to do."

"You'll always have work to do. It can wait. Come on."

She shook her head and followed. It was the same old Nico, with the wicked gleam in his eyes. Taking his hand, they climbed the steps to Puntan Dos Amantes—Two Lovers Point. The concrete and stone steps were still there but the admission booth to pay the entrance fee was gone.

"Is the cliff even safe?"

Nico rolled his eyes. "It's rock, and it's been standing here for centuries. I think it'll be okay, just be careful you don't trip on the loose pieces."

This was where they had gotten engaged. The jutting peak over Tumon Bay was revered in Chamorro culture as a symbol of love. The walk up to the top was normally easy, but the concrete pathways had sustained some damage. Still, Nico helped her up so they could stand in the spot where he had proposed to her. She remembered that day vividly.

"Isn't this where two lovers jumped to their deaths?"

"That's not how we see the story."

Sitting on a rock, she looked out at the sea, its impossible blue crashing against the black rocks in clouds of white foam. It was one of the most beautiful places she had ever seen. The sun was lazily dropping toward the horizon and a cool breeze brought in the smell of salt and jasmine. She had been begging Nico to bring her here for months, but he'd always found an excuse not to go. He had been holding out on her.

"Tell me, how do you see the story?"

"Once upon a time, when the Spaniards ruled Guam, there was a wealthy Spanish aristocrat who married the daughter of a great Chamorro chief. They were royalty on this island. They had a beautiful daughter who was admired for her beauty, dignity and charm. Her father arranged for the girl to be married to a powerful Spanish captain."

Nico sat down beside her and draped his arm around her shoulders. She leaned into him, picturing the young girl dreading an arranged marriage to a man she didn't know.

"The girl was so upset, she ran away from home and found this secluded spot where she could cry in peace. Here she met a Chamorro man, a warrior from a modest family. They fell in love."

She turned to him. "Let me guess—Daddy was really upset."

He rolled his eyes and she suppressed a grin. Nico loved telling fables from Guam.

"He forbade her from seeing her lover and threatened to kill him. So at sundown, she came here to see him again. But her father— and the Spanish soldiers—followed her. The lovers found themselves trapped on the edge of the cliff. To surrender would mean death for the young man and a life of misery for the girl. Because now that she had known true love, she could never give herself to another man."

Anna gazed out at the calm sea, picturing the young couple standing at the edge of the world.

"So the lovers tied their hair into a knot, looked at each other, kissed a final time then leaped over the edge."

Anna knew the story, but she'd never heard it in quite this way.

"Their souls were entwined in life, and in death, so they could be together for eternity."

Then he knelt down.

"You were always such a hopeless romantic. You refused to bring me here just so you could propose to me that day."

Nico laughed. "You caught that, huh? I knew from the day I met you that I wanted to marry you, Anna. And I knew I'd propose to you here, where my people believe souls are entwined for life. This is where I wanted us to make a commitment to each other."

"Well, it worked. Seems no matter how hard I try, I can't get away from you," she said lightly.

Anna looked out at the sparkling water, thinking of the two lovers who chose to plunge to their death just so they could be together. The love of a lifetime. Her sister Caroline had lost her husband, and with him her desire to love again. *If I'd lost Nico...* Without any hesitation, she would've given her life for his. If he asked her to stand on the edge of this cliff and take a plunge with him, she would. She already had. *He's right here. Neither one of us died with Lucas, so why should our love?*

He took her hand. On that day he'd given her a pearl ring in an antique silver box. The box had been in his family for generations and the pearl was to signify their new life on the island. She'd loved that ring. The only times she'd taken it off to put it back in the antique box was when her fingers swelled during pregnancy, and then again after Lucas died. Nico held out his palm, the ring cradled in it.

"Anna, here and now I want to entwine my soul with you forever. Will you be my wife again?"

They were the same words he'd said to her the day he proposed, and her answer was also the same.

CHAPTER TWENTY-ONE

"Captain Atao, your deployment is up in two days."

Anna had been catching up on her patient charts in the nurses' station but turned when she heard Dr. Tucker's voice. She did some quick math and realized Linda was right. How could she have forgotten? She'd been counting down her hours since she got there.

"We're fully staffed here—I have orders to extend your deployment if you'd like to stay, but I understand if you want to go."

It had been two days since their trip to the house in Tumon but Anna and Nico hadn't told anyone besides Maria that they were back together. Nico wanted to tell Nana in his own way once things had calmed on the island, but he'd spoken to Maria right away. She had successfully avoided Anna since the breakfast at Nana's house despite Anna's persistence in looking for her.

"I would be willing to stay. I want to oversee Emma coming off the ECMO." The baby had been doing remarkably well.

Linda nodded and Anna could swear her eyes were teary. "You should be here to hear that baby coo and cry."

Anna couldn't wait for the moment when Aurelia got to hold her healthy baby daughter. She wished Kat could've seen it too. "When does the congresswoman leave?" she asked Linda.

"Her plane is in two hours. The staff is gathering in the lobby to say goodbye to her."

Kat had been scheduled to leave days ago, but Luke had to return or face AWOL charges so she was stuck waiting for a seat on an outgoing plane. Commercial airlines still weren't flying in and out of Guam and only cargo planes with limited passenger space were using the one available runway. Anna would feel much better once Kat was gone. The island's sole OB, Dr. Li, had quit months ago and while Dr. Balachandra was a good general practitioner, early pregnancy complications were not for the generalists to handle. After everything Kat had done for Guam, her safe return to DC was essential.

Anna followed Linda to the main lobby, where cake and coffee had been laid out.

Maria was there and Anna made a beeline for her.

"Before you say it, yes I've been avoiding you."

Anna made a hard stop. She had thought of several ways to apologize and to beg for Maria's forgiveness, but her mouth was bone-dry and all she could do was open it stupidly.

"I never meant to hurt you," Anna croaked. How did you tell a woman *I'm sorry* for taking away the love of her life?

Maria bit her lip and Anna's heart lurched. "Nico was mine once and I let him go. I'll be paying for that mistake for the rest of my life. I just hope you won't throw away your second chance."

Anna hugged her, and Maria hesitated but then buried her face in Anna's shoulder. Anna understood Maria's pain. Giving up Nico had killed her inside. That was a fact she now accepted. That gnawing feeling, like an ulcer had been eating away at her, was gone, replaced by the calm she'd first felt on the island. The feeling of peace.

"I'm sorry to interrupt."

Anna and Maria turned to find Governor Tom in a suit and tie. It was the first time Anna had seen him dressed so formally. His eyes stayed on Maria, as if he was silently asking her if she was okay. Maria nodded, and only then did he clear his throat. "I'm going to make a little speech, and I'm wondering if you ladies would join me."

Anna realized that Maria was also looking sharp in a black dress and short maroon jacket. She, on the other hand, was wearing wrinkled scrubs.

Anna shook her head, but Maria grabbed her hand and pulled her along. Nico had appeared and he placed his hand on the small of Anna's back, a silent reassurance that nothing was amiss.

Tom gave a short speech thanking Kat and all the relief workers, medical personnel and volunteers. He turned to Maria, who thanked everyone for helping open the hospital "by hook and by crook."

Then she turned to Anna. "And now I need your help making sure that this hospital will continue to stay open and take care of all of you. I'd like to offer Dr. Anna Atao the position of chief medical officer at the new Lucas Memorial Hospital. Please join me in requesting that she accept the position."

It was a good thing Nico was behind her because Anna felt like she might fall over.

She had not been expecting that. He was grinning mischievously. She raised an eyebrow. "How long have you been planning this?"

Maria answered for him. "A few days, and don't worry, we had the governor call your supervisor at the surgeon general's office and clear you to stay for two months."

Nico touched her shoulder. "You can try it, see how it works for you."

A roar went up from the crowd and someone managed to start a "We want Anna" cheer. Cheeks red, she stood with a frog in her throat, wondering what to say. Did she want that job? She and Nico had studiously avoided talking about their long-term plans. Would he follow her to California? Nana was never going to leave the island, and with her cancer, Anna already knew what Nico needed to do. He wouldn't abandon his mother.

And then it hit her. This was his way of keeping her here. It was her turn to make a decision. Would she stay or go?

Crash!

Before she could process what had happened, Nico was on top of her, covering her as pieces of concrete rained down on them and water gushed into the foyer.

"Everybody out!" he shouted, though no

one needed encouragement. People were rushing for the exits, and Nico pushed Anna in that direction, but she resisted.

"No, we have to get the patients from the top floors. We can't leave them behind." A piece of the exterior wall had caved in. Who knew what else was coming down?

"I'll go get them," Nico said.

Anna was on his heels. She wouldn't leave without her patients; she had to make sure Emma was okay.

Maria ran to the announcement system, which they had just gotten up and running this morning, to encourage anyone who could walk without assistance to get outdoors. The fire alarm was unfortunately not fully functional.

It was a maddening process, but all the medical personnel understood it. Those who could walk got out first. That would clear the hallways for them to carry out those who couldn't. No matter how many times Anna had been through situations like this, she could never look the bedridden patients in the eyes. Thailand had been the worst. They'd had to leave some patients behind when the building collapsed too fast to get them out.

But that wasn't going to happen today because every able-bodied man and woman in the community had come running back into the hospital to help carry stretchers, wheelchairs and patients attached to machines. They were willing to risk their own lives for others.

Once everyone was out and there was no more falling debris, Nico and Maria walked back into the building to survey the damage. Anna joined them and squared her shoulders when Nico gave her an exasperated look and pointed to the door.

"If you want me to be the CMO of this crumbling heap, I'm going to be here, for better or worse."

Maria failed to suppress her smile. Even under the circumstances, Nico's glare was priceless.

He eyed the source of the wall cave-in. "I'm no engineer, but my guess is that crack in the foundation we've been worried about stressed a load-bearing wall. The water was from a pipe burst." Nico's voice was weary, and Anna knew he was blaming himself.

Maria swore under her breath. "That's where the water must have come from during the hurricane. I haven't been able to get a structural engineer in to check it out."

"The more immediate problem is what we do with the patients," Anna chimed in. "The battery backups on the machines won't last long, especially the ECMO. Emma and the burn patients need to be in a sterile environment."

The DMAT and PHS teams were already erecting tents a safe distance away from the hospital. Nico rubbed his neck. Anna touched his arm, but it was Maria who had a solution in mind.

"Here's what we do—see if the congresswoman can lean on the base commander to send the army corps of engineers to do an assessment. Bruno said his friend at the base told him they're there doing repairs."

Nico snapped his fingers. "Good. Maria, while we see if the Army can spare someone, you check if the governor knows anyone at the fire department—they're responsible for condemning buildings, so they have to know someone who can do assessments."

"I'll go talk to Kat," Anna volunteered, trying to shake the sinking feeling that there was another disaster in store for them.

ANNA DIDN'T LIKE Kat's face when she finally found her in one of the tents. She was whiter than the bedsheet she was lying on. Vickie was beside her, holding her hand.

"What's wrong?"

Dr. Balachandra was tending to her. "She started cramping. I did a pelvic exam—she's bleeding."

A cold dread spread through Anna's veins. "Do we have a portable ultrasound?"

Dr. Balachandra nodded. "One of the volunteers is getting it for me. We left it in the hospital."

"Kat, how're you feeling?"

To her credit, Kat cracked a small smile. "Great timing to have a complication, huh? Alex is going to kill me."

Anna grabbed her hand. "We're going to take care of you." She was not going to let anything happen to Kat. Not after everything the woman had done for them. The volunteer rolled in the ultrasound machine and they lifted Kat's shirt to apply the conduction gel. Anna let out a breath when they saw the fetal heartbeat. She wasn't a trained ob-gyn and her ultrasound skills were basic. She needed a specialist. Dr. Balachandra peered at the screen with her.

"We don't see anything wrong with the baby."

Kat breathed a sigh of relief but Anna exchanged a glance with Dr. Balachandra. Bleeding and cramping together was a bad sign, but they didn't have the expertise to make a diagnosis.

"Was Kat able to call the base?" Maria breezed in and stopped short when she saw what was going on. She slapped a hand to her mouth.

"What's happened? What do you need me to do?" Trust Kat to worry about everybody else.

"You take care of yourself right now, Kat," Anna said firmly, but of course the congresswoman was already sitting up, gazing expectantly at Maria who shot Anna an apologetic look.

"Sorry, Tom said the guy from the fire department who did assessments died in the tsunami, so we have no other choice."

Maria explained the situation to Kat, who promptly pulled out her phone to call the garrison commander in charge of base logistics.

Anna stepped aside to work her own contacts to find an OB who could help them over Skype. She finally got hold of one who told her they'd need to do more tests. Anna returned to the tent to find Kat was still on the phone with the base.

"I understand, Commander, but I must say that when I return to DC, I'm going to talk with the armed services committee chairman, who is a friend of my father's. I'll have to convey your utter lack of compassion in a time of crisis." Maria and Dr. Balachandra were staring at her in awe, and despite the acid churning in her stomach, Anna had to take a second to admire Kat.

"Well, I'm glad you can spare someone, after all. We'll expect him within the hour."

"Okay, everyone out." Anna was firm. "Dr. Balachandra and I need to take care of Kat."

Vickie stood to leave but Anna waved her down. Kat would need her sister in case they had bad news.

"What's going on?" Vickie's voice was laced with worry. "I thought the baby was fine."

"The baby is fine, but we need to do an internal ultrasound to see why you're bleeding. I have an OB from Hawaii on the line."

Anna reactivated the connection with the OB and turned her phone so Kat could see him. He directed Anna as she did an internal

ultrasound, instructing her on how to take
measurements using the machine.

"Unfortunately, the portable ultrasound
does not have the sensitivity I'd need for a
full diagnosis," he said when the test was
complete. "If she were Stateside, I'd send her
to Maternal-Fetal Medicine to get her cervical length properly measured, but I think she
is likely experiencing cervical incompetence.
I recommend you do a cerclage." The OB's
crackly voice cut through the room.

Anna's heart dropped to the soles of her
feet. They weren't equipped to perform this
surgery on a pregnant woman. At least when
they operated on Emma they had a proper
facility. In addition to not having properly
trained staff, they didn't have a sterile OR.
This was not something she had ever done or
been trained to do and judging by the panic
in Dr. Balachandra's eyes, he hadn't, either.

"Can we transport her?"

The OB considered this. "If that's the only
option, keep her on bed rest and see if you
can get a medical transport right away."

Anna motioned to Vickie, who was already
on her phone. They had missed their scheduled flight waiting to make sure everyone
made it out of the hospital. Kat had refused

to ask someone to drive them to the airport in the middle of the evacuation.

As they exited the tent, Vickie turned to Anna, her voice filled with fear. "There are no flights out for two days. They're saying it's only supply planes that can't carry people."

Heart thumping, Anna forced herself to take some deep breaths. "Let's go talk to Maria about medical helicopters."

They found Maria, who started to apologize for her earlier blunder. Anna explained the situation.

"CNMI was badly hit too, so between all the relief organizations, we only have two medical helicopters." The Commonwealth of the Northern Marianas was a group of neighboring islands that were also a US Territory and the only major land mass near Guam. Maria wrung her hands. "They're running twenty-four hours, but they have a priority list of patients. I will ask because Kat is a congresswoman but…" She looked from Vickie to Anna.

Anna didn't wait for her to continue. "I know. The critical patients go out first. Kat's condition is urgent, but the heart patients, stroke victims and people with head injuries take priority."

Vickie put a palm to her forehead. "And knowing Kat, she wouldn't want to cut in line."

Nico joined them and Anna brought him up to speed. "Then we do the surgery here," he said.

"Nico!" Anna stared at him, flabbergasted.

"Look, I'm no doctor and I know you'll say we don't have the resources, but that's the whole point of this hospital. When people can't get off the island, we have to find a way to get them the care they need. That's why I built the surgical suite with telemedicine capabilities so you can get a specialist to talk you through things."

"Nico, it doesn't work that way. I've never done a cerclage and neither has Dr. Balachandra. We can't take such risks with Kat's life—or her baby's. We nick something the wrong way, and she could bleed out."

But he wasn't listening. She recognized the stubborn jut of his chin, the pressed lips and concentrated frown. It was the way he'd looked when they found out they couldn't get Lucas off the island.

She grabbed his arm. "Nico, this is not the time to prove a point. Kat has done a lot for us—we can't play with her family."

He shook off her arm. "This is not about making a point. Kat's life is no more important than any other person's. Just like we did everything we could to save Emma, we will do what's necessary to save Kat."

Then he strode away and all Anna was left with was the red-hot anger that rose in her belly. Nico was wrong; he was trying to prove something to her, and his stubbornness would get Kat killed.

She turned to Maria. "Make the call, see if you can get Kat on a list or get a new helicopter for her." She asked Vickie to call the base and anyone she could think of in Washington, DC. Maybe Luke could commandeer another helicopter.

Anna was going to get Kat off this island if it was the last thing she did.

CHAPTER TWENTY-TWO

NICO DIDN'T KNOW whether to consider it good news or bad news. The army engineer was a stand-up guy who not only brought equipment to survey the damage but also a small crew that could work to repair it. The bad news was that there was a crack in the foundation, probably caused by the tsunami and exacerbated by the hurricane. The good news was that the crew could seal it, shore up the wall that had fallen, and the rest of the building was stable. They recommended fixing the foundation and letting it dry before bringing anyone into the building. So the hospital would be out of commission for at least two days.

While the men went to work, Nico checked in with Maria. There was rain in the forecast, but no storms. The DMAT and PHS teams had plenty of tents to house the current patients, especially if they could use the lawn space closer to the building.

The main problem was preparing the surgical facility for Kat and finding a generator for the ECMO machine, ventilators and other medical equipment that were about to run out of batteries. The generator the DMAT team had brought was low on gas and there were no propane tanks left on the island.

"We have to bring the patients in." Nico told Maria. "The engineers said the building is still solid, and we can put them on the west side, away from the damaged section." There were solar panels on the roof that had been repaired, so the hospital itself had electricity.

"Nico, the man said it's not safe to have people inside while they're repairing the foundation in case something goes wrong."

"We don't have a choice. We can keep them outside as long as possible, but Kat needs surgery. She's not getting off the island."

Maria chewed on her lower lip. "Tom says if we say the word, he'll override the priority list for the medical transports."

"What should we do?" He'd always valued Maria's judgment and he knew his judgment was colored by Anna.

"Mrs. LaCosta had a stroke and she needs out. She's next on the list. You remember Ryan Louis? That kid who scored the touchdown in the last game against CNMI? He needs neurosurgery." She was conflicted, and so was he.

"It's not the right thing to do, Maria. We can't play with people's lives like that."

She sighed wearily. "I know. But if something happens to Kat, Anna will never forgive you."

He didn't need to be reminded of that fact. While they had reconciled, he and Anna hadn't talked about her moving back to the island. They needed some breathing room before making that decision. It had been Maria's idea to offer her the CMO position, but he'd had the same thought days ago when they'd first discussed it. He'd gone to Tom to ask him to call the mainland to see if they would consider extending her deployment.

But he'd watched Anna's face when Maria made the announcement. Nico hadn't wanted to do it publicly, but Maria had insisted that Anna would hear the encouragement of the crowd and get swept away. Instead she'd looked panicked. Like the reality of her decision to be with Nico was crashing down on her.

"We have to show Anna that she's wrong."

Nico spent the next hours talking to every doctor who had arrived on island and each relief organization that had the capacity to bring people in. Nobody was an ob-gyn and everyone agreed that while losing the baby would be a horrible outcome for Kat, there were more urgent situations on the island. Some people who had suffered semiserious injuries days ago were now in critical condition due to the ongoing shortages of drugs and medical supplies. The Red Cross had set up a field hospital on the other side of the island and medical command was sympathetic with Nico but couldn't offer any more support. They had even fewer doctors, nurses, supplies and surgical facilities than he did. They were using a tent for their surgical suite with bare-bones equipment.

But he had to find a way to save Kat's baby. His marriage depended on it.

IT WAS PAST midnight when Anna finally saw Nico again. She was with Baby Emma, who was breathing on her own after being weaned off the ECMO. Emma, Troy and Aurelia were the only ones with Anna in the eerily quiet NICU.

"How is she?" he asked.

Anna sighed. "We won't be able to tell for a few more days. She's come off the machine well, she's breathing on her own and her heart is pumping. Now we just have to see if it can stand the workload, and make sure she doesn't get an infection." That was one of the big reasons they'd brought Emma inside, despite the ongoing repair work.

"Can I hold her?"

Anna smiled at Aurelia. She wanted the other woman to be able to hold her baby without Emma being attached to machines. She held up her finger, then worked inside the incubator to cap off her IV line. Emma would continue needing intravenous medications, so they couldn't take the line out, but Anna could disconnect her temporarily. Checking to make sure Emma was oxygenating well, she also disconnected the tube in the baby's nose.

Picking up the little baby, Anna felt her wiggle and move in her arms. It had been well over five years since she'd held a baby like this. Anna was having trouble counting the exact number of days. The little movements of Emma's body should have seized her with panic, but all she felt was happiness. Emma gurgled, her little arms and legs working furiously, like she was excited to be awake and off the machines. She was alive and wanted people to know it. Nico was beside her, ready to take the baby from her if she wanted. His eyes plainly said what was in her heart. She had paid the penance for Lucas's death.

Handing the baby to Aurelia, Anna watched the young woman kiss her daughter, letting the tears flow down her cheeks. Emma reached up to touch her mother's face with her chubby hands, and Aurelia kissed them.

"Thank you." Troy said the simple words with such deep emotion that Anna's tears flowed with his.

Emma's wails had them all laughing. "I think after days of IV nutrition, she's ready for her mommy." Anna smiled at Aurelia and touched Nico's arm so they could leave and let the parents enjoy their baby.

On the way out, she instructed the nurse to put Emma back in the incubator after a few minutes. She wasn't totally out of the woods yet.

"You did it," Nico whispered and pulled her into his arms. Resting her head against his chest, she felt the beat of his heart. She needed him to hold her, to not have to deal with the flood of emotions on her own.

"Holding Emma like that..." Her voice cracked.

Nico stroked her hair, "I know you've always wanted a big family."

And she still did. Somewhere in the past five years, she'd lost track of what she wanted out of life, what the future would hold for her.

"I still do."

"It's not too late for us," he said softly. His lips were soft against her ear, his voice pleading. He'd told her that as an only child, he'd always wanted a house full of kids. When they renovated the house in Tumon, they'd converted one big room into two smaller bedrooms. *Two girls and two boys.* But what would happen if she had another baby with a heart defect, or God forbid the child fell and had a head injury? The mortality rate for children under five years old was high in Guam. Injuries that children on the mainland recovered from couldn't be treated on the island.

"I can't go through what happened with Lucas again. Or with Emma. And look at Kat now. If we were on the mainland, even in the middle of a disaster, a cerclage would be a routine procedure." She stepped out of his embrace. Nico had a way of making her feel like anything was possible, but she lived in the real world.

"I know what you've been trying to do here, but you can't possibly get every single specialist you ever need right when you need them." He looked pained, and she understood. They were back where they'd started. The reason she'd left to begin with.

"Anna, look around. Five years ago a hospital like this would have been impossible. If people like us, people who can make things happen, leave for the mainland, life will never improve here. Together we can make this community whole."

What was she supposed to say to that? That despite working in poorly resourced areas for five years, in extreme situations, she still hadn't come to the point where she was okay with it? That she was willing to sleep on cots, expose herself to the worst diseases in the world, eat MREs for months on end, but she still couldn't bring herself to face the notion that someone she loved could die and she wouldn't be able to save them.

"I can't sacrifice any more."

"I'm sorry to interrupt." Both Nico and

Anna turned to see Maria standing there. She was wringing her hands, and the stricken look on her face told Anna she was there to give them bad news.

CHAPTER TWENTY-THREE

MARIA HELD NICO back as Anna rushed into Kat's tent.

Nico closed his eyes. If something happened to Kat, there was no hope for him and Anna. He had to act.

Maria touched his arm. "Her husband and father have been calling in a number of favors. Tom's gotten a call directly from the White House. He's willing to use executive privilege to get Kat on a transport. There's one on the way back from dropping a patient in Hawaii. She can go out in an hour. Tom wants us to decide what's best."

He squeezed his eyes shut. If only it were so easy to figure out what the right thing was. The words were on his lips to ask Maria to make the call to Tom, but he stopped himself. The triage process was in place to protect people. If he intervened, he was playing God.

"Why don't you just ask Anna what she wants to do?" Maria suggested.

"No!" The last thing he was going to do was burden Anna with this decision. If something happened during transport or whoever was next in line got bumped and died, Anna would never stop blaming herself. But if Kat stayed on Guam and had a bad outcome, Anna would never stay there. She would leave just like she had with Lucas. This was his only chance to show her he could take care of her and their family and the people of the island. He had to. He wasn't going to abandon them the way his father had.

"We need to get her off the island." Anna snapped off her gloves. "We can't tell on the ultrasound what the exact problem is, but we're hoping that the cerclage will help. She needs a proper hospital with better diagnostic equipment to figure out what's going on."

"There's no way to get her off the island," Nico said simply.

"I've been thinking..." Dr. Balachandra stepped toward them, tapping a finger to his chin. "Dr. Atao, you already have Emma in the hospital. What if we opened a surgical suite and had one of the Stateside OBs talk us through the procedure?"

Anna shifted on her feet.

Nico opened his mouth to encourage her,

but Dr. Balachandra continued. "I've delivered a lot of babies, and I've dealt with uterine prolapse—I think I can do this. It's her best chance, if we put her on a transport, who knows what might happen on the way."

"I can get an OR suite sterilized," Maria chimed in.

Anna shook her head. "I'm not willing to risk the surgery. We don't even know if it's the right procedure!"

"I'm taking the risk, Dr. Atao, all I need you for is to assist and monitor the baby, but this is not on you."

Anna flashed her eyes at Dr. Balachandra. "It's not about blame, it's about doing what's best for the patient and making sure we don't let our personal desire for heroics affect our decision-making."

Nico stepped back. Did she think that's what he was doing? Or what she'd done when she operated on Lucas?

"These are unusual circumstances, and it requires creative thinking," Maria said carefully.

Anna didn't have to say it out loud for Nico to know what she was thinking. It was the way things always seemed to work on Guam. And she wasn't wrong. There was greater acceptance here for the fact that not everything could be fixed. But as a woman of modern medicine, Anna would never acknowledge that.

"I'll go start setting up." Maria left with Dr. Balachandra in tow.

"I think this is the wrong thing to do," Anna said ominously. Nico's stomach churned. Was he making the right call? If something happened to Kat and Anna found out later that he hadn't told her about the transport, she'd never trust him again.

Her eyes were dark, weary from the stress of the last several days. He wanted nothing more than to pull her into his arms and tell her everything would be okay.

But the sinking feeling in his stomach told him he was going to lose Anna again.

CHAPTER TWENTY-FOUR

ANNA CHECKED THE clock in the OR. One thousand, nine hundred and seven days and ten hours since she'd felt the tremor that shook her hands now. Kat had been anesthetized. They had a nurse anesthetist and a trauma surgeon who were pulled into the surgery because of who Kat was and the frequent calls from her father, a powerful former senator who had gotten the White House involved.

Her gloved hands twitched as she helped Dr. Balachandra drape Kat and push her legs into position. Kat attached the fetal monitor so they could continue watching the baby's progress. Since giving Kat a fluid bolus, the fetal heart rate had come up.

Kat's husband was on his way to the island. How would Anna face Alex if things didn't go well? After all Kat had done for her, how would she tell him that she couldn't even save their first baby?

"Dr. Atao?"

She snapped her attention back to Dr. Balachandra. "I'm sorry."

"I asked whether you were satisfied with the fetal heart rate and ready to begin."

No I am not. This is a crazy idea, just like me doing Lucas's surgery was a desperate plan. Kat could die on the table. She could bleed out. We shouldn't be doing this.

"Let's do this." Her voice sounded remarkably calm.

A volunteer who looked like he was about to pass out held up a tablet computer so the OB in Hawaii could watch and direct them. Dr. Balachandra inserted the speculum and began.

"The bleeding is really heavy—I'm having trouble seeing." Dr. Balachandra couldn't hide the anxiety in his voice. Her own pulse pounded through her body, the normally cold temperature of the OR unable to stop beads of sweat from prickling her forehead.

The trauma surgeon gave him some suggestions for controlling the bleeding. The beep of the fetal monitor pulled Anna's attention. The baby's heart rate was still okay but it had dropped. She checked Kat's vital signs. "We need to give her some blood—her heart rate is rising and pressure is dropping."

They only had one unit of blood on hand. Normally for a surgery like this, there would be several, but blood was yet another item that was in short supply on Guam. Yesterday they had done a blood drive in the hospital, but it took time for the Red Cross to test and replenish their inventory.

She didn't need to tell Dr. Balachandra that he didn't have much time to stop the bleeding.

"She might have cysts that are causing the bleeding." The disembodied voice of the OB from Hawaii broke in.

"Okay, I'm in, suctioning now."

The whole thing lasted twenty-six minutes but it might as well have been twenty-six hours. Once Dr. Balachandra was done, they slowly brought Kat out of anesthesia. She'd been given as light a dose as possible to protect the baby. She was woozy but seemed to be doing well.

"You're trembling."

Nico put his arms around Anna as she exited the OR. She let him hold her, her body both cold and hot.

"She'll be okay. You guys did it."

Anna had done nothing. "I wish we hadn't had to do this here."

"Alex has arranged a medical transport for her. He'll be here in seven hours."

Anna hoped they'd done the right thing. After seeing the bleeding, even the mainland OB had his doubts as to whether they'd made the right diagnosis.

"This is just like it was with Lucas. No way off the island." Anna muttered, her chest burning. "It'll always be like that—when we need to get off, we can't. No way out."

Nico tightened his hold on her. "Anna, I need to tell you something."

The hesitation in Nico's voice put her nerves on edge. She pushed away from him so she could look him in the eyes. *Now what?*

"I lied to you earlier. Kat's father called the White House and they put pressure on Tom to move Kat up on the priority list for medical transport. We had a helicopter that was leaving in an hour. I made the call not to ask Tom, to avoid bumping someone off the list. So there was a way off the island. I know you don't believe it because of what happened with Lucas, but there's always a way. It's just about making the right choice."

Anna staggered and hit a wall behind her. She leaned against it for support. Nico reached out for her but she slapped his arms away.

"You had a way to get her off the island?"

"Anna, if we had, the person who would've missed his turn was a thirteen-year-old with a bleed in his brain."

She glared at him. Kat would never be high on a medical triage list for transport. While her situation was bad, it could be managed. At worst, she could lose her baby, but they could save her life. The kid with the brain bleed would die without neurosurgery. Anna knew he'd made the right decision. That was what disaster triage was all about, making sure those who most needed care got it first. And yet she couldn't suppress her anger.

"That was a decision you should've let me make."

"I couldn't." His eyes pleaded with her. "I didn't want to put the responsibility on you. I asked Dr. Balachandra to make the call."

"Don't you get it, Nico? The responsibility is mine, whether or not I want it." She sank to the floor and pulled her knees to her chest, burying her head in her arms. The stress of the past few days was catching up with her.

"Hey, it's okay. You guys saved Kat and her baby. She'll be fine." Nico stroked her hair. It felt so good to have Nico share the burden with her. When it was Lucas, Nico had deferred to her medical judgment for all decisions. At the time, she had been driven to save Lucas at any cost.

"You don't have to take on everything. Kat is our collective responsibility. Not yours alone."

She lifted her head and rested it against the wall. "I know you can't leave. You have an obligation to fulfill for your family, and I get that. You need to take care of Nana."

He hung his head. "It's not forever, Anna. My obligations, as you call them, won't last long, especially if Nana isn't getting treatment. Maria can run this hospital once it's fully operational. I won't have to be here physically to help. Can you stay with me for a little while? So we can work this out together?"

Could she?

"Dr. Atao, you need to come right away," the nurse shouted down the hall. Anna was on her feet in a flash and Nico followed close behind.

She rushed into Kat's room, where the

trauma surgeon and Dr. Balachandra were opening up IV lines.

"She passed out and the fetal heart rate has dropped."

The portable ultrasound machine had already been set up. Anna did an internal ultrasound. The baby's heart was beating, but way too slowly. Dr. Balachandra began a pelvic exam. "The sutures are intact, but she's bleeding."

Someone left to rouse the Hawaiian OB to see if he had any ideas.

An alarm on the fetal monitor began beeping incessantly. "The heart rate is only fifty... now forty-five...now forty-one...now forty." Anna closed her eyes. She didn't need to keep reading to know what was happening. Kat was losing the baby.

Minutes later, there was no heartbeat on the monitor. Anna didn't try to stop her tears. What was she going to tell Alex when she saw him?

"We have to get her to the OR and do a D and C."

"I'll do it," Anna said wearily.

Both the trauma surgeon and Dr. Balachandra stared at her. "You don't have to. Unfortunately, I've done a lot of these."

"No, I should be the one," Anna insisted.

"No!" Nico's harsh voice cut through the room.

HE DIDN'T KNOW if it was Anna's pale face, the haunted look in her eyes, or the boneless way in which her shoulders sagged. But a realization had hit him with more force than the tsunami itself.

Anna needed him to be the strong one. She would keep sacrificing herself until she had nothing left to give. This time he would be the strong one. He would do what needed doing.

He wrapped his arm around her. "Dr. Balachandra, please perform the surgery." Anna fought against him but he held on to her and firmly guided her to his and Maria's office. There was a cot there that he'd been using. He set her on it. "I want you to sleep."

She shook her head. "Nico, are you crazy, this is not the time to sleep! I need to take care of Kat, talk to Alex when he gets here, I need to—"

"I've got it, Anna. I will talk to Alex. The other doctors are more than capable of helping Kat. They'll take care of her, I promise."

"No, Nico, you don't understand." She

threw back the blanket he'd covered her with, eyes flashing. "It's too late. It's too late for Kat, and it's too late for us."

She walked out and he didn't stop her. There was nothing he could say that would keep Anna on Guam. It was up to him to choose what he wanted more.

CHAPTER TWENTY-FIVE

"Nico! I'm glad you came by. I was going to bring this by the hospital. I made your favorite, *alåguan*."

Nico sighed. He was in need of some comfort food, and the warm, soupy dish of rice and coconut milk would hit the spot. He sat at his mother's kitchen table, a small Formica contraption that fit only two chairs. They had never needed anything bigger; it had been just the two of them for the longest time. He knew how Anna viewed this house. It was dated, full of things that belonged in the seventies.

It wasn't that Guam didn't have modern comforts. The influx of tourists brought money to the island; there were five-star resorts, fancy malls selling the finest goods, and anything someone needed could be flown or shipped in. Yet most of the indigenous people lived like his mother: in small houses with crumbling roofs and walls. The per capita income was half that of the general United States.

Guam was a strategic outpost for the United States, a "gateway to Asia." Beyond the military base, there would be no investment in Guam by the federal government. The people needed to improve their own lives. *I made a promise to the community that I would be here, be the man my father never was.*

"Look who's here."

Nico turned to see Tito on crutches. "Finally washed up, huh?" Nico teased.

"Yeah, you were gonna leave me for dead in that field hospital. Lucky for you, I charmed one of the cute nurses and she took good care of me." He winked at Nico and Nana slapped him on the arm.

"You sit too. I'll give you a bowl."

Tito grinned and sat in the chair Nana had vacated. "Yeah, my house is, like, gone. The roof is in the neighbors' yard, my bed is on the road. Dude, my ATV disappeared. I'm okay with the house, but my ATV, that's rough, man. What's a tsunami gonna do with an ATV? It ain't even a water vehicle."

Nico grinned. Tito's silliness was just what he needed right now. Tito slurped some food into his mouth. "Nana…" He kissed his fingers. She smiled and patted him on the head.

Tito regaled them with stories of the "other" field hospital where he had been transferred when the hurricane came. He had apparently hit on every single available nurse and a few patients, one of whom had turned out to be eighty years old, which Tito didn't know because he was heavily medicated at the time.

"I told Tito he could stay in your room until his house is repaired."

"It'll be just like when we were kids." Tito grinned. When they were younger, Tito's parents had gone through some hard times and had to go live in a shelter. Tito had come to stay with them and he and Nico had slept in Nico's double bed together for more than a year while his family got back on their feet. At the time, Nana would not hear of Tito going into foster care or staying at a shelter. They'd been like brothers ever since.

"Nana, he's going to break my bed." Tito was an easy three hundred pounds.

"Hey, don't be jealous just 'cause you can't have this body. I work hard to keep it in this shape."

"I haven't seen you here in a week," Nana said to Nico, ignoring the men's friendly bickering. "I figure you'll be back in your house in Tumon now that you and Anna are together."

She certainly hadn't bothered easing into the conversation. But it was long overdue. Nobody could keep a secret on Guam, and his reconciliation with Anna was already the talk of half the hospital. Except he wasn't sure they were truly back together.

"It's complicated, Nana."

"It always was between you two."

"Listen, man, if I were you, I'd hightail it to California. I hear they got houses with swimming pools and hot tubs, just like a resort but in your house. And yo, the hot tubs are, like, my size."

He wouldn't tell Tito that that was exactly what Anna's house was like. She described her mother as well-to-do, having improved her financial status with each divorce. When he'd gone to find Anna there, he'd had to triple-check the address to make sure he hadn't pulled up to a hotel. His entire neighborhood was the size of that one house. It had a swimming pool, hot tub and tennis courts. It was any wonder Anna hadn't fainted and demanded an immediate divorce when she saw the house in Tumon. He'd never known houses like her mother's. When she showed him into their house, he'd nearly left, figuring Anna was better off without him. Nico would never be able to give her such a luxurious lifestyle.

"Nico, have you considered your decision? I know you love her, and it's hard not to get caught up in the emotions of seeing her again."

"Nana, I'm not going to be happy without her."

"And you're not going to be happy with her. She doesn't want what you want from life. You must decide what you're willing to give up for her. Your home? Me?"

He sighed wearily. "I'm not going to abandon you, Nana, you know that. But you could be a little less stubborn. What's wrong with going to the mainland for treatment? Trying to fight this thing rather than admit defeat?"

"Nico, how many times must we have this conversation? I don't want to die alone in a strange place. I was born here and I will die here. This is my community, my family. Look at Anna—has she had any peace being by herself all these years? If she'd stayed, you two would have a house full of children by now."

He couldn't disagree with his mother. Just

like he couldn't undo the past. Nana took Nico's hand in hers. "If you want to go to California with her, I will give you my blessing. I want you to be happy, my child."

He buried his face in her hand. "Nana, what am I going to do without you?"

Tito wrapped his arms around Nico and Nana. "You don't worry, coz—I'm gonna be here for you and Nana. I'll take care of her when you're gone, Nico. Something happens to you, Nana, you're never gonna be alone."

They stayed in the group hug a few moments longer, just like old times. He knew Nana truly meant what she said just as surely as he knew that the island was his soul.

His life was here.

CHAPTER TWENTY-SIX

THE OPERATION SHOULD have only taken twenty to thirty minutes, but forty-eight minutes later, Dr. Balachandra was still in the OR with Kat. Anna knew there was no point in pacing. She also knew that Nico had been right in not letting her do the procedure. As a physician, it was her job to stay above the fray, to remain unemotional so she could make clear decisions.

The hospital was eerily quiet. The army engineers recommended waiting another day before letting people into the building, so the tents outside still held all the patients besides Kat and Emma. So much had happened in just a few days.

"Anna, there you are." She turned to find Linda Tucker walking purposefully toward her.

"Linda." They had dispensed with formalities a few days ago. Something about having to watch a woman perform surgery on an infant after her own had died on the table put things in perspective for the otherwise staunch rear admiral.

"I want to tell you that I have approval to extend your time here, but there is also an opportunity in Puerto Rico if you'd like to go there instead."

Was it written all over her face? The knot in her stomach twisted.

Linda placed a hand on her arm. "You know, sometimes you need distance from a situation to figure out how you feel about it."

Right, that's what she'd done the last time; put distance between her and Nico, between her and Lucas. And ultimately, she was back where she'd started. With a choice between Nico and her sanity.

"Do you think I could request personal leave?"

Linda didn't look surprised at the request. "Why don't you contact your supervisor at the surgeon general's office? From what I understand, you haven't had a lot of time between deployments. I dare say it might do you some good."

Linda turned to leave then stopped. "For what it's worth, I think you're one of the finest doctors I've had the pleasure of working with. What happened to your son might have happened anywhere in the States. Your skills are better than most of the doctors I've met. Sometimes, no matter what you do, a patient can't be saved."

Anna knew Linda was right. She'd lost her fair share of patients in the last few years, a side effect of working in extreme situations, but she hadn't developed emotional attachments to them.

The OR door finally opened and a nurse wheeled Kat out. She was unconscious but only had an oxygen mask on her face. She was breathing on her own. Anna nearly collapsed with relief. Kat hadn't died.

Dr. Balachandra emerged into the antechamber and took off his gloves, mask and cap. Catching a glimpse of Anna through the glass door, he gave her a thumbs-up. When he came out, Anna accosted him.

"The procedure went fine. She's stable, no complications." Anna exhaled and the doctor continued. "I'm no expert at these things, but for what it's worth, I think she would've lost the baby anyway. The bleeding was coming from the uterus. I think she had a partial placental abruption."

Anna thanked Dr. Balachandra and went

to see Kat. Vickie was already by her side. "How is she?"

Vickie shrugged. "I think she's still groggy. Is she okay?"

Anna nodded and checked her vitals just to be sure. "She's just resting."

Vickie nodded. "Alex is on his way. He checked in with me a few minutes ago, using an in-flight phone. He's been delayed a bit."

"It takes a while to get here. He must be climbing the walls."

"He is. He got rerouted to Osaka. Luke is meeting him there to helicopter him over here. I don't think I realized just how remote this place is."

Caro had once said that. When Lucas was first diagnosed, Anna's sister had offered to fly over but she was in the middle of college exams and when she realized the flight alone would take twenty-one hours, she'd balked. Anna left Vickie with Kat and found an empty room. One thing she regretted doing the last time she was on Guam was isolating herself from her family.

"Oh, my God, Anna, I've been trying to call you for days. Where in the world are you?" Anna filled her sister in on everything that had happened in the past twelve days.

She and Caro were close even though they'd been going in different directions the past five years. While Anna wallowed in her grief, Caro had made sure to call and email every few days to check in, even when Anna didn't respond.

Anna hadn't had a chance to check her email during this deployment, but she knew there would be at least a dozen messages. Caro was now a lawyer but instead of lining her pockets doing corporate law the way their fourth stepfather had, Caro was working for an advocacy organization lobbying for more funding for autism. It had become her calling when her own son was diagnosed with autism. Anna loved her precocious nephew, Ethan, but knew raising him by herself was hard on Caro. Two years ago, she'd lost her husband in Afghanistan and Anna felt guilty for not being around more to help. Like Anna, Caro put on a brave front but she was still hurting.

"Are you crazy? What's gotten into you?" Anna held the phone away from her ear so her sister's screaming voice wouldn't blow out her eardrums.

"I'm not staying, Caro. It's time to come home."

"Anna...where is home?"

"What do you mean?"

"My home is in Washington, DC, but it's not defined by where I live. My home will always be wherever Ethan is. What about you?" Ethan was now a second grader.

Anna sat on the floor, pondering Caro's question. Where was her home? Five years ago it was on Tumon Bay. For the past five years, she'd been a nomad.

"California, I guess."

"Mom's house?"

The automatic "no" was on her lips. Her mother's houses had never felt like home. The latest acquisition was a McMansion she'd bought after a substantial divorce settlement. The monstrosity, with its high ceilings and modern decor, felt too impersonal to ever be home. Anna had all of one suitcase that she left in one of the five guest rooms. It wasn't even home base between deployments. She preferred to go stay in Caro's two-bedroom Capitol Hill town house and share a bed with Ethan. The house smelled of food, there were toys on the floor, pictures of her and Caro and Ethan on the walls. It felt like home. But it wasn't exactly Anna's.

The only home that had truly been hers was on Tumon Bay. The house that was currently crumbling with an inch of water covering the ground floor. She looked down at the pearl ring on her finger.

"I guess it's time to figure out where home is."

ANNA HAD GOTTEN so exhausted waiting for Alex that she finally went to Nico's office to catch some sleep. Kat had woken up and Anna had to tell her what had happened. Considering everything, Kat took it well. Anna was the one who barely held it together. She had to call on every ounce of professionalism she had not to cry like a baby while delivering the news.

Kat wrung her hands and asked how long it would take Alex to get there, then asked to be left alone. Anna knew very well that Kat would grieve in private. She didn't want to burden Anna with her sorrow. Anna's only solace was that Vickie assured her she wouldn't leave Kat's side until Alex got there.

She opened the door and stopped short. Maria and the governor were in the office. Anna could've slapped herself. Nico had told her he shared the space with Maria.

"Sorry about that." She went to close the

door, Maria and the governor were in an intense discussion.

"No, Dr. Atao, please come in, I was just leaving."

"Please call me Anna. I think we're past all formalities, Governor."

"Likewise, please call me Tom."

As soon as he'd left, Maria sank into her chair.

"I interrupted something, didn't I?"

Maria nodded.

"Tom wants me to date him. Seeing all this death and suffering, he's suddenly like, 'let's seize the day, who knows what tomorrow might bring.'"

Anna nodded. It was a normal feeling after a disaster. People who were affected looked at the devastation around them and took stock of all the opportunities they'd wasted. Impulsive decisions were very common. Then it struck her. Nico had almost died after the hurricane. Had she made a hasty call in her emotionally charged state?

Maria's face clearly told her she had turned Tom down.

"Too soon?" Anna asked sympathetically.

Maria nodded and Anna's heart crumbled. She'd taken away Maria's happiness, and for what? She and Nico were in exactly the same place as before.

"Maria, Nico and I... I'm not sure..."

Maria's eyes widened. "You're going back, aren't you?" Anna flinched at the judgment in her voice.

"I know, I'm an awful person, and it doesn't make a difference that I never meant any of it to hurt you. I'm so sorry. I wish I had never deployed here or that I'd quit before coming back because nothing has changed."

"It wasn't all a waste."

"What?"

"You've found peace with what happened here. This time when you leave, don't slink away. Say goodbye."

Goodbye. It hadn't been easy to sneak away the last time, but it had felt like the clear choice. Her bones ached and she suddenly felt like the weight of the world was on her shoulders.

Maria stood. "I have to go check on the engineers. Why don't you get some sleep? You look like you could use it."

Anna didn't need to be told twice. Maria paused at the door before she left. "I also sometimes wish you had never come back. Nico had those divorce papers on his desk ready to go. We would've married and I would have lived happily ever after."

Anna swallowed. She deserved much worse than that and Maria deserved better.

"But Nico wouldn't have been happy, and in time I would've noticed. And I wouldn't have noticed how hot our *maga'låhi* is." *Maga'låhi* was the Chamorro word for governor, but Maria made it sound like a term of endearment.

Maria had let Anna off the hook, but the only thing Anna could think about was the divorce papers Maria had pointed out. Once Maria was out of sight, she went to Nico's desk and flipped through the pile of papers, easily finding the ones she wanted. Reading through the text, she noted that there was a blank next to the disposition of the Tumon house. There was a holder with a dozen pens sitting right there on the desk. Since her leave was approved, she could go out on the next flight, perhaps on the same one as Kat. Her deployment was officially over in a few hours.

Her hand quivered as she held the pen.

CHAPTER TWENTY-SEVEN

NICO HAD NEVER met a man as intense as Alex Santiago. Physically, Nico and Alex were evenly matched, yet Alex managed to stare him down. "How is my wife?"

"She's doing well. She just had breakfast and is sitting with her sister. I'll take you directly to her." Nico looked back at Luke Williams, who gave him a wide grin and nodded reassuringly. Nico had met Luke earlier, when he'd piloted Kat onto the island. When they got to Kat's room, Alex didn't hesitate; he went right to her and kissed her unabashedly.

Nico turned to Luke. "Is he always like that?"

"The first time I met him, the guy wanted to throttle me just for talking to Kat."

Nico smiled, imagining the scene. "I never thanked you for bringing the ECMO machine. It meant a lot to Anna to be able to save that baby."

Luke pinned him with his startling blue eyes. "No problem, man, I was glad to do it. What you're doing here is pretty incredible."

"That's high praise coming from someone who is literally putting his life on the line to serve our country."

Luke waved his hand. "There are hundreds of thousands like me, but it takes a lot to build something out of nothing. If I could do anything with my life, I'd want to do something like this. To bring medical care to people, to better their lives… That's the way to live."

"You're pretty young, and healthy," Nico said pointedly. "You can do anything you want."

"If only it were that easy."

Somehow, Nico knew what he meant. "Family obligations?"

Luke nodded. "Following in my father's footsteps. How about you?"

"Trying not to follow in my father's footsteps."

The two men watched Alex and Kat break off their impossibly long kiss.

"Tell you what, I would give up anything to have that kind of love." Luke gestured to Alex

and Kat; despite their tears, they were looking at each other like nothing else mattered.

ANNA MADE HER way to Nana's front door.
She'd woken this morning to find that Alex
had arrived and Nico had already explained
what had happened, taking the brunt of Alex's
anger. Still, she had gone to see Alex and Kat.
While he wasn't happy, he seemed to care
more about the fact that Kat was okay. For
her part, Kat seemed to accept what had happened. When Anna apologized to her, she'd
looked up and said, *Sometimes fate deals you
a blow and you have to roll with it. Dwelling
on it means you can't move forward.*

She wished she could be as strong as Kat
but Anna also didn't want to repeat her own
mistakes.

Since everything seemed under control
at the hospital, she'd decided to come here
before her flight off the island later today.
Normally the PHS worked at the speed of
molasses to get paperwork approved but her
leave orders came through in record time.
Linda had pulled some strings so Anna could
leave with Kat; otherwise, she could be stuck
on Guam for days or even weeks.

Rapping on the door, she stood back and

waited. Nana smiled widely when she saw Anna and invited her in. Tito was there, recuperating from his femur fracture.

"Hey, no offense, Anna, but I still have PTSD from you yanking on my leg that night. Jeez, I thought I was gonna die."

"Sorry, Tito, it had to be done to save your leg."

"Well, for that I guess I can forgive you. The ladies don't like one-legged men so much."

Anna smiled. She'd forgotten how Tito made her smile. As if sensing a serious conversation brewing, he made an excuse about needing a nap and disappeared into his room.

Nana made tea while Anna sat at the Formica table. She remembered the first time she'd visited this house. Nico had been a little embarrassed, making a point about how his mother refused to get rid of her old things even though he offered to buy her new stuff. Anna had been charmed. She would've given anything to have grown up in a home with so much personal history. Instead, her mother had bought new things every time they moved. At Nana's house, there were still crayon marks on the table from when Nico was a child.

Nana set down two steaming cups. "You've

come to say goodbye." She wasn't a woman to mince words.

Anna nodded. "I didn't want to leave like I did the last time. And I want to thank you for the quilt, and for giving me closure on Lucas's death."

"You were not the only one who needed the closure. We all needed to grieve for him, and we couldn't do it without you."

Anna nodded, looking down at her teacup. It seemed the only thing she could do these days was cry. Nothing made sense anymore, no decision felt right.

Nana patted her hand. "I'm sorry to see you go."

"I'm sorry I messed things up between Nico and Maria. I tried to talk to her. It was never my intention…" What could she possibly say? "I wish I had quit my job and never come back. Then Nico would still be engaged to Maria. They'd be happy."

"That was my hope. But even if you hadn't come, that's not what would've happened."

Anna looked up. Nana's face was weary. "I've been asking Nico to send you the divorce papers. Your mother said she had an address he could use, but he's been holding on to them. I think he was planning to go to California to see you one last time. He has never stopped loving you."

"I would've signed the papers if he'd sent them. Then maybe I wouldn't have ruined Maria's life."

Nana shrugged. "Maria is a smart, beautiful girl. All the bachelors on the island want to marry her. She'll be okay. I hear even the governor is sweet on her. It's Nico I worry about. He will never be the same without you."

Anna knew where this was going and she had braced herself for it. Nana would try to talk her into staying. She would argue a case for compromise or make a deal with Anna. It was what she'd done when Anna had expressed her discomfort with living in Nana's house after they'd gotten married. Nana had suggested they find a home of their own. It was what had made her and Nico decide to buy their own house. Then Nico, in his typical *make things happen* fashion, had bought the house in Tumon without telling her. But not before he got Nana's blessing. One thing Anna could never fault in Nana was how much she loved her son. She would sacrifice her own happiness for his.

"You need to go in order for things to work out," Nana said softly.

Wait, what? She had settled in to hear a lecture about why she shouldn't leave Guam. Nana wanted her to go? But Anna nodded, like it was unquestionably the right decision.

"Please come to California and get treatment. It's only for a short time—you'll be back on the island before you know it."

Nana smiled and stood. Giving Anna a hug, she patted her back. "I've had a good life, Nico has made me very proud. I'm okay here at home."

Anna had lost track of how many tears she'd shed during the past few days. And she had yet to say her most painful goodbye. Alex and Kat were leaving on the helicopter with Luke in just over an hour. Anna was going to catch a ride to Japan with them. She'd never get off Guam if she had to wait for a commercial flight here. The airport still only had one working runway.

She returned to the hospital and said her goodbyes to Maria and Bruno after running into them in the lobby. The other woman hugged her and cried. Even Bruno was a big baby, sobbing uncontrollably.

Then it was time to see Nico.

She knocked on his office door.

His eyes were red when he opened it, and

the hurt in his face pierced her soul. He held up her ring and the divorce papers. "I see you've signed these."

What could she say? She had left them on the desk so she wouldn't have to say the words out loud. A part of her wanted to leave like she had last time. It always seemed easier in the moment, but she'd learned the hard way that she'd regret it for years to come.

"I gave you the house in Tumon. Whatever money you get from the insurance, put my half into this hospital."

"I couldn't care less about the money. I want to rebuild that house with you."

"And I want us to have a life away from this island."

He held out his arms and she went to him. They had said everything they ever needed to say to each other. There was nothing left to do but to say goodbye.

He bent his head and cupped her face. His lips were soft and light on hers. It was like the first time he'd kissed her, his lips seeking permission. She didn't hesitate. This was the last time she'd get to be with the man she loved, and she wanted every last touch she could get. She stood on her tiptoes to get closer to him and deepened the kiss. His love flowed into her heart, like it always did. She tasted salt and didn't know if it was from her tears or his. She ended the kiss to sob into his chest and he held her tight.

A rap on the door broke their embrace. Maria looked in, her face pained. "I'm really sorry, but everyone is loaded into the chopper and Luke has to get going."

Anna nodded and Nico grabbed the duffel she'd dropped on the floor. They walked to the helicopter and he handed her bag to Vickie. Alex was sitting next to Luke in the copilot seat to make room for Anna to sit in the back. Vickie held out a hand to help her climb in. Anna looked down as the helicopter rose.

Nico pressed a hand to his heart then to his lips, and blew a kiss at her.

CHAPTER TWENTY-EIGHT

"I SAY THIS as a woman who formerly loved you and still cares about you..."

Nico looked up to see Maria standing there with her arms crossed. *Uh, oh.* She had that look in her eyes, the one she got when she was about to give him a long lecture.

He moaned. "I don't need this right now."

Although each day since Anna had left felt like a struggle to get through, two months had gone by and he'd been busy getting the hospital fully operational. Things had come together in large part thanks to the governor and to Lieutenant Luke Williams, both of whom had become close personal friends of his. Luke had managed to get himself assigned to Guam, and both men had put in some hard labor when they weren't at their day jobs to help get the hospital up and running.

"You're going to hear it!" Maria said. "I am done with seeing your mopey face around here. I have work to do, a hospital to run, and we've hired and fired two CMOs in less than six weeks. I need you to snap out of it."

Nico couldn't help but crack a smile. Maria was being a friend, and despite her bluster, he could see the worry lines etched in her forehead. "Listen, Miss Bossy, haven't I done everything you've asked? It's not my fault the CMOs can't cut it here."

"Right, especially after you keep riding them for not performing miracles like our famed Dr. Atao."

She took a seat across from him and softened her tone. "Listen, I know this hasn't been easy for you, but maybe it's time you really said goodbye to her. We just hired this really cute nurse for the ER…"

"Maria!"

"What, you think I'll be here waiting for you? I've got several dates lined up."

"Would one of them be our *maga'låhi*?" Even Nico hadn't missed the way Tom doted on Maria, following her around like a lovesick puppy.

She raised a brow and looked at him sideways. "I'm not ready for him yet."

He bit his tongue before he said something

that would get him a new lecture. The last thing he had a right to do was give love advice to Maria.

"You're right. I need to start focusing on my family. Nana has a phone consultation with that oncologist you found in California."

Maria nodded. "I checked his credentials— he's really good. And if it works out, he's willing to come here once every two months for exams and consultations on Nana's case and any others we want to give him. He'll do the rest of his work remotely. He's not cheap, but if we have a few more patients, I think he's worth it."

Nico thanked Maria, then drove home to Tumon Bay. The house was still a disaster and barely habitable, but he was slowly making progress. He'd managed to pump out the water on the first floor and dry it out. The next step was to fix the roof. Maybe he'd get out of Maria's hair and spend some time working on the house.

After Anna left, it had felt right to move back in there. He couldn't explain it to himself or Nana, but he wanted to fix it. Five years ago, he hadn't been able to face the house that only held memories of Anna, but now something felt different. It wasn't just their house, it was also his. A labor of love. It was the first place that belonged to him, the first big purchase he'd made. All his. He remembered how he felt when he signed the papers to buy it. At the time, he had no idea whether he was making the best decision or the biggest mistake of his life. But the house had turned out exactly as he'd pictured it would. Until Lucas's diagnosis, he'd been able to make his wife happy there. He'd been able to provide for her. For the first time in his life, he'd felt like he could do anything he wanted.

This was his house, and he wasn't going to sell it. He was going to use the insurance money to rebuild it and make a home for himself. With or without Anna.

He went to the kitchen and took out a bottle of beer from the refrigerator that he'd gotten working just last night. The kitchen wasn't fully functional yet because the plumbing had been damaged. Tito had promised to come by on the weekend and help him repair it now that his leg had healed.

Nico opened a drawer to retrieve a bottle opener and caught sight of the divorce papers. He'd shoved them in the drawer when he'd gotten home the day Anna left and hadn't touched them since. Her ring was back in the little silver antique box in the dresser upstairs.

Everything had changed, yet nothing had.

CHAPTER TWENTY-NINE

Something was wrong. I'm out of air! *Anna tapped her air gauge wondering how she could've been so irresponsible. She was still sixty feet underwater. She wouldn't make it back to the surface. There wasn't enough air. Her lungs burned as she looked for Nico. She needed his emergency regulator; that was the only way she would get back up to the surface safely. But he wasn't there. Where did he go? He was her diving buddy, he was supposed to be beside her in case there was an emergency like this. But Nico was nowhere to be found. Her goggles filled with water, making it hard to see. Then she started sinking; her body was getting heavy as she released her last breath. She was going in the wrong direction.*

"Anna, it's nearly five o'clock and you're still not dressed."

Anna woke with a start and rubbed her eyes. Her pulse was racing and her skin was damp. *That dream again.* She looked at the Star Wars clock on the wall. It had been 3,068 hours since she'd left Guam. She'd had the same dream 126 times and it never got better.

"You okay?"

Anna eyed Caro, who was balancing a laundry basket in one arm and dressed in a black cocktail dress with a long strand of double pearls. Caro didn't usually wear black because she thought it was too stark against her pale blond hair and light blue eyes. But it worked today.

"Sorry, I took an afternoon nap and must have forgotten to set an alarm."

"Ethan has been playing drums all afternoon, how did you sleep through that?"

Anna had no idea. Shrugging, she pulled herself up and hit her head on the top bunk. After she'd been there a month, Ethan decided it was too hot to sleep in the same bed as Aunt Anna and asked his mother for a bunk bed.

"What time are we supposed to be at Kat's house?"

Caro slapped her own head in obvious frustration. "Anna, get it together. We aren't going to Kat's, we're going to former Senator Roberts's house for Kat and Alex's anniversary dinner, remember? I'm your plus one and I'm already dressed. Come on, the baby-sitter will be here any minute now."

Anna groaned. "Can't we skip it? I'm not up for a stuffy function."

"You haven't been up for much in the past four months. I think it'll be good for you to get out and socialize. Plus, you know it's good for me to meet Kat and her father. He's still a pretty powerful figure in Washington and I hear he has a new nonprofit that I want to talk to him about."

Anna rubbed her eyes. Her sister was a lobbyist and meeting Senator Roberts was a big deal for her. There was no way Caro would agree to call in an excuse. Besides, Anna hadn't seen Kat since they'd returned from Guam. Kat had personally called several times to check on her but Anna had taken the lazy way out and returned her phone calls with upbeat emails. It was easier to fake it in writing than to try and make herself sound convincing. Kat seemed to be doing okay with everything, but Anna knew she should find out for herself. She owed Kat that much.

She stepped into the shower and picked up Ethan's Power Rangers foam soap can. Perhaps because she didn't have children, she didn't understand why it was charming to spray foam all over yourself. Caro had done Anna's shopping when she'd first gotten back, buying soap, moisturizer and all the feminine essentials, but she'd stopped a few weeks ago and firmly told Anna that she needed to go get her own supplies. Anna hadn't gotten around to it, or too much of anything else. What was the point?

After returning from Guam, she'd taken a few weeks of leave, then quit her post with the PHS. At Caro's insistence, she'd emailed some of her colleagues inquiring about job opportunities, and there had been several offers. One of her former medical school classmates had insisted she join him at his private family practice in Bethesda, Maryland. That lasted a week before she got tired of hearing parents with perfectly healthy children try to convince her that their kids needed speech therapy because they weren't speaking ten languages by age five.

Finally she'd agreed to take some shifts at the local community health center in the Southeast neighborhood of DC. People who came to those clinics had no health insurance or were on Medicaid, the public insurance for the very poor. Gunshot injuries were common at her clinic, and so were old ladies struggling with their diabetes. But even that wasn't enough to make her feel whole. Her heart felt like it would spark and cough but then it died again, like an engine out of fuel.

Caro's banging on the door made her turn off the shower. She stepped out and wrapped herself in a towel.

"What am I going to—" Anna couldn't even get the question out before Caro held up a stunning silvery dress. She and Caro weren't the same size; her sister was only five foot two and more petite than Anna. This dress was new and in Anna's size. In her other hand, Caro held a pair of silver-and-black heels. Also in Anna's size.

"Caro. I'll pay you back for these." While Caro lived comfortably, she didn't exactly make a ton of money and Washington, DC, was an expensive city, especially when she had to pay for private school and special therapy for Ethan.

Caro shook her head. "It's okay, sis. You've been taking care of me my whole life—I can take care of you for a little bit." Misty-eyed, the sisters hugged each other. "You know, I'm sorry you're hurting, but I have to say that I love having you living with me."

Anna nodded. Guam was so far away that she'd only seen her sister once while she'd been married to Nico, at their wedding. Nico had his family but she also had hers.

Oh, Nico. He had emailed to check on her more than once. She had taken him out of email jail and answered, letting him know she was doing well. But her messages were perfunctory.

He, on the other hand, sent regular updates with pictures of the hospital. The day she left, all the patients had been moved back in. The hospital was officially open for business and Nico was working on getting a grant to buy a medical helicopter so they could have access to transport when they needed it. He had taken a step back from the administrative side to give Maria a chance to run things. Anna suspected he'd also made the move to give Maria a chance to move on with her life. Nana's symptoms were starting to get worse, but she was as stubborn as ever. Tito had texted to let her know that Nico had moved back into the house in Tumon and was fixing it up. Nico hadn't mentioned it to her and Anna hadn't asked.

Maria had also emailed, with the same updates on how well the hospital was coming along. The island was slowly recovering and coming back to life. People were fixing their houses, keeping the hospital busy when they fell off roofs or accidently hammered their hands. After going out on a few dates with other men, Maria had finally accepted Governor Tom's invitation to have dinner at one of the fancy tourist restaurants.

Stepping into the dress Caro had bought, Anna looked at her reflection in amazement. The last time she'd worn a fancy dress had been when she went out to dinner with Nico to celebrate her pregnancy. That had also been a silver dress. Nico loved the way the color brought out her eyes.

"Sit down. I'm going to do your hair and makeup." She let Caro fuss with her, and they reminisced about the way they used to sneak into their mother's room when she was out and try on her fancy jewelry and makeup.

Eventually, though, Caro grew serious. "Anna, I'm worried about you. You're welcome to stay here as long as you want, but a few shifts a month at the community center is not how you operate. You're used to working sixteen-plus-hour days, I've never known you to take naps in the middle of the afternoon. It's time to rebuild your life."

Anna sighed. Her sister was right, but she didn't have a clear path. Where was her home? As much as she loved Caro and Ethan, she couldn't live with them indefinitely.

"Listen, my neighbor is putting her house up for sale. How about you get yourself a job and buy it. We can break down a wall in between and make a secret door. Ethan would love that." The thought made Anna smile. Their favorite house growing up had been an old town house in San Francisco that had once been a bigger home before it was divided into two units. However, the original owners had left a small panel connecting the two houses through one of the closets. Anna and Caro used to sneak through that access panel when the owners weren't home and use it as their own private retreat. They'd gotten caught several times, but the owner was a sixty-five-year-old woman who had never had children. She'd yell at them for sneaking in, then feed them milk and cookies.

"Do you know what happened to Mrs. Chambers?" Anna had lost track of the older woman when she went on deployment.

"She died two years ago. You were in Liberia and I couldn't get ahold of you for so long that I forgot to tell you. I didn't make it to the funeral and of course Mom couldn't care less. Poor woman, she died alone. The mail carrier noticed no one was clearing her mailbox and raised the alarm. Her sister was scheduled to visit her the following week and never even got to say goodbye." Anna took a sharp breath. If Nico left Guam and Nana died before he got a chance to see her again, he'd never be able to live with himself.

After situating the babysitter, Caro hurried them out of the house and into her little Mini Cooper. It was a twenty-minute drive to the former senator's mansion in McLean. They arrived and were buzzed in through an imposing set of wrought iron gates. There were a number of cars already in the driveway and adjacent parking area.

Anna struggled up the stone steps to the front door. She couldn't remember the last time she'd worn anything other than sensible shoes; the heels were going to take some getting used to.

Kat opened the door and hugged Anna for a long time. "You've been avoiding me." She put a hand on her hip and Anna smiled sheepishly.

"I'm sorry, I just haven't been up for socializing with anyone."

"Well, if you had called me, I could've told you the good news that I'm expecting again." Kat was grinning and Anna's eyes widened.

"Oh, my God, Kat, that's so wonderful." Anna realized she was speaking loudly and looked over Kat's shoulder. She couldn't be too far along and Anna wasn't sure if she was sharing the news with everyone yet.

"You were a little late and Alex and I couldn't contain ourselves, so we just told everyone else."

"Kat, you have no idea how happy that makes me."

"I'm ten weeks along and so far everything is perfect."

Seeing the exuberance on Kat's face, Anna felt her own spirits lift.

"You know, Anna, life goes on, but you have to let it. I'm not saying what happened to you is something you easily forget, but you have to let yourself go back to living. Try again."

"Hear! Hear!" Caro chimed in.

It wasn't as if Anna hadn't thought about it. When she was with Nico in that house in Tumon, when they had almost rekindled their marriage, she had been ready to move on. Maybe she would've gotten pregnant and it would have been a sign that she was ready to restart her life, to go back to the plans she'd made before Lucas died.

During the drive over, she'd thought about Caro's idea for her to buy the house next door. If she went back to working full-time as a private physician, she could certainly afford it. She hadn't spent any of her PHS salary over the past five years, so she even had the down payment. Perhaps that was the answer. She could still have a family, just not the one she pictured.

They walked through the kitchen and into the great room. "See, this feels like a home," Caro said. "I'm going to take some pictures and text them to Mom's interior designer, tell her this is how real people live." Anna suppressed a smile as Caro motioned with her eyes toward the plush leather sofa that looked cozy and comfortable. Their mother's house had a leopard print, funky-shaped sitting *thing* that she called a couch. Anna once made the mistake of sitting on it to read a book. Her tailbone was sore for days.

They had a brown leather couch in the house in Tumon. She and Nico had saved up to have it shipped from the States. Anna had wanted something big enough for them to cuddle on when they watched movies together. The waterlogged couch was gone now, but the house was still standing.

Kat and Alex's entire family was gathered: Kat's parents, Alex's mother and Vickie, who gave Anna a hug.

Kat introduced them to her father, the former senator who was highly recognizable with his shock of white hair and bright blue eyes. Caro didn't waste any time bending his ear with her autism advocacy. Kat's mother, Emilia, pulled Anna aside. The woman was an older version of Kat with the same blond hair and slim figure.

"I want to thank you for taking care of Kat on Guam."

Anna frowned. "No, Mrs. Roberts, I want to apologize that we weren't able to get her off the island in time to save the pregnancy. I'm glad all has worked out well, but I wish I could've done more, especially after all your daughter has done for the Chamorro people."

"Anna, you have got to get over it." Alex's voice boomed behind her. She turned to find him holding out a glass of red wine. He handed it to her. "Listen, I know I was spitting mad when I got to Guam, but not at you. I was just frustrated with how long it took me to get there. These things happen and you did the best you could."

That was exactly the point. It had taken forever for Alex to get to Kat's side in a time of crisis. That's how it always was on Guam. If she lived there, all she would ever have was Nico.

"That's right." Kat had joined the conversation. "I could just have easily been hit by a bus crossing North Capitol Street. Have you seen the potholes there? It's a wonder I don't trip and fall and get run over."

Alex put an arm around her. "How about I come carry you across every day?"

Kat rolled her eyes. "Oh, no, Mr. Overprotective, I already catch a lot of flak for how many times a day you walk over on thin pretense to check on me." She turned to Anna. "I haven't yet shared the news with my staff, but they all suspect something's up because Alex insists on personally delivering decaf coffee every afternoon."

They both laughed and Anna found herself joining in.

The senator had made his famous pot roast and they all sat around the large kitchen island to eat. Kat's parents took turns telling the story of how Emilia had burned the very first meal she'd ever cooked for a dinner party and the senator had saved her by making his now famous pot roast. Bill Roberts kissed his wife as everyone passed around plates and food. Despite the grandeur of the house, it was a cozy family meal. Not unlike the ones Nana hosted in Guam.

"Do you miss politics?" Caro asked the former senator. Anna hadn't followed the full story but remembered that he had divorced Kat's mother before Kat was born and had reconciled with her right before he lost the election a couple of years ago. Senator Roberts had been a powerful member of the Senate Appropriations Committee, but he'd seemingly given it up for love.

The former senator smiled broadly and shook his head. "I thought I would go nuts not being in the Senate, but as it turns out, a lot of people can use a former ranking member of the appropriations committee. I don't think there's a single think tank or lobbying firm that doesn't want a piece of me."

"Including me," Caro said brazenly.

Roberts laughed good-naturedly. "Your firm I will call back, now that I know you. I'm picking and choosing who I consult for. Has to be a worthy cause. Kat's been a big influence on me. Seeing what she's done for the people of Guam is inspiring me to do better. I think I can get more done out of Congress than I ever did from within."

Anna could see the pride in Kat's eyes as she stood to give her father a hug.

"Actually, Anna, Dad had a good idea when I told him about Nico's new hospital."

At the mention of his name, Anna's heart gave a kick.

"Right. Actually, my son Walt, who's now in California, works for a consulting firm that focuses on telemedicine. Are you familiar with the concept?"

Anna nodded. "More than familiar. We used it on nearly all my deployments, and even in Guam recently. Everything from low-tech phone consulting to video chats to sending X-rays and CT scan results off-site for expert readings. It's been revolutionary for remote areas."

Tapping his finger on the granite counter, Roberts jumped in. "Yes, but this is different. Robotic technology that lets an off-site surgeon perform a procedure."

Anna closed her mouth. She'd heard about medical robotics but the technology seemed so futuristic she hadn't thought much of it.

"The FDA has just approved a model for surgery. It's an adult-only model but the company is already in the process of getting approval for their pediatric attachments."

The doorbell rang. "I'll get it," Kat volunteered and stood. Anna hardly noticed; she wanted to hear more about the machine.

"How does it work?" Vickie asked.

"Basically, you have, say, a cardiac surgeon sitting in his home in South Dakota. He has one half of the technology and he controls a surgical robot. The other piece is in a place like Guam. He can do the surgery any time it's needed, without having to leave his home. That's the future. Right now the company has facilities around the country where their trained surgeons go because the equipment isn't mobile enough for home use yet. The idea is the same—a surgeon can do a surgery from hundreds or thousands of miles away."

"But so much of surgery is touch, how something feels. Being able to see where a bleed is coming from. How can you do that remotely?"

"That's the beauty of this—it uses virtual reality technology. The surgeon has these gloves that he or she puts on. The gloves let you manipulate things remotely and the machine sends signals to the gloves that the doctor is wearing so that he or she feels what's going on, on the operating table. You wear these glasses that connect to the camera on the other end so you see what a surgeon would see if they were right there."

"It sounds so space-age. The price must be exorbitant," Vickie said.

Roberts nodded. "It is. But—and this is what I want to talk to you about, Anna—the company can't sell the product without having real-life testimonials. They're willing to do a rent-to-own program in exchange for some PR."

Anna's throat was so tight, she could barely speak. The machine would be great for Nico's hospital, but it still didn't solve all her problems. And now that she'd been with Caro and Ethan for so many months, how could she ever leave them? "I think Nico would be very interested. You should contact him."

"He already has."

Anna froze at the sound of his voice. It couldn't be. She was hearing things, or dreaming while wide-awake.

"Anna…" This time there was no mistaking his voice. No one said her name like that. She spun around and sure enough, there he was.

Standing in the great room looking like he'd been there all along.

She nearly fell off her chair as she flew into Nico's arms. He held on to her tightly and suddenly everything felt like it should. The deep, gnawing ache in her heart eased. She was in Nico's arms, where she belonged, and he was holding on to her like he'd never let her go. The entire room was talking at once but Anna didn't hear any of it.

Lifting her head, she gazed at him. "You're here," she said in disbelief.

"I learned my lesson, Anna. This time, I've come to get you. And I'm not leaving unless you're with me. Whatever it takes, however long I need to stay, we're going to be together."

Her eyes widened but she didn't get to ask him more. The crowd had gotten impatient and Caro separated them so she could hug Nico. The two of them had always gotten along. After Caro was done, Kat got in for the hugs. Alex slapped Nico on the back and made the introductions to Kat's parents. Anna noticed Luke lingering in the background in battle dress uniform. He was standing with his feet shoulder-width apart, arms crossed, a big smile on his face.

"You brought him here, didn't you?"

Luke grinned. "I got myself a gig in Guam, so I've been stationed on base for the past few months. This guy has been bringing down the entire island with all his moping. People were begging me to bring him to you. Tito even started a tin can fund at the hospital and people were throwing in quarters and nickels to buy him a ticket off the island. I managed to get him a ride as my plus one on a military transport."

Anna smiled. "Thank you."

The senator insisted the new arrivals sit and eat, but Luke excused himself, saying he had to leave to see his father who lived in the DC area.

"You're General Williams's son," Roberts exclaimed.

Luke nodded. "Yes, sir."

"I know your daddy from my time on the appropriations committee. He's a tough man."

Luke smiled. "Don't I know it, sir."

"You one of his twin boys?"

"Before you ask, sir, I'm the screwup."

The senator laughed. "You must be the younger one, then. Last time I saw the general, he told me all about how you boys were at Westpoint. Your brother graduated with honors, and you..."

"Barely scraped through."

Roberts gestured toward the combat patch on Luke's arm. "You've served our country, so in my book, you've done well. Tell your daddy I said hello. And that he still owes me one."

"Yes, sir."

Luke said his goodbyes and left.

"Nico, there's plenty of food here for you." Emilia removed a plate from the cabinet. Nico shook his head. Excusing himself from the group, he pulled Anna into the hallway. Kat pointed them to a study off the foyer so they could talk privately.

As soon as they were alone, he pulled her into his arms and brought his mouth down on hers. She wrapped her arms around his neck and kissed him back with everything she had. For the first time since she'd come back from Guam, it didn't hurt to breathe. He tasted of coffee and smelled like soap. When they came up for air, she buried her face in his chest, needing to feel the rise and fall of his body to believe that he was really there.

"I can't live without you, Nico. I've tried, but I can't."

"I'll give it all up for you. I can live in California—I'll go back once a month to be with Nana, I'll do whatever it takes. But the one thing I can't do is live another minute without you in my arms."

They were words she'd longed to hear. Caro's laughter filtered in from the other room, but looking into Nico's eyes, Anna couldn't imagine a life without him. He was willing to give up everything for her. "I can't do that to you, Nico. I know what the island means to you. You won't be happy leaving Nana there. I'll be okay. I'll go back and work at the hospital with you and Maria. As long as I'm with you, it doesn't matter where we are."

They looked at each other and laughed. "We're quite the pair, aren't we?" Nico said.

"You'll be miserable if you're not on the island."

"And you'll be anxious every minute you're there."

CHAPTER THIRTY

ANNA BLEW OUT a breath. Of course nothing could be easy or actually work as it was supposed to.

Nico smiled. "Ethan, how is it that your aunt Anna can fix people, yet she can't figure out that you have to turn the piece to make it fit?" Giggling, Ethan took the T-shaped Lego block and attached it to the replica of the White House they were building.

Ethan had taken to Nico right away, latching on to him with a fierceness that made Caro cry at night, wondering whether Ethan was starving for a male role model. For his part, Nico showered Ethan with love and attention. Anna didn't have to imagine how good a father he'd be. When they'd had Lucas, Nico had changed just as many diapers as she had and had given him just as many baths.

"Uncle Nico, pass me the piece for the outside balcony—I think it's supposed to face the Washington Monument." Anna marveled at the architectural complexity of the project. Caro had explained that Ethan's psychologist had recommended building with Lego as a way to build both his cognitive and fine motor skills. The box that the Lego came in said it was designed for children five years older than Ethan, and yet he could do it with more ease than Anna. The extra play therapy that Caro had invested in was really paying off.

Anna remembered when Ethan was first diagnosed two years ago. One of Caro's biggest problems had been which specialist to choose; there were hundreds of them in the Washington area. There were none on Guam. Ethan had a good chance of growing up to be a successful adult. His autism was not going to hold him back. But if Anna had had a child with Ethan's needs while living on Guam, she'd have nowhere to turn. The schools on the island were marginal at best. Every governor promised to invest in the education system, health care, roads, housing… The list went on but hardly any of it ever got done.

Nico had been in DC for three months now, and they still hadn't decided what to do. With her usual graciousness, Caro had given them her bedroom and was sleeping on Ethan's bottom bunk so Anna and Nico could have some privacy. Yet they avoided the elephant in the bed between them, both content to enjoy being with each other, pretending they were like any other happily married couple. Maria was handling things with the hospital, and Nana was doing well. Nico had no urgent need to return.

Watching Nico play with Ethan, Anna realized that this is what she'd always wanted. To have Nico be a part of her life, just as much as she'd become a part of his. But that wouldn't be possible if they lived on Guam. Caro couldn't journey with Ethan that often. He was afraid of small spaces; the plane ride alone would be torture. Not to mention the cost of airfare. Then there were all his appointments with the therapist. Now that she'd been living with them for more than half a year, Anna couldn't imagine a life without them.

Her thoughts were interrupted by a knock on the door. Caro was out taking a night to herself thanks to her free babysitters, so Anna opened the door.

A gray-haired lady stood on the stoop.

"I'm sorry, I was looking for Caroline. You

must be her sister, Anna. I see the family resemblance."

Anna nodded as the woman extended her hand. "I'm Edna, I live next door. Caroline mentioned you might be interested in buying my townhome."

With a glance at Nico, Anna nodded again but stepped outside, closing the door behind her. "Ethan is really engrossed in a game," she said to explain her rudeness in not inviting Edna inside.

Edna nodded. "Yes, best not to disturb him. I spoke to Caroline a while ago when my son first asked if I'd like to move close to him. He just found me this nice condo in Phoenix, right by him, so I really need to sell my house in order to buy it. She mentioned you might be interested. Do you have a minute to come see it now?"

Anna looked back at the door.

"If this is a bad time, it's not a problem. It's just that one of the other neighbors also wants to buy it. I guess word spreads around, but I know it would mean so much to Caroline to have you right next to her. She could use the help with Ethan. Poor girl never gets out. I tried to watch him once, but he's a handful for me. I see you and your husband know just how to get along with him."

Caro hadn't dated since Ethan's diagnosis. The list of babysitters who were willing to take care of Ethan was small, and expensive. It would be nice if she could be here for Caro.

She opened the door and stuck her head in. "Nico, I'm going to the neighbor's for a second. Will you two be okay?"

"It's okay, Aunt Anna, he's much better at this than you are. Take your time."

Smiling, Anna closed the door and followed Edna into her home. It was a mirror image of Caro's house and Anna could definitely afford Edna's price. She even found the closet where they could make a gateway to Caro's house for Ethan.

"I don't mean to rush you, dear, but the other folks have already made me an offer. If you can match their price, we have a deal."

Washington, DC, was almost eight thousand miles away from Guam; a third of the way around the earth. She and Nico had briefly talked about the idea of living in Hawaii, where they could catch direct flights to the island. From DC, they'd be lucky if they could make it with just two connections. Most of the flight paths required at least three connections and well over twenty hours in transit. They'd never be able to split their time. But what was the point of living in Hawaii? Nico wouldn't have Nana and she wouldn't have Caro and Ethan.

"I'll buy it," Anna said.

ANNA HADN'T BEEN gone for more than ten minutes when Nico's cell phone rang. He made sure Ethan was busy with his blocks and went to the kitchen to answer it.

"Maria, *Hafa Adai.*"

"*Hafa Adai*, Nico. I'm sorry to call you like this, but you must return home."

Nico's heart stopped. Had something happened to Nana? To the hospital? Last he'd checked, there were no storms expected anytime soon, but he knew that could've changed overnight.

"Maria, please—"

"Nana collapsed. She's okay now, but she said she got dizzy and fell. The phone was too far away for her to reach. Lucky that Tito came home and found her. He brought her to the hospital."

Nico's stomach hardened. He never should've left Nana alone, especially not for this long.

"What does Dr. Balachandra say?"

While they had a whole new team of physicians at the hospital, Nico trusted Dr. Balachandra the most and Maria knew that. She would've made sure he was the one to see Nana.

"He said it's hard to tell what's going on with her cancer, but that's the likely cause. He wants you to talk to your mother about having the tests that oncologist recommended on the mainland."

Nico rubbed his neck. The oncologist they'd hired could only do so much over video chat. He'd recommended Nana come to his hospital in Los Angeles for further testing and possibly surgery. He wouldn't even prescribe any medication without the tests. One of the disadvantages of the mainland was that the doctors were all worried about people suing them. Nana wouldn't hear of going to California. Not even for tests.

"I'll get on a flight as soon as I can."

"She's asking for you, Nico."

Maria transferred the phone to Nana and Nico chatted with her. Nana was putting on a good show, but Nico heard the fear in her voice. She didn't want to die alone.

"I'll be there, Nana, you hang in."

As soon as he hung up, he powered up

Caro's computer to look for flights, frantically searching the websites for the combination of legs that would get him home as quickly as possible.

"Nico?"

He turned to find Anna standing behind him. "Ethan was all alone in the family room. What's going on?"

He closed his eyes. Ethan seemed so independent, he'd forgotten that the boy needed to be supervised at all times. "Is he okay?"

Anna nodded. "Why did you leave him alone?"

Nico filled her in on everything that had happened with Nana. Anna braced herself against the desk. "I'll come with you," she said softly.

He wanted more than anything for her to be with him, but what could she do there? He'd seen the price of flights. They cost more than the monthly salary he drew from his work at the hospital. And that was just one way. Besides, Anna had tried to convince Nana to go to California and she'd refused.

"It's going to take twenty-six hours to get home," he said dejectedly as he clicked through to buy his ticket.

"I know," Anna whispered softly.

"That's the point you've been making, isn't it? That my home is too far away."

She nodded. "See how you feel now, trying to get to Nana? That'll be what our lives are like. You can't go back every month. It's not practical. And if something happens to Nana like it just did, you'll never forgive yourself if you can't make it home in time."

He knew she was right. There was no real choice. Anna circled her arms around his neck and sat in his lap. Burying his head in her shoulder, he took a deep breath, memorizing the feel of her body against his, her scent, the softness of her skin. The flight he selected was leaving in three hours.

CHAPTER THIRTY-ONE

"I DON'T UNDERSTAND why Nico isn't here to help you." Caro grunted as she struggled to lift a coffee table up the front porch steps of Anna's town house. Ethan sat on the stoop playing a video game.

"Uncle Nico is gone for good." Trust Ethan to cut to the heart of the matter. Caro set down the table and Anna blew out a breath.

"This thing is ridiculously heavy," Caro complained. Anna had found the table at an antiques sale along with several other pieces for her new home.

"Why hasn't Nico been back? It's been almost a month."

What was she supposed to say? The phrase *it's complicated* was invented to describe her and Nico. Anna had gotten a full-time job at the community clinic where she had been working. It was the same kind of work she enjoyed when she'd been working for the PHS but without the crazy hours and with the stability of home. Instead of a secret passage, she and Caro had opted to make a whole doorway so they could more easily pass between the houses. Ethan was thriving having his aunt so close by. His "safe zone" had doubled. Caro had never been happier. She was even dating now that she had a reliable sitter.

Anna had everything she needed. Except Nico. Before her heart held pain and suffering inside it, suffocating her. Now there was a big gaping hole that she knew would never heal.

"Maybe it's time for me to move on with my life. Without Nico."

Nico hammered the final nail onto the roof. There were a few minor repairs left but the house was in functioning order. Now all it needed was new furniture. That was Anna's department. Or had been. Aside from the furniture in the bedroom and Lucas's old crib, nothing had survived. He hadn't been able to bring himself to throw out the crib. Instead he'd stored it in the shed.

He climbed down the ladder and stepped back to admire his work. It hadn't been the same, resurrecting the house without Anna. But he'd done it.

"You gonna bring that ladder back for

352 MENDING THE DOCTOR'S HEART

me before I fall through this crappy roof, or what?"

Nico shook his head at Tito who was perched on the roof with his legs hanging over the side. He moved the ladder so Tito could come down. He'd been repairing the chimney. Tito worked as a handyman around the island and had been helping Nico get the house back in order.

Tito dusted his hands. "Yo, this could be such a sweet bachelor pad. I'm thinking black leather couches on the main level, big flat-screen TVs. That new nurse in the ER has a friend. I'm just saying, bro, we can live it up here."

Nico patted Tito and shook his head. The last thing he wanted to do was date. He'd learned his lesson with Maria. There was no point in trying to get over Anna. It wasn't going to happen. Besides, he had another plan, one which he should've put in place a long time ago. It was time for him to be a man and do what was right for his family.

CHAPTER THIRTY-TWO

"NANA, WHAT DID you put in here? It weighs a ton." Tito huffed as he loaded the suitcase onto the conveyor belt.

"You need to exercise some more, Tito. Young man like you should be able to lift that," Nana scolded.

Nico ignored them as he stabbed the end button on his phone. He'd been trying to reach Anna on her cell; it had been going straight to voice mail for a day. She hadn't answered any of her texts or emails, either. Had she done something drastic again like sign up to go work in Syria? He pulled up Caro's number on his phone. It was a decent hour in DC, so if Anna was just avoiding his calls, he wouldn't embarrass himself.

"Hello?" Caro sounded groggy. It was early morning on a Saturday in Washington, and Nico remembered that she liked to sleep in on the weekends.

He handed his passport to Nana so she

could finish checking them in, waving to Lando behind the counter.

"Caro, it's Nico."

A loud shriek on the other end of the line made him pull the phone away from his ear. "Shh, Ethan, it's okay," came Caro's soothing voice. "Nico, I'll call you back," she said, hanging up.

"You all are really late. I can't guarantee your bags will make it, but I'll call the gate to hold the plane. They're boarding now." Lando handed over their boarding passes then exited the ticket counter and put up a closed sign amid the moans of the passengers behind them. Lando was an old family friend. He was the son of Nana's best friend from high school. That was practically family.

"Come on, I'll take you to the front of the security line."

Nana hugged Tito, who started sobbing. He squeezed Nico as Lando yelled at them to hurry. They ran through the terminal to security. Lando took them to the VIP lane and spoke to the security guard at front. Nico's phone rang.

"Caro, where's Anna?"

"What do you mean? You don't know where she is?"

Nico's heart came to a stop. "Why would I know where she is?"

Before he could hear her response, the phone was unceremoniously taken from him by the security guard. He put the phone in a plastic container already on its way through the X-ray.

"Shoes off, smart guy. You're lucky Lando vouched for you. I don't let anyone cut."

Nana was already through the metal detector. Nico took off his shoes and belt and slapped them onto the conveyor. He stepped through the detector, grateful it didn't go off. As soon as he got to the other side, he picked up his phone, but Caro was gone.

Where's Anna?

He knew he'd taken too long to convince Nana to go to the mainland. Almost eight weeks had passed since he'd seen Anna. Unsure of whether his plan would really work, he hadn't told her what he was planning. He was going to show up at Caro's door and surprise her. The big hiccup had been Nana, who wanted to attend her "last" fiesta in Talofofo. Each of the villages in Guam held its own festival each year. Nana was the church organizer for the fiesta and didn't want to let the congregation down. The concession had been that Nana had gone to California for her tests. The next battle would be getting her to agree to the surgery the oncologist recommended. Nico figured the small delay wouldn't make a difference given how long they'd already waited. But what if he was too late?

He was about to try Caro again as he followed Nana to the gate. There was a woman in red walking in his direction. He could've sworn it was Anna. It seemed he couldn't stop thinking about her and seeing her everywhere. The woman passed right by him and Nana. *Wait.*

"Anna!"

She halted and turned. Leaving her carry-on bag, she ran toward him. He met her halfway, his arms automatically reaching for her. He held on to her tightly, kissing her with everything he had. Every day they'd been apart, all he could think about was this moment when he'd get to hold her in his arms. Whatever happened, he wasn't going to let her go. They were done being apart.

"You're the other half of me, Anna. I'm not a whole man without you."

She lifted her head, eyes shining. "I couldn't stand being apart anymore."

Something was different about her. Be-

fore his brain could process what it was, she
stepped back.

"Anna! Look at you!"

Nana had caught up with them and she
hugged Anna.

"You shouldn't be traveling in your condition."

Nico frowned. What did Nana mean? Anna
put a hand to her belly and then it dawned on
him. "I'm only four months along. It's perfectly safe to travel. But I'm having the baby
in DC. I came to get you." She looked at Nico,
then Nana. "Both of you."

"Would Nico and Teresa Atao please make
their way to Gate 23? Your flight is about to
leave."

They all looked at each other and laughed.
Nana put a hand on Nico's arm and nodded.
Nico pulled out his phone and called Lando,
explaining what he needed. He held the phone
away from his phone as Lando screamed at
him about the impossibility of his request.
Nico gestured to Anna and Nana, who made
their way to the gate. When they got there,
the gate agent was standing in the doorway,
holding out her hand for Nico and Nana's
boarding passes. Nico shook his head and
motioned to the desk where another agent

was on the phone. He looked at Nico, rolled his eyes and hit some buttons on the computer.

"These flights are usually full—how did you get me a ticket so last minute?" Anna asked.

"Nana's transferring her ticket to you."

Anna stared at Nana. "No! I'll catch the next flight. You need to go…"

Nana shook her head. "I'm going to stay here and let the Lord take care of me. The only reason I was coming was to reunite you two, that's what I prayed for. And look, here you are." She put Anna's hand in Nico's. "I never want to see either of you without the other. Understand?" They both nodded and hugged Nana.

The desk agent hurried toward them and asked Anna for her passport. After verifying it, he gave her a boarding pass.

"So, is Caro ready for houseguests?"

Anna shook her head. "She doesn't need to be." She wiggled her eyebrows at him and gave a mysterious smile. "I have a surprise for you, kind of like the one you gave me on our wedding day."

CHAPTER THIRTY-THREE

"WHERE IS MY *NETA*?"

Anna watched Nico greet his mother through the crowd of passengers at the airport. She smiled as she heard his annoyed, "What, you don't give your own son a hug anymore?"

Nana shook her head and put one hand on her hip. "Don't you know, my granddaughter trumps you!" Then she spotted Anna and raced toward her, stopping a few inches short, as if she were afraid to come any closer. She put her hands on her cheeks, her eyes shining.

"Oh, my precious little baby."

Anna held out her arms and transferred the wriggly infant to her grandmother's arms. "Here you go, Teresa, meet your namesake."

Nana kissed the baby on her head. "May you have every happiness in the world." Nico put his arm around his mother. "We're so glad you came."

Anna nodded in agreement. Seeing the

tears in Nana's eyes and the grin on Nico's face made her heart swell.

"Well, it's not like you left me any choice. Were you in on this plan, Anna? To torture a poor old woman by sending her pictures of her granddaughter and saying I could only see her if I traveled halfway around the world?"

Anna smiled, wisely staying out of the argument that was about to ensue between mother and son. Their initial plan had been to take the healthy baby girl to Guam to meet Nana, but Nico realized that holding the baby out as a carrot would be the only way to get his mother to the mainland. The oncologist Nico had been working with said that Nana could easily live another ten to fifteen years if she got surgery. Her cancer hadn't metastasized and she was generally in good health. But Nana was the most stubborn woman on the planet and still refused. Until she saw pictures of Baby Teresa and realized there was something for her off the island.

"Come on, Nana, it's time to take you home," Nico said.

A MONTH LATER, they were all at Senator Roberts's house. Kat's mother had insisted

on having a dinner for all of them. Kat and
Alex had been living in Virginia but had recently bought a town house in DC so Kat
could come home between meetings to check
on her five-month-old boy, who was only four
months older than little Teresa. Kat's mother-
in-law looked after Baby Kyle during the day.
That arrangement was what had given Anna
the idea to entice Nana to the mainland.

Nana had been horrified when Anna told
her that she'd soon have to leave little Teresa
in day care so she could go back to work.
That had been the final straw that compelled Nana to get on the plane. Since she
arrived, Nana had been taking care of both
Teresa and Ethan. Caro had stopped using
her after-school babysitter once she saw how
well Ethan reacted to Nana's cooking. Both
Anna and Caro finally had the mother they
never had. Nana spoiled everyone, and Anna
enjoyed every minute of it.

"Welcome!" the senator boomed as he
opened the door. Introductions were made
and the senator called Emilia over to keep
Nana and Baby Teresa company.

"You two, I need with me," Roberts said
mysteriously. Anna looked at Nico, her pulse
kicking up a notch. They'd been in talks with

the senator for months. He was helping them broker a deal with the medical robotics company.

Ushering them into his study, the senator grinned widely. "We have a deal!" Anna clapped her hands and Nico shook the senator's hand vigorously. "Thank you, sir, you have no idea what this means to us."

The robotics company had FDA approval for a remote surgical robot and had a cadre of trained surgeons. As Anna and Nico had suspected, the technology cost way more money than the hospital, or even the government of Guam could afford. The former senator had been working on a deal where Kat would promote the technology using her media contacts and the hospital would allow televised surgeries that the company could use to sell it to other places around the world. The company had made some concessions, but the price was still too high. Tom had tried to work with the legislature, but with the infrastructure repairs needed after the tsunami and hurricane, even his hands were tied when it came to getting more money from the Guam Treasury.

For the past few weeks, Roberts had been trying to sweeten the deal by working his contacts in the military to secure a lucrative contract in exchange for the company giving the surgical robot to Lucas Memorial Hospital for next to nothing. The deal would enable the hospital to do many routine surgeries.

Anna knew that no matter how well Maria was running the hospital, Nico could never be satisfied unless he did what he'd set out to do: bring first class care to the island. Now it was finally happening.

Nico had been working hand in hand with the former senator, using his contacts to makes sure the OR suites were equipped to accommodate the robotic surgeon.

"You want to call your partner and tell her?" the senator asked.

Nico nodded and Roberts pushed a phone toward him. Before he'd left Guam, he'd made Maria a full partner in the hospital rather than just an employee. That way she was able to make some of the major decisions without him. He hadn't made any promises to return. They were taking it a day at a time. Nana's surgery and the birth of Baby Teresa had kept them too busy to really think about how they were going to work things out long-term.

Maria answered on the second ring. Before Nico could get a word out, Anna heard the other woman's excited voice on the line.

Anna pressed the speaker button so she could hear what Maria was saying.

"I can't believe how fast news travels around here. He only proposed like five minutes ago. How did you find out so soon?"

"Maria, this is Anna, what're you talking about?"

There was a pause and then they heard laughter and a slight crackle as Maria put them on Speaker, as well.

"Hi, Nico and Anna. This is Tom. Maria and I are getting married."

Now it was Anna's turn to squeal. The only fly in Nico and Anna's happiness had been whether Maria would be okay. She'd been suspiciously quiet about how her relationship with the governor was going. Even Nana didn't have much gossip. Anna had wondered whether they were just being discreet because he was a public figure or whether things hadn't worked out and Maria was too embarrassed to say anything.

Anna had worried about Maria, and she knew Nico had, too, so the news filled her with joy. She was about to congratulate Maria when the other woman's gleeful voice burst through.

"Okay, so I know Baby Teresa's little but

I want you to be at my wedding. I want Nico to be my man of honor."

"Your what now?"

Anna suppressed a grin as Nico made a face at her.

"Man of honor. It's like a maid of honor, only for guys."

Before Nico could say anything he'd regret, Anna jumped in. "He'll be there, don't worry. He'll even wear a pink tux."

Nico made a face. Anna mouthed, "You owe her," and he wisely kept quiet.

"I want all of you here. You two, Nana, and I want to meet Baby Teresa. Promise me, Anna."

She closed her eyes. Teresa was only seven weeks old. Anna had gotten her tested for everything under the sun—so far the little girl was totally healthy—but she wasn't prepared to make a trip to Guam so soon.

Nico saved her from making any promises by giving Maria the news about the deal. Anna stood back as they all discussed the details, including the timing and transfer of funds. Since Tom was in the room, the senator used the opportunity to hash out some of the details he needed to get the contract drawn up.

Anna returned to the kitchen and took Teresa from Nana, using the excuse of having to nurse the baby to get a private moment with her little girl. Looking down at her pink face, feeling her wriggling body, Anna knew she had everything she ever wanted. She kissed her baby on the head. Teresa smelled a little like sour milk, just as Lucas had.

"I'll do whatever I need to protect you, baby girl. I'm not going to make the same mistakes over again."

Nico joined her. "You know, it doesn't matter where we live, as long as we're together. The only thing that matters to me is my family—you, me, Teresa, Nana, Caro and Ethan."

Anna lifted her face so Nico could kiss her. In the twenty-four weeks they'd been together, Anna hadn't had any nightmares. And that was the way it was going to be for the rest of their lives. She was never letting go of her family.

EPILOGUE

"WELCOME HOME!"

Anna smiled at Nico. "I can't believe you rebuilt it."

Nico put his arm around his wife and daughter. "I knew that one day I'd bring you back here and you'd look at this place—"

"And feel like I was home." Anna gazed in wonder at the house in Tumon.

"Come on, Teresa, I've got a surprise for you." Nico had come a month ahead of them to finalize the installation of the robotic surgeon and give Maria a hand with all the new contracts they had to negotiate.

When they stepped onto the porch, he suddenly turned and lifted Anna off her feet. "Nico!"

"Mama baby!"

"Yep, Teresa, I'm carrying your mama like a baby. This is how I always carry her into the house." They watched Teresa toddle inside.

Anna wrapped her arms around his neck and kissed the little crook between his ear and jaw.

Once they were over the threshold, he set her down. Anna gasped. The house looked totally different from the last time she'd been there. Not only had it been cleaned up, but Nico had also bought new furniture. There was a kids play table instead of a coffee table next to the brown leather couch—almost identical to the one that had been destroyed in the tsunami. He showed her around the kitchen, then took her up the stairs. She stopped when Nico turned into what had been Lucas's nursery. She'd painted it in soft blues and decorated his crib with a nautical-themed bedspread.

"Mama!" Teresa held out her chubby little arms as Anna stood frozen outside the door. She lifted her daughter, taking comfort in her softness. She followed Nico inside.

Her heart leaped into her throat as she took in the room. Nico turned and raised his brows, his eyes seeking her approval. It was Lucas's crib, now with a pink and purple hand-knitted blanket inside. The walls had been painted in cream and pink stripes. Teresa squealed as she spotted Miss Molly, her favorite teddy bear that Anna knew they'd left behind in DC. Anna set her down in the crib and watched her girl giggle as she pressed Miss Molly's tummy to hear the sounds the bear played.

"It's a duplicate," Nico mouthed.

Anna circled her arms around his waist. "Thank you, Nico."

"This is home too, you know."

She nodded. It was. They'd made a home in DC but standing in the house she and Nico had shared, listening to the sound of the sea lap against the shore, and Miss Molly's squeaky voice telling them it was time for tea, this felt like home too.

ANNA HELD TERESA by the hand as she dropped flower petals down the aisle. The flower girl could barely walk, but she was trying her best to make her aunt Maria proud. When they finally got to the front of the aisle, Anna picked her up and stood by Nico. He bent down and kissed his wife and daughter on their heads. Nico was wearing a hot-pink shirt with cream linen pants. Anna was also in a hot-pink dress to match the one Teresa was wearing. While Teresa was in a cream-colored dress with a hot pink sash that Nana had sewn, Anna's entire dress was made with yards of hot-pink taffeta offset by a cream-colored sash.

She and Nico exchanged knowing glances. They deserved to be dressed in hot pink and frills after making Maria wait until Teresa was almost a year old before agreeing to come for the wedding.

Tom was dressed in a tuxedo and appeared nervous. Anna and Nico had checked in on him earlier and he'd been a basket case, worried that Maria would come to her senses and realize she was too good for him. Nico had assured Tom that he'd had the same thoughts on his wedding day and Anna had shown up anyway.

Anna looked out at the audience and smiled when she saw Nana sitting on the bride's side with Tito. Another reason they'd made Maria wait was that Nana needed to recover. Her surgery had gone well, but she needed follow-up treatments. Just a month earlier she had received a remission certificate from her oncologist, a proclamation that she was officially cancer-free. The postsurgery radiation and chemotherapy had been hard on Nana but she'd borne it all with a smile, realizing that every day she survived meant one more milestone she got to witness with her *neta*. First smile, first crawl, first step, first time she said *guela* when calling out to Nana.

The wedding march had been playing for a few minutes, but there was no sign of Maria. Tom glanced anxiously at the door, as did the priest. They were in Agana, in the church that Tom belonged to. His parents were in the front pew and shifted in their seats.

"I'll go see what the hold up is," Anna muttered, handing Teresa to Nico. Lifting her skirt, she went down the aisle and to the antechamber where Maria should've been waiting. Luke Williams entered the church. He was wearing his Army Class A's. Anna knew every single girl at the wedding would be swooning over him all afternoon.

"Have you seen Maria?"

"What? No! I got held up at the base and just got here. They're shipping me out. I thought I'd missed the wedding."

"Help me find Maria."

Anna ran to the little room that was being used as a bridal dressing area. Maria was seated in a chair talking on the phone. "No, call Dr. Balachandra and tell him to examine her. She won't let anyone else do it. Got it? What else? Oh, come on! I'm supposed to be getting married, I can't come over right now."

Luke tapped her on the shoulder and gestured toward the chapel. Maria put the phone on Mute. "Remember that leaky drainpipe we keep having a problem with? Guess what? Now where am I going to find a plumber on a Sunday?"

"Hey, Maria. I got it."

She looked gratefully at Luke.

"But listen, I have to say goodbye."

"What!" Maria frowned at him.

"I'm heading back to the mainland."

"I thought your daddy pulled some strings so you could be here awhile."

He shook his head. "He called to say something's come up with my brother. I've got to go. But I'll go deal with the drainpipe. It's your big day."

Maria stood and gave him a hug and Anna did the same. They both extracted a promise from him to keep in touch. After Luke left, Maria got back on the phone.

"Maria, you're supposed to be walking down the aisle." Anna plucked the phone out of her hand.

"At this rate, I'll be on the phone while poor Tom waits for me in our wedding bed."

Anna quirked a brow. "The hospital is that crazy?"

"We still don't have a CMO, so guess whose life is a living hell?"

"What happened to that last doctor?"

"She quit. I've offered the position to Dr. Balachandra, but he won't take it, either. Says it's too much pressure." She eyed Anna. "There's only one person who can do the job."

Anna backed away. "Oh, no, I live in Washington, DC." But even as she said the words, the image of the house in Tumon flooded her mind. "Now's not the time—let's get you married. Tom's probably having a heart attack."

Grinning, Maria stood. "Good, I don't want him taking me for granted. Let him sweat a bit."

Anna adjusted Maria's wedding gown. Maria's father had died a few years ago so she was walking down the aisle alone. Her gown was a traditional dress with a beaded bodice and a full skirt and train. The white cloth set off Maria's brown skin beautifully. Anna returned to her spot beside Nico, nodding at Tom to let him know everything was okay.

This time when the organ started up, Maria was marching down the aisle, her smile so brilliant that she lit up the entire church.

They had written their own vows, and as they went through the ceremony, Anna remembered the words she and Nico had said to each other when they were married.

Anna, I promise to love and care for you, to do everything in my power to make you happy. I give you my heart and soul, to have and to hold, until death do us part.

Nico had been with her in DC for well over a year. Not once in that time had he pressured her to come back to Guam or discuss their long-term plans. He'd helped her finish furnishing the house in DC. Nana had accepted Caro and Ethan as her own family, and Nico loved Ethan just as much as he loved Teresa. Together, they had made a home in DC, but something had always been missing and Anna knew what it was. His heart was in the house in Tumon. That was obvious from the smile on his face when he'd brought them over the minute they landed yesterday.

Once Tom and Maria were married, they exited the church beneath a shower of rice and flowers. There was a small reception at the community center. As Maria got ready to leave for their honeymoon, Anna held out her hand.

"What?"

"Give me your phone."

"What?"

"You're officially off duty. I'll take the calls from the hospital."

Maria's eyes widened. "Don't get too excited, it's only for six months." Nico had come up behind her and watched Maria give Anna her phone.

"Are you sure about this?" he said when Anna explained her plan.

Anna nodded. "It won't be easy but we can do it. I'll work at the hospital for half the year and then go back and work at the community center part-time over their busy summer months."

"The best of both worlds."

Anna nodded. "Our baby girl will be lucky to have two homes. She'll have the love of her cousin Ethan and meet a whole bunch of new family members here on Guam. We have a few years to figure out how we'll handle school. Let's just take it a day at a time."

Nico wiggled his brows. "You know, we can give her some more siblings to keep her company. We can easily fit two cribs in Teresa's room."

Anna smiled and let her husband lead her away, back to their home.

* * * * *

LARGER-PRINT BOOKS!

GET 2 FREE LARGER-PRINT NOVELS PLUS 2 FREE MYSTERY GIFTS

Love Inspired®

Larger-print novels are now available...

LILP15

LARGER-PRINT BOOKS!

GET 2 FREE LARGER-PRINT NOVELS PLUS 2 FREE MYSTERY GIFTS

Love Inspired®

SUSPENSE

RIVETING INSPIRATIONAL ROMANCE

Larger-print novels are now available...

LARGER-PRINT BOOKS!
GET 2 FREE LARGER-PRINT NOVELS PLUS
2 FREE GIFTS!

⟨H⟩HARLEQUIN®

super romance®

More Story...More Romance

READERSERVICE.COM

Manage your account online!

- Review your order history
- Manage your payments
- Update your address

---

*We've designed the
Reader Service website
just for you.*

Enjoy all the features!

- Discover new series available to you,
  and read excerpts from any series.
- Respond to mailings and special
  monthly offers.
- Connect with favorite authors at
  the blog.
- Browse the Bonus Bucks catalog
  and online-only exculsives.
- Share your feedback.

Visit us at:

ReaderService.com

RS15